*

"Great stuff . . . Our hero has but to look at a piece of human bone and, like Sherlock Holmes, can tell everything about the person to whom it belonged. Since he knows more about hominid phylogeny than Sherlock did, he can look at a tibial fragment 113 millimeters long and say, 'This one was nearly forty. And Japanese. And built like a wrestler, say 145 pounds.'" —*New York Times Book Review*

*

"He writes riveting mysteries, where nasty things happen and the smell of gunfire is in the air. . . . Cozy, yes, but count on there always being greed, death, sex, and assorted villains."

—*Denver Post*

*

"Aaron Elkins is one of the best in the business and getting better all the time: when his new book arrives I let the cats go hungry and put my own work on hold till I've finished it."

—Elizabeth Peters, author of
The Snake, the Crocodile and the Dog

*

Please turn the page for more reviews . . .

*

"He not only makes one think how interesting it would be to be an anthropologist, he almost persuades one that a certain amount of fun could be had out of being a skeleton."

—Sarah Caudwell, author of
The Sirens Sang of Murder

*

"A pleasure . . . sit back and enjoy . . . while wallowing in all that deliciously obscure and newly learned information."   —*USA Today*

*

"Aaron Elkins's anthropologist detective, Gideon Oliver, has dug out a niche all his own. A latter-day Dr. Thorndyke, he's a forensic whiz known as 'the skeleton detective.' Show him a few bones and he'll not only describe who died, and from what, but how he or she lived."

—*Detroit News*

*

*

"Elkins writes with a nice touch of humor . . . Oliver is a likable, down-to-earth, cerebral sleuth."

—*Chicago Tribune*

*

"At last a new detective has come along that looks to small clues, however inanimate, to discover what a man looks like and what his customary behavior might have been. . . . It is when Gideon uses a few charred scraps of a human body to describe a man, his height, weight, age, and smoking habits, that a new Sherlock Holmes rises before us."

—*Houston Post*

*

"Murder, a singular detective, a winning supporting case, humor—what more could we want for a mystery?"

—*Chicago Sun-Times*

*

AARON ELKINS

DEAD MEN'S HEARTS

THE MYSTERIOUS PRESS

Published by Warner Books

A Time Warner Company

MYSTERIOUS PRESS EDITION

Cover design by Krystyna Skalski
Cover illustration by Mary Ann Lasher

The Mysterious Press name and logo are registered trademarks of Warner Books, Inc.

 Mysterious Press books are published by
Warner Books, Inc.
1271 Avenue of the Americas
New York, NY 10020

Visit our Web site at
http://pathfinder.com/twep

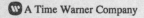 A Time Warner Company

Printed in the United States of America

Originally published in hardcover by The Mysterious Press.
First Mysterious Press Paperback Printing: April, 1995

10 9 8 7 6 5 4

Acknowledgments

The impetus for *Dead Men's Hearts* came from a curious forensic case described to me, alone with some interesting speculations, by my old friend Professor Charles F. Merbs of the Anthropology Department, Arizona State University.

Other forensic experts who cheerfully gave advice and information and generally did their best to keep Gideon Oliver honest are Professor Michael Finnegan of the Department of Sociology, Anthropology and Social Work, Kansas State University; Dr. William D. Haglund of the King County Medical Examiner's Office; Professor Kenneth A. R. Kennedy of the Section of Ecology and Systematics, Cornell University; Dr. Robert B. Pickering of the Denver Museum of Natural History; and Professor Ted A. Rathbun of the Anthropology Department, University of South Carolina.

A number of Egyptological experts from the Royal Ontario Museum also pitched in to the extent that they were needed (desperately): Dr. Lyn Green and Gayle Gibson-Kerwin of the

Education Department and Alan Hollett of the Egyptian Department freely shared their expertise. Roberta Shaw of the Egyptian Department was especially helpful on Amarna art. Dr. Elene Kolb of Seattle provided assistance in the areas of linguistics, history, and morale.

And particular thanks are owed to Dr. Barbara Mertz for her example, her no-nonsense scholarship, and her roaring good company on the Nile.

Anyone who has had the good fortune to visit Chicago House, the Egyptian headquarters of the University of Chicago's Oriental Institute, will probably wonder if that venerable and respected institution is the model for Horizon House. It isn't. To put it simply, I needed a fictional archaeological center situated on the banks of the Nile in Luxor, so that's where I put it. The fact that Chicago House beat me there by sixty years is an accident of history.

The heart of the dead man is weighted in the scale of the balance, against the feather of righteousness.

The Ancient Egyptian Book of the Dead
Translation by R. O. Faulkner

Chapter One

"All right, then, explain Drbal's Phenomenon," Bruno Gustafson demanded.

"Um . . . Drbal's Phenomenon?" Gideon said.

"The fact," Bruno said, his ruddy face aglow with the pleasures of scholarly debate, "that if you leave an old razor blade in the Great Chamber of Cheops' pyramid, oriented exactly north–south, in twenty-four hours it comes out sharp as new. This is a known fact, proved by Drbal. He could shave two hundred times with the same Gillette Blue blade."

"Oh," Gideon said, "that Drbal." He sipped his Scotch-and-water. "Well—"

Bruno's wife saved him, for the moment at least. "I thought it was Khufu's pyramid," Bea Gustafson said matter-of-factly.

"Same guy," Bruno said. "But the thing is, it could have been anybody's pyramid. Drbal made himself a mint selling little cardboard razor-blade sharpeners shaped like pyramids. Czechoslovakian patent number 91304. Don't ask me why I remember."

"Fascinating," Rupert Armstrong LeMoyne said, beaming over his white wine. "Absolutely fascinating."

That had been about the level of Rupert's participation so far. This, Gideon thought, was understandable behavior from the University of Washington's vice-president for development in the presence of Bea and Bruno Gustafson of Walla Walla, the alumni couple whose contributions to the school had been $150,000 in each of the last two years. Gideon also understood why the Gustafsons had been treated to a string of receptions over the past two days, had been given twelfth-row seats smack on the fifty-yard line for Saturday's sell-out game between the Huskies and Arizona, and were now being entertained with drinks and hors d'oeuvres in the faculty club bar, prior to being escorted upstairs for dinner.

What Gideon didn't understand was what *he* was doing there. He and Julie.

"What do you suppose accounts for it?" asked the fascinated Rupert. "Vibrations or something?" Rupert's academic training, long in business administration, was a little short in the sciences.

"Well, that's an interesting question," Bruno said. "I think that the idea is that a pyramid shape is like a, well, like some kind of a, a—"

"Resonator," Bea said. "This fried mozzarella is wonderful, don't you think so, Julie?"

"It certainly is," said Julie, who hadn't had the opportunity to say very much thus far.

"Resonator, right," said Bruno. "For different kinds of— well, unknown frequencies from different parts of the, um, uh, cosmos." He seemed to realize this was a bit weak. "Did you know that if you keep yogurt in a pyramid-shaped carton it just about never spoils?" he added, by way of strengthening his argument. "Known fact. They sell it that way in France. I'm thinking of test-marketing it here. Cheops' Yogurt, what do you think? I don't see how it can miss."

Rupert shook his head appreciatively back and forth while he swallowed a mouthful of cracker and pâté preparatory to speaking.

Just fascinating, Gideon said to himself.

"Just *fascinating*," Rupert said. He dusted his lips with a cocktail napkin. "Well, if everyone is ready, suppose we trot along upstairs to dinner?"

On the steps, he and Gideon brought up the rear.

"Rupert, what am I doing here?"

"Shh, they asked for you specifically."

"They probably want me to endorse Cheops' Yogurt. You know, I just might do it."

"Gideon, don't be funny, please. It makes me nervous."

"But only if he meets my price."

Rupert's fingers dug imploringly into his upper arm. "Gideon, be *good*. It's not his fault if he's a little odd."

Bruno Gustafson was certainly a little odd. Jolly, redfaced, and sociable, he was one of those businessmen who didn't have any business in particular. He had built (and lost) fortunes in plastics, in metal fabrication, and in food services. Reputedly a onetime pal of Spiro Agnew's, he had been ambassador to Suriname (or was it St. Kitts?) for a few months during the Nixon administration. Now he developed commercial real estate in eastern Washington, dabbled in dairy farming, and pursued obscure studies in Egyptology, or rather on the loony fringes of Egyptology.

Gideon had met him three or four times, at one university function or another, and each time Bruno had eagerly peppered him with one crackpot theory or another. Last time it had been the proposition that the pyramids had been built as huge protective baffles by Egyptian priest-scientists who had discovered how to utilize the energy of the Van Allen belts by transporting it to earth along ionized laser beam paths. A slight accident in calculation, Bruno had told him, had created a momentary overabundance of power that had knocked the planet off its axis in 3001 B.C., prematurely ending experimentation along this line.

Despite all this, or possibly on account of it, Gideon had taken a liking to Bruno. He liked his energy and his amiableness, he liked his open-handed philanthropy, and he liked the enthusiasm with which he'd attacked Egyptology, even if he'd made straight for some of its nuttier byways.

He liked Bea Gustafson too. An intelligent, feisty, pintsized woman about Bruno's age—sixty or sixty-one—she had made a fortune of her own as an investment manager, and was obviously an equal partner, or maybe a little more than an equal partner, in the Gustafsons' current financial activities. They made a good team: one the visionary, the dreamer, the man with the big but fuzzy ideas; the other the clear-eyed, no-nonsense realist who kept their feet on the ground and their cash flow positive.

Once upstairs, Rupert led the way to a table at the big window and arranged for Bruno and Bea to sit facing eastward, looking out over a spectacular view that took in Lake Washington with the floating—and occasionally sinking—Evergreen Point bridge in the foreground, and, farther off, the thrusting, jagged wall of the Cascades, glinting with an early layering of snow.

The setting wasn't wasted on Bruno. "Some view," he said appreciatively. "Right out over Husky Stadium."

But as soon as they were seated, he was back to his subject, addressing them all. "Did you know that in 1799, Napoleon asked his men to leave him alone inside the Great Pyramid for a few minutes, just like Alexander the Great did, back in—whenever it was. And when he came out he was white as a ghost. When they asked him about it, all he did was shake his head and tell them he never wanted to talk about it again. No one's ever been able to explain it."

"If it smelled the way it did when I was there," Gideon said, "I think I might be able to explain it."

A smaller man might have taken offense, but Bruno merely laughed his happy laugh. "Okay, but there's *some* kind of energy there. Explain to me why, if you wrap a wine bottle in a damp newspaper and stand on the very top of the pyramid, and hold it up above your head, and the conditions are right, sparks come out of—"

"Honey," Bea said, "give the poor man some rest. Let's go get our food, and then make your pitch."

It was Mediterranean buffet night at the faculty club. Julie and Gideon found themselves facing each other across the salad section of the buffet table, over platters of hummus, cold stuffed grape leaves, and feta-cheese-and-tomato salad.

"Not that I'm not having a good time," Julie said, "but have you figured out what this is about yet?"

Gideon shook his head. They'd been wondering since Rupert had called to ask them to dinner. Gideon taught at the university's Port Angeles branch, sixty miles and a half-hour ferry ride from the main campus in Seattle, and didn't ordinarily come into the city more than once every two or three weeks. Julie, a supervising ranger at Olympic National Park's Port Angeles headquarters, got in even less frequently. It had been six months since their last meal at the faculty club. And never before had they gotten an invitation from Rupert LeMoyne.

But this had been more like a summons than an invitation, and Rupert had been firm about Julie's attendance as well. "The Gustafsons would like her to be there too," was all he could, or would, say.

"Whatever his pitch is, you'd better say yes," Julie told him, ladling yogurt dressing onto her salad, "or poor Rupert is liable to disintegrate right in front of us."

"Well, you know, he has a tough job," Gideon said charitably.

Back at the table, Rupert turned the wine list over to Bruno, who proved unpretentiously knowledgeable. A bottle of St.-Emilion and another of Oregon Pinot Gris were chosen to go with the main course, the black-tied waitress was sent on her way, and business was gotten down to.

"I'll bet you've been trying to figure out why we asked Rupert to bring you two along today," Bruno said.

"Not at all," Gideon said. "It's nice to be invited."

"Well, we have a proposition to make. Rupert, you listen up too."

Rupert listened up.

"What we have in mind, Gideon—why don't you explain it, hon?"

"Sure," Bea said. "We'd like you—"

"We being the Horizon Foundation," Bruno said. "I'm on the board, you know."

"We'd like you," Bea said again, "to be part of a project—"

"This has been in the planning stages for over a year," Bruno said.

"Honey," Bea sang, "if you want to explain it, go right ahead."

"No, no, you go ahead."

"All right, then." She waited a moment to see if he meant it, then went on. "The foundation is going to do a documentary—"

"You're going to like this," Bruno got in, then flinched back into his chair under the force of Bea's scowl and let her finish.

Gideon didn't like it.

The Horizon Foundation was a nonprofit, Philadelphia-based institution that endowed archaeological projects around the world, among them the work of the famous Horizon House in Luxor. When the foundation's board of directors had concluded that the Horizon House endowment was in need of beefing up after thirty years of inflation, Bruno had come up with the idea of a promotional and educational video on their activities. More than that, he and Bea had volunteered to underwrite it. The Gustafsons, who made yearly visits to Egypt anyway, would be going there at the end of November—in six weeks—to accompany the documentary crew that would tape *Reclaiming History: The Story of Horizon House*.

So far, so good. But what they were asking now—the "pitch"—was that Gideon come along to serve as one of the narrators; a sort of color-man, according to Bea, who would provide general information on ancient Egypt and its inhabitants to balance the drier, more specialized presentations by Horizon staff members. In return, and on the assumption that he would refuse personal remuneration, they would be pleased to make a token donation of $25,000 earmarked for the anthropology department. Over and above their annual contribution, naturally.

"Why, that's *extremely* generous," Rupert burbled. "Gideon, that being the case," he said slyly, "I think we might see our way after all to getting you that Grenz X-ray unit you've been asking for. You could find all those foreign particles you're always after. What do you say?"

"I don't think so," Gideon said reluctantly.

Even Julie looked surprised.

Well, he was flattered, Gideon explained, but his field was Pleistocene evolution, not Egyptology; his sole claim to hands-on experience in the latter was three weeks in Egypt, during which he'd helped measure and analyze a skeletal collection from the Twelfth Dynasty. He'd spent almost the whole of it in the dingy basement of the Cairo Museum, escaping only the final week for a whirlwind tour by Volkswagen bus into Upper Egypt, hoping to make it to Luxor, but getting only as far south as Abydos. He'd stopped at all the *de rigueur* monuments—the pyramids, Memphis, Saqqara, Beni Hassan—sometimes three in a day, and by the time he'd staggered out of the last one, they'd all started to look alike to him. Now, six years later, they were little more than a blur.

Other than that, the only thing he'd done in Egyptology was to teach a couple of classes in it while the regular professor was on sabbatical, but as he didn't have to tell them, that hardly made him an expert, and besides, it had been years ago. Getting up in front of a camera and talking about Egyptology would make him feel like a fraud, he said, and an interloper besides. Why not turn to a recognized expert in the field?

"I'll tell you why," Bruno said, "first, because there aren't as many recognized experts as you think, and second, we're not doing a movie for professional anthropologists, we're doing it for businessmen who might want to give a few bucks, and for high school students who might want to learn a few things, so we don't need any fancy scientific gobbledygook. What we need is someone personable, someone who can talk in front of a camera in understandable language."

"Yes, but—"

"Look, it also doesn't hurt that you happen to be Gideon Oliver, *the* Skeleton Detective. That'll catch people's attention. How many Egyptologists are celebrities?"

A reference to the nickname that had clung to him like a barnacle since his first publicized forensic case was not the best way to win Gideon over. He scowled down at his plate. "I'm not—"

"I don't think you should reject this too hastily," Rupert interjected.

"For what it's worth," Bea said, "it was Abe Goldstein's idea."

Gideon looked up sharply from the chunks of shish kebab he'd been pushing around with his fork. "What was Abe's idea?"

"That you do some of the narration. He was still chairman

of the board then, and as soon as the subject came up, he said you'd be perfect for it. Right, hon?''

"Absolutely right," Bruno agreed.

For the first time, Gideon's resistance weakened. Abraham Irving Goldstein, then already near retirement, had been his professor in graduate school, his mentor, his father-figure (or grandfather-figure), and finally his friend. His death from a kidney infection four months before, at the age of eighty-one, had left a space in Gideon's life, and Julie's too, that no one else would ever fill.

And narrating a film was exactly the sort of thing Abe would have come up with for him; something to get his nose out of the dusty alleys of Pleistocene hominid taxonomy. Abe had never stopped nagging Gideon—gently, to be sure—about spending too much time in the library stacks and skeletal labs, and too little among people who still had some flesh on their bones.

"Abe really wanted me to do it?" he said softly.

At this sign of wavering, they laid it on: The project would take only two weeks. His work would be undemanding. Nobody was expecting prepared presentations, they simply wanted him to respond to the interviewer's questions in a relaxed, conversational manner; after-the-fact editing would smooth everything out. It was doubtful that he'd be needed for more than an hour or two a day, so there would be plenty of time for sightseeing and relaxation.

Besides that, another good, old friend of Gideon's was going to be involved too. Since Phil Boyajian would be in Egypt researching one of his travel books anyway, they had talked him into coming along to handle the logistics, a guarantee of smooth sailing and good company.

"Well—" Gideon said.

And, let's see, had they forgotten to mention that a leisurely week-long cruise up the Nile would be part of it, so that scenes could be shot at el-Amarna, Dendera, and other wonders of ancient Egypt? Phil had already lined up one of the posh Nile riverboats for their exclusive use.

Gideon laughed. "Are you sure we're talking about the same Phil Boyajian? Editor of *Egypt on the Cheap*? I know this guy. He doesn't exactly believe in posh."

"Listen," Bea said, "when I go to Egypt I go posh, and anybody who goes with me just better get used to it."

"Well——" said Gideon.

And, oh yes, Bea added, there was more than enough room for two on the cruise ship, and at Horizon House as well. They would be delighted if Julie could come too, assuming she could get away.

Would that, she asked disingenuously, be something they might possibly enjoy?

Naturally enough, that sealed it. Julie and Gideon didn't need even to glance at each other to consider whether two winter weeks on and around the Nile would be something they might possibly enjoy. It beat his going alone, that was for sure. He raised a few pallid objections for form's sake—his class schedule would have to be adjusted, for one thing—but Rupert waved them airily aside; no problem at all, these things could be taken care of, leave it to him, not to worry.

When Julie said that she didn't think that changing her vacation schedule would create any difficulties either, the matter was settled, and a few minutes later they were toasting the coming expedition with glasses of Pinot Gris.

"Here's to a great documentary," Julie said.

"Here's to a new Grenz X-ray machine for Anthropology," said Rupert.

Bruno laughed. "Here's to a couple of weeks of fun in the sun, let's not forget that part of it."

"Amen to that," Bea said. "Here's to all of us sitting together at another table in a few months, sipping wine, and watching the sun set over the Nile."

"I'll drink to that," Gideon said with a smile. But his feelings were mixed. Here's to six solid weeks of cramming on ancient Egypt, he thought.

Chapter Two

Clifford Haddon paused in mid-sentence, placed his glass of Scotch on the side table, and rose to shut the windows behind him. Even with them closed, the din was maddening. Eighteen years in Egypt and he had yet to get used to the unremitting noise. When he'd first started at Horizon House, the nights had been almost tolerable, but ever since some public-relations *wunderkind* had come up with those unspeakable sound-and-light shows at Karnak and Luxor Temple—one three-quarters of a mile north of Horizon House, the other three-quarters of a mile south—the racket along the Corniche was unending from morning till midnight. If you asked him, Luxor's traffic was as deafening as Cairo's and getting worse all the time.

He snorted. The Egyptian view of automobile horns, as conveniently fatalistic as the Egyptian view of everything else, was that they were meant to be used, or else why have them? And use them they did, with a vengeance. No polite little bip-bips on the streets of Luxor or Cairo or Alexandria. Six endless, excruciating seconds—that was the mean time any individual horn blared; he knew because he had taken the time to establish it empirically. They blew their precious horns on any pretext whatever: to let off steam, to express high spirits, to impress other drivers, to intimidate those pedestrians foolish or desperate enough to try make it from one curb to the other, and, he had no doubt, to satisfy the universal desire to add their two cents to the general pandemonium lest Allah not mark their presence.

He returned to his chair and resumed his seat. "Have you ever thought," he mused to the three people seated in armchairs near the fireless fireplace in the austere, vaguely baronial room known as the gallery, "what a wonderful country Egypt would be—"

"—if not for the Egyptians," said one of them, a blonde woman of thirty-five with one bare leg draped over the arm of her chair.

Haddon scowled, having remembered too late that Tiffany Baroff had been at his side a few days before, when he had produced this witticism while showing a group of visiting Austrian scholars over the grounds.

"Exactly," he said grumpily as he resumed his seat, averting his eyes from the vulgarly swinging leg, on the knee of which he had perceived one of the Donald Duck plastic strips that she used to cover her frequent scrapes and scratches. When had archaeologists begun looking like overgrown tomboys?

And Tiffany, was that a name for an archaeologist? She herself preferred TJ, but to his mind that was more preposterous still. Tiffany was her name, such as it was, and as far as he was concerned, they were both stuck with it.

Not that she looked like a Tiffany. Now Helga, that would suit her, or Edwina. Big-boned, knobby-kneed, impertinent, and relentlessly, aggravatingly healthy, she was given to baggy tan shorts, baggy men's work shirts (worn with the tails out), and ankle-top sneakers of a startlingly pneumatic appearance. All in all, she looked more like a forward on a ladies' field hockey team than the supervisor of field activities for one of the world's oldest Egyptological institutions. And not only the supervisor of field activities, but his chief assistant. And not only *that*, but the likely heir to the directorship when he himself was forced to step down the following year on reaching seventy.

Over his dead body. No grubbing field archaeologist who couldn't tell the difference between demotic script and abnormal hieratic was going to run Horizon House if he had anything to say about it. Certainly not one named Tiffany, with Donald Duck patches on her knees.

"Shall we get down to business?" he said. He stroked his crisp, silvery beard. "It seems we're going to have to adjust our schedule for the next few days."

Tiffany's tanned leg stopped swinging. She watched him warily. On her right, Arlo Gerber, head of the epigraphic unit, had a vaguely apprehensive look in his eyes, but was there really anything extraordinary about that? On Tiffany's other side, Jerry Baroff, librarian and registrar (and Tiffany's much-to-be-pitied husband), puffed his pipe and also looked the way he always looked, which was to say elsewhere.

"As you know," Dr. Haddon went on, "we poor scholars are at the mercy of our old friend Forrest Freeman, the Orson Welles of *cinéma archéologique*, who has been encumbering our normally simple and unassuming lives for several days now, in connection with the making of a manifestly unecessary, exasperatingly time-consuming, and extraordinarily expensive documentary film—not, of course, that the expenses involved would be of any concern to its sponsors, the estimable Beatrice and Bruno, among us at present for their annual laying on of hands and imperial—"

He paused. "Yes, Arlo?"

"Actually, they're not making a film. It's a videotape."

"Oh, yes? How interesting."

"I only meant that it's not as expensive as making a film."

"Thank you. Will all please note that the record has been set straight."

Beneath Arlo's absurd little mustache his mouth quivered and set. He examined his rather grubby fingernails. Dr. Haddon recognized the all-too-familiar signs of resentment and offended dignity. A man of exquisite sensibilities, Arlo Gerber.

"May I continue now?" Dr. Haddon said. "I met with Forrest for some time this afternoon to discuss changes in our schedule. It seems they have run into a conflict with the visa authorities, and must cut their time with us by several days. You can readily imagine how disconsolate I was at this news.

"Now: our original schedule called for two more days here at Horizon House, to be followed by a flight to el-Amarna, whence we were to embark on a *luxurious* week-long cruise back up the Nile to Luxor—a Nile cruise, heaven help us!—stopping at various and sundry sites recalling the many Horizon House triumphs of yesteryear. Then we were to conclude with another five days of filming—I beg your pardon, Arlo, of *videotaping*—in and around Horizon House."

He frowned at Tiffany, whose leg had begun its impatient and recriminatory oscillations again. What an unfailingly irritating woman she was. Really, it wasn't as if he didn't know perfectly well that he was repeating something they had already heard. But with this group, one couldn't repeat things too many times. Say it often enough, and anything was possible. Tiffany might actually stop arguing, Arlo might say something pertinent, and Jerry might even be caught at a rare moment when he was inadvertently paying attention to what was going on around him.

Not very likely, any of it, but one had to try.

"And now there's going to be a change?" Jerry asked.

Well, there you were.

"Yes, Jerry. In order to meet the new time constraints el-Amarna has been eliminated from the schedule. We will start the cruise at Abydos instead, saving several days. And our departure from Horizon House will now be the day after tomorrow, one day after we are joined by Gideon Oliver, that well-known paragon of scientific decorum and reserve. That will eliminate a day here at Horizon House, and one additional day will be pruned after we return. Naturally, certain activities will have to be abbreviated or eliminated. For one thing, Jerry, they obviously can no longer spend an entire morning in the library. I hope two hours will be sufficient."

Jerry's shoulders lifted in a vague but acquiescent shrug. "Sure, I guess so. I don't even know what I can tell them that'll take two hours."

"Very good. And Arlo? Three hours in your section?"

Arlo nodded in a removed sort of way, as if these details were beneath him. Still piqued, the man was. "Very well, if that's all that can be spared."

"Very good. And I fear we had better eliminate the visit to WV-29 entirely, inasmuch—"

"Oh, now, wait a minute—" Tiffany's leg was snatched gawkily back over the arm of the chair. Her dirty, size-ten sneaker swept across the low table in front of her, knocking Jerry's pipe out of the ashtray and making him sit up with a start, alert if only for the moment.

Tiffany leaned forward, staring grimly at Haddon. "I don't believe this."

Excessive though it was, this response did not surprise him. WV-29 was archaeological shorthand for Western Valley 29, the twenty-ninth site to be located in the arid, dismal, little-visited side-canyon of the Valley of the Kings just across the Nile. It was also Tiffany's pet project, now in its fifth season of excavation, and she had entertained fond hopes of showing it off for posterity.

"Believe me, my dear," Dr. Haddon said, "I'm more distressed about this than you are. But think about the time involved. A ferry across the river, a van to the valley floor, a fifty-foot scramble up the hillside with all that camera equipment—Forrest felt—"

"Balls, Forrest doesn't have anything to do with it," Tiffany said. "It's you. You just don't give a damn whether the site's included or not."

Dr. Haddon considered pouring himself a bit more Scotch, but decided against it despite the provocation. He knew from sad experience that more than three fingers, when combined with the pills he now took to battle the various decrepitudes of age, would make him a sorry man in the morning.

With some effort, he dredged up a kindly smile for her. "Not so, my dear. The fact of the matter is, I argued mightily with Forrest, suggesting that Horizon House be the documentary's sole location, thereby eliminating the cruising time in its entirety. Unfortunately, the masterful Forrest exerted his contractual—"

"Are you cutting the time they're going to spend on your Middle Egyptian generative grammar paradigm?"

"*That*," he said crisply, "was never scheduled to take more than two hours in the first place."

"So they're getting two hours of syntactic analysis that

nobody has given a damn about since 1932," Tiffany blurted, "but you're not going to let them near our one and only working excavation?"

Now he was annoyed. "Excavation of what?" he said testily. "Tell us, just what is there to see up there? What is this wondrous WV-29 that consumes so much of our resources? The long-lost royal tomb of Queen Tiy? Of Akhenaten himself?" Damn it all, there she'd gone and made him lose his temper.

"No," she said, her face settling into the irritating sulk that heralded one of her little lectures. "It's not a long-lost royal anything. It was a common, everyday workers' village with absolutely nothing in it of royal interest. Just ordinary, average people not worth bothering about."

He eyed the Scotch bottle once more: Teacher's Highland Cream, purchased at extortionate cost, but well worth it when compared to the barbaric Egyptian spirits. Perhaps under the circumstances he could allow himself the merest driblet more. He poured, sipped, and felt better for it.

"My dear Tiffany, I'm quite aware—"

"The purpose of modern Egyptological research," she went on automatically—and why wouldn't it be automatic, considering the regularity with which she trotted out this tiresome and misinformed harangue?—"isn't to uncover more royal burials, more royal stelae, it's to reconstruct the broader—"

"—the broader social and cultural institutions of ancient Egypt," Dr. Haddon supplied. Tit for tat.

"—and—" Tiffany faltered momentarily, but only momentarily. "Yes, that's right, but as long as we continue to pay more attention to interpreting, and re-interpreting, and re-re-interpreting the goddamn *objects* that come out of the ground than we do to the real knowledge that comes from careful stratigraphic excavation—"

"Yes, yes, Tiffany, I know, but time had to be found somewhere. Forrest is in complete accord with the decision, and I really don't see what I can be expected to do about it."

Apparently, neither did she. She made a disgusted motion with her hand and folded her arms. "The hell with it," she muttered and subsided, defeated.

Dr. Haddon cleared his throat. "Now, if no one has further objections, I should like to discuss a few related matters to make sure there is no misunderstanding." He paused. "*Are* there any objections?"

Jerry Baroff dipped his chin and passed the back of his hand over his mouth to hide a yawn. Tiffany stared morosely at the floor, no doubt framing the rebuttals and counterstatements she wished she'd made. Arlo Gerber, turtlelike and opaque, offered a convincing impression of a man giving his attention to some unpleasant digestive happening. Whether from malice or constitutional deficiency, Dr. Haddon's audience appeared to have sunk into impenetrability.

Abruptly, Dr. Haddon suffered one of his increasingly frequent sinkings of the heart. The thought of ending his long career—he who had worked alongside Aldred and James—with this sorry crew as his companions in the pursuit of knowledge weighed heavily on his aging shoulders. Just look at them. What was going on in those closed and brutish minds?

Was anything?

Chapter Three

How did people like Clifford Haddon get that way, Arlo Gerber asked himself as Haddon prattled away. So full of themselves, so in love with their own voices, so certain that any remark that came to their lips would fall on ears eager to catch every shimmering phrase. Haddon didn't converse, he delivered speeches, self-indulgent and meandering, thickly interlarded with previously worked-out gems of wit. Comments and questions were brushed aside as so many bothersome obstructions to the grand narrative flow.

Had he really worked under this man for five years now? It seemed impossible; five years of thankless production, five years of Haddon's endless strutting and petty despotizing. On the other hand, it had also been five years of evenings blessedly his own, five years during which his interest in Eighteenth Dynasty jewelry, avocational to begin with, had blossomed so joyously and unexpectedly. First there had been a brief, diffident note on his observations that had been published in the *Journal of Egyptian Archaeology*, then two papers as his confidence increased, and finally a contract with the University of Wisconsin Press to produce a comprehensive monograph, complete with his own color photographs.

That glorious day had come two years ago, and by now *Personal Ornamentation from the Time of Akhenaten* was well on the way to completion, the photographs almost completed, the text more than half-done. With luck and perseverance, another year would do it. He had no doubt that it would be the making of his career, that it would get him out of this parched and backward country, out from under Haddon, and into a respectable academic post in the United States. Someplace civilized, with soft, moist summers and a little snow in the winter; someplace with clouds. Virginia or Maryland sounded nice.

But how unfortunate this news of a schedule change was. Arlo had been hearing rumors about some jewelry of interest in the storage cabinets at the el-Amarna Museum, and he had hoped to use the visit as a way of examining it for himself, but now—

"—for which I am relying on you, Arlo," Haddon said out of the blue.

Arlo straightened up, scrambling for something to say. For all Haddon's shabby faults, the older man still had the ability to tie his tongue in knots.

"I beg your pardon . . . I wasn't . . ."

Haddon spoke with exaggerated patience. "I am relying on you, Arlo, to see to it that Forrest Freeman's video production does not result in a distorted, typically sensationalized program in which Horizon House's genuine accomplishments are trivialized or oversimplified to suit the television mentality. As a trained photographer yourself, you are in a position to work closely with them in the day-by-day editing—"

"But I don't know anything about making a documentary. I don't know anything about video. It's a completely different field, as different as . . . as—"

"Nevertheless, I'm depending on you. We're all depending on you, Arlo."

"But—but even if I *did* know something about it, how in the world could I tell them what to do? I don't have any authority—"

"Authority?" Haddon snatched the word out of the air as a frog might snatch a bug. "By which you mean the power to elicit compliance?"

"Well . . ."

"Well, now, Arlo," Haddon said, and the pedantic,

glossily genial overtones were unmistakable. A set piece was on the way. "It seems to me," he said, crossing his legs more comfortably, "that there are essentially four types of authority . . ."

Arlo slumped bleakly in his chair.

". . . four types of authority. First there is the authority of *com*-pe-tence, in which one's power to influence others derives from one's knowledge and abilities. Second, there is the authority of *con*-fi-dence, achieved only when one has won the trust and reliance of one's associates. Third, there is the authority of *char*-ac-ter, built on the strength of one's personal integrity. And fourth—" Haddon's lip curled, his voice dropped dismissively. "—there is the authority of *po*-*si*-tion, which has nothing to do with achievement or expertise, but derives solely from the perquisites of title and office, and evokes—at best—mere com-*pli*-ance. Ahem."

What an absolute schmuck Haddon was, Jerry Baroff thought; not rancorously, but with something close to admiration. It was amazing, the old guy just never let you down. Every time you thought he might actually be going to say something different—something original, for example, or something nice about somebody else, or something responsive or even helpful—he managed to come up with another dose of the same old crap. Arlo, the poor fish, was getting Lecture Number 94, the one Haddon usually reserved for any staff member dumb enough to mention in his presence that he was having trouble getting the Egyptian antiquities authorities to go along on something or other.

And the old bugger was in prime form, especially considering that he was drunk as a skunk, or pretty well on the way. Only the windup remained now, the part where he leaned forward keenly and said: "Now tell me, young man, just which type of authority do *you* lack?"

Haddon leaned keenly forward, eyeing the cringing Arlo. "Now suppose you tell me," he said with quivering beard, "just which kind of authority do *you* lack?"

For a man who prided himself on observing the vagaries of others with tolerance and detachment, on not letting people get under his skin, Jerry was ready to admit that he'd met his match in Clifford Haddon. Usually Haddon, who didn't even pretend to take any interest in Jerry's domain of library and collection administration, let him go his way in peace, but in the past few days he'd seen more of the director than in most months, and he was beginning to get a glimmer of why Tiffany, who had to deal with him every day, needed a neck massage about three nights a week and got that look on her face when his name came up. Still, if you looked at it right, you had to admit the guy was funny. Sometimes you just had to laugh out loud. Which, not intending to, he did.

Haddon turned to look sourly at him. "Something amuses you?"

Jerry raised his hands apologetically, one of them holding the pipe. "Sorry, Dr. Haddon, no offense. Something just struck me funny." He shrugged amiably, grinned at Haddon, and stuck the pipe back in his mouth.

Dr. Haddon's retort was interrupted by the appearance in the arched doorway of a wiry, dark-skinned man in turban and long, loose dirt-stained *galabiya*, who appeared to be in a state of mild, pleasurable excitement. This was in itself an extraordinary occurrence. It was one of Dr. Haddon's rules that outside workers were not to enter the living quarters.

"What the devil—" he began.

"Moomy," the man announced, and was silent.

"Moomy," Dr. Haddon echoed after a moment. "What the devil is moomy?"

"Moomy," the man said again. "In back."

Dr. Haddon had no choice but to ask for help from Tiffany, the only one among them who knew more Arabic than was required to issue an instruction or hold a rudimentary conversation. She asked a brief question. The man replied volubly.

"He says he found a mummy while he was cleaning up," Tiffany explained.

"A *mummy*?" Dr. Haddon exclaimed incredulously. "Here on the grounds? Impossible."

Tiffany asked several more questions and received lengthy answers. "Apparently what he's found is a skeleton, or at least some bones. He thinks they're human."

Dr. Haddon waved the idea away. "Absurd. Where?"

"In the old storage area behind the laundry."

"The—what in heavens was he doing in there?" Dr. Haddon glowered at the man. "You! What were you doing in there?"

The man grinned and nodded. "Moomy, yes. No problem."

"He said they were following your instructions, cleaning everything up for the moving pictures," Tiffany said.

"Yes, of course, but I didn't mean the old storage area, for God's sake. Does he think they want to—oh, what difference does it make?" Haddon rubbed wearily at his eyes. "Go and see what he's talking about, Tiffany. Nobody's been back there for ages. It's probably what's left of some dog that got in."

As Tiffany left with the Egyptian, Dr. Haddon turned to the others. "I'll keep you from your beds for only a few minutes more," he said, yawning. "Now, what was I saying—"

TJ escaped into the night with a sense of having made it just in time. Another thirty seconds of Clifford Haddon's arch and simpering posturing, his petty meanness and insincerity, and she would have burst. *Tell me, just what kind of authority do you lack? . . . Believe me, my dear, I'm more distressed about this than you are . . .* Aaaargh.

She realized she was overbreathing—Haddon did that to her—and made herself take a deep breath and slacken her stride. "Slow down, Ragheb," she said.

The Egyptian, who was leading the way over the dark, curving, hibiscus-scented paths with his powerful flashlight, obeyed.

Damn Haddon, he had gotten to her again. She was still fuming. It wasn't simply because of the schedule change—although that would have been enough—but because of his uncanny ability to set her off just by being himself. She was not an emotional person. She hated emotional people, and she hated herself when she blew up, the way she had back there. What had been the point? How many times had they been over the same ground, and where was it ever going to get them? But Clifford Haddon, like no other person she had ever known, could turn her into a ranting screamer just by opening his mouth. It was amazing, really. Sometimes, especially when he'd been at his Scotch, he could set her teeth on edge just by walking into a room. Those smarmy, prissy speeches, that horrible little pharaoh's tuft of beard, that narrow-minded, self-righteous . . .

And why was it only her? That was what was so frustrating, that nobody else ever blew their stack. Haddon hadn't aced only her out of the picture, after all; he had cut the time that Jerry would have to show the library as well, and what had Jerry's reaction been?

Duh, sure, chief, what else?

No, that wasn't fair. Jerry wasn't dumb, she knew that, he honestly didn't give a damn. He was probably glad of the change. Leaving him out of it altogether probably would have made him happiest of all. It was too bad she couldn't be more like her easygoing, take-things-in-his-stride husband when it came to dealing with their despicable boss, she thought, not quite meaning it. But thank God he was always there to provide TLC and propping-up after one of her sessions with Haddon. She'd probably need some tonight.

A few steps ahead of her, Ragheb stopped at the warped and leaning metal gate of an unroofed, stucco-walled enclosure jutting out from the rear of the laundry building. Her eyes had gotten used to the darkness now. Even without the flashlight she could see the welter of junk through the open gate: corroded bed frames, a toilet bowl broken in two, knotted tangles of filthy, moldering clothing, some rust-cankered, mysterious engine parts reputed to be from a 1925 motorcycle.

Ragheb waited for her to precede him. He spoke English. "Moomy in here, madam," he said politely.

Unexpectedly, she caught herself hesitating. Out here, at the furthest perimeter of the Horizon compound and of the city itself, shielded by the bulk of the buildings, the familiar traffic sounds from the Corniche were muted and distant. The civilized aroma of bougainvillea and hibiscus from the well-planted grounds was faint, the ashy, primeval smell of the vast, unseen Eastern Desert strong and mysterious. Even the familiar, friendly Ragheb was suddenly exotic and inscrutable. A rare, chill breeze from the desert eddied about her, raising the tiny hairs on the back of her neck.

"Well, then," she said, and her own too-loud voice made her start. "Let's just see what we have." Firmly, she led the way into the enclosure.

Thirty seconds later, grim-faced, she told Ragheb to go back and get Haddon.

Chapter Four

They came scurrying in a line behind the director, who had commandeered Ragheb's flashlight and made for the storage area double-time, his bearded chin well out ahead of his feet, a man who intended to set things straight, by God.

But when he reached the enclosure, he lost impetus. Standing at the entrance, swaying a little, he flashed the light from mound to mound of junk. "Well then, where is it? Don't keep us in suspense."

TJ used her own penlight to direct his larger beam to the sandy ground near a rough, oil-stained workbench built into one of the corners. There, next to two rusted five-gallon cans of congealed roofing tar, one of them on its side, a stained, dun-colored, unevenly globular object gleamed dully in the artificial light.

Jerry was the first to speak. "A skull. I guess there isn't much doubt about its being human."

"There's more than the skull," TJ said. She bounced her thin line of light to other objects scattered in an eight- or nine-foot radius over the junk-littered ground: a snarled, grisly clump consisting of a scapula and humerus held together by a few tattered shreds of ligament, the entire mess caught up in a twisted, filthy *galabiya*; a thigh bone with the ends gnawed away; a sacrum and an innominate bone, also held together by a few threads of fiber. A few feet from the skull was what appeared to be a turban, collapsed and filthy. Near the sacrum was a cracked, curled sandal.

"An Arab," Jerry said. "The jackals must have been at him. There's still some dried flesh left, but not much."

Arlo shivered. "I wonder how long he's . . . it's been here."

"Who knows?" Jerry said. He leaned over, peering at the femur, hands on his knees. "Ten years, twenty years . . ."

"Impossible," Haddon said curtly. "This area was in regular use until—when was it?"

"Until the big rains five years ago, so they've been here less than that," TJ said. "Five years at most. And I doubt if the jackals can get into the compound. Dogs, more likely, or those monster rats."

Arlo's face, pasty at the best of times, was distinctly greenish in the light from the flashlights. He looked away as Haddon shone his light directly onto the skull.

"Who is it?" the director demanded, sounding thoroughly aggrieved. "How did he get in? What the devil was he doing in here?"

No one answered. "Nobody'd better touch anything," Jerry said.

Haddon's lips turned down. "Perish the thought."

"And I think we'd better notify the police."

"The *police*?" Haddon turned on him. "Good God, Jerry, have you ever dealt with the Egyptian police? Why would we want to drag them into this? This—this person has been dead for years and no one's missed him yet, have they? I think it's clear enough what happened. The poor beggar got in here somehow, hoping to find something worth stealing in the collection and had the misfortune to die *in flagrante delicto*. Claimed by the Grim Reaper in the very act of plunder."

His light darted erratically through the jumble of discarded objects. "Ha, see that piece right there? He must have come in here—"

"Why *here*?" TJ said. She waved her own smaller beam over the mounds of debris. "What would he want in here?"

"Now how would I possibly know that? Who knows what was in the heart of a dead man? Perhaps he heard someone coming and ran in here to hide. Perhaps he was hiding until nightfall, when he could make his, er, getaway more easily. Whatever it was, he simply had the bad luck to die in the interim.''

"Of what?" TJ persisted. "Old age? Gallstones? Guilt?"

"Whatever the reason," Haddon said sweetly, "we can rest secure in the knowledge that the unfortunate gentleman is in the arms of Osiris and beyond caring what we make of him. I hardly see the need to stir things up at this late date, and particularly not *now*, with the Gustafsons here, busily putting their noses into every corner, not to mention that accursed camera crew. And don't forget the anticipated arrival of the man known to one and all as the Skeleton Detective tomorrow evening. God in heaven! No, it seems to me it would save a great deal of commotion all around if we simply disposed of his remains without bothering anybody.''

"You're kidding!" TJ exclaimed.

"With dignity, of course," Haddon added.

"We could bury him right in the compound," Arlo volunteered, earning a surprised glance from Haddon. It was not common for Arlo to address the director without having been spoken to first. "In the northeast corner, where Lambert used to bury his garbage. Nobody uses it anymore.''

"Do I understand you to be volunteering for the assignment?" Haddon asked.

"I—I only meant that I agree with you.''

"I can't begin to tell you," said Haddon, "what a source of comfort that is to me.''

Jerry, who had been going quietly through his pipe-lighting ritual, exhaled a lungful of fragrant smoke and shook out the match. "Dr. Haddon, we've got a corpse right in our backyard. We don't know who he was, we don't know how he died, and we don't know what he was doing here. The police have to be called. There's no two ways about it.''

Haddon wavered. Despite the coolness he dabbed at his forehead with a handkerchief. "I take your point, Jerry," he said with surprising mildness, "but I hardly see any hurry—''

"And don't forget, Ragheb knows all about it.''

"And if Ragheb knows, everybody knows," TJ said.

Haddon opened his mouth to reply, closed it again, and arrived at a decision he didn't like. "Yes, all right, you're probably right," he said, wearily passing a hand over his eyes. The Scotches had finally caught up with him. "We'll call them from the house." He made a frustrated little gesture with the flashlight, pointing the way for their return. They went back the way they'd come, with Haddon in the lead and Arlo bringing up the rear.

"But what a time for this to happen!" Haddon muttered bitterly as they entered the main building.

"All the more reason to take care of it right now," Jerry said sensibly. "Maybe they can wrap the whole thing up by tomorrow. By the time Oliver gets here it'll be forgotten." He found the proper page in the tiny local telephone directory, picked up the telephone, and handed them both to Haddon.

Haddon took it without enthusiasm. His face was gray. "Wrap something up by tomorrow? The Luxor police? Don't make me laugh. We'll be lucky if they *get* here by tomorrow."

He was quickly proved right. The receptionist at the police department regretted that no English-speaking official of sufficient rank to attend to this most serious matter was currently available. The morning shift would report at 8 A.M., however, and at that time a responsible investigator would be dispatched to Horizon House at once. Personnel at Horizon House were instructed to secure the grounds.

Haddon hung up with a slurred laugh. He seemed about to fall asleep. "At once. That means . . . that could mean anywhere from eight A.M. to eight P.M. Well, I don't see how it can be helped. I'm going to b- . . . to bed, and I suggest the rest of you do the same." He took a deep breath and headed for the door to the patio, off which the living quarters opened. Partway there he listed, managing to right himself with the help of the wall.

At the door he turned, steadied himself against the jamb, and fixed them with a quizzical and suspicious gaze. "I don't suppose . . . don't suppose any of *you* know anything ab- . . . about this?"

Tiffany shook her head.

Arlo shook his head.

"Who, me?" Jerry said.

Haddon nodded gravely. "Good night to all," he proclaimed, drawing himself up, "and to all a good night." A moment later they heard a clatter as he stumbled against one of the wicker chairs on the patio.

"The man's swacked again," TJ said.

"Swozzled," agreed Jerry. "One of these nights he's going to fall in the fountain and kill himself on his two A.M. rounds."

"He makes rounds?" Arlo asked. "At night? I knew he was an insomniac, but——"

"You don't see him," Jerry said. "Your window faces the other way. He prowls around till two or three in the morning, talking to himself and falling over stuff."

TJ was shaking her head. "You know, it's really not that he drinks that much. It's the interaction with the medications he's on that does it; that stuff for anxiety, or depression, or whatever he takes. I'm surprised he can see straight."

"Now what in the world does *he* have to be depressed about?" Arlo asked. "We're the ones who have to work for him."

Jerry laughed. "If you had to be Clifford Haddon, you wouldn't be depressed?"

"You certainly have a point there," Arlo said, pressing his eyes with his fingertips. "Well, I guess I'd better get to bed too."

"Not me," Jerry said, stretching. "I left Forrest and his crew over in the annex with some six-packs and pizza, and I bet they're still there. I know I could use a couple of beers."

"God knows, so could I," TJ said fervently.

"You can say that again," said Arlo after a moment's reflection.

Chapter Five

Whatever aura of mystery had hung over the storage enclosure the night before, it was not in evidence in the dusty, flat 9 A.M. sunlight of the next morning. The enclosure looked like what it was, a squalid, fifteen-square-foot pen crammed with the household and workplace castoffs of years. Most of it—the shabby, anonymous clothing, the moldy automobile cushions, the time-grayed newspapers—was peacefully disintegrating. Some—the broken toilet bowl, the warped plastic coat hangers—would be around for future generations of archaeologists to potter blissfully among.

Major Yussef Saleh and Sergeant Monir Gabra of the Qena Governate Police, Criminal Investigation Division, had been pottering for half an hour. They were not blissful. They had located, in addition to the bones found the night before, the other half of the pelvis, a few long bones and ribs they took to be human, and several irregular smaller pieces that they thought might be human hand or foot bones. They had found no signs of foul play and hoped they would not; sorting through the broken tools, discarded utensils, and rusty, unidentifiable pieces of metal in search of a probable blunt or pointed instrument of death was a task neither of them cared to think about.

Following proper police procedure, the bones had not been

disturbed until they had been photographed and their positions sketched and described. Then, kneeling on a cracked rubber mat that they had found among the junk, they delicately turned over the skull.

After a moment, the two men looked at each other with puzzled expressions.

"Yes?" Clifford Haddon glanced up, not pleased to be interrupted. When he saw that it was Major Saleh, his tone became more cordial. "Ah, yes, Major, may I help you?"

"Will you come with us, please?"

Haddon stiffened. Spots of deeper color popped out on his pink throat. "Come with you—where?"

"To the storage enclosure," Saleh said. "I would like to ask you about something if you can spare a few minutes."

"The—" The spots disappeared. "Oh, yes, certainly. Of course, Major." He stood up and looked at TJ. "Will you come too, please, Dr. Baroff?"

"Certainly, Dr. Haddon," TJ said, formality for formality. The object, she supposed, was to impress the Egyptian police with the businesslike decorum of Horizon House. Well, what they didn't know wouldn't hurt them.

She closed the budget file on which she had been briefing him so that he could continue to delude the visiting Gustafsons into thinking that he had his finger on the pulse of Horizon House's operations, and rose to join them. She knew perfectly well why Haddon had asked her to come along. He was afraid the officers might ask him something he didn't know the answer to—which covered one hell of a lot of ground—and he wanted TJ, who took her administrative role as assistant director seriously, at his side to bail him out.

Well, fine. Anything was better than sitting alone in a room with him, trying to explain item after item, none of which he knew anything about, but on all of which he was maddeningly ready to lecture her at mind-numbing length.

"You've found something, then?" Haddon asked the major as the four of them followed the network of flower-bordered gravel pathways to the storage enclosure.

But Major Saleh wasn't there to answer questions. "This area, it has not been used in how long?"

"Five years," Haddon said. "That's correct, isn't it, Dr. Baroff?"

"Right, everything in it was ruined in those colossal rains."

Saleh nodded his remembrance. With Upper Egypt averaging a fraction of an inch of rain a year, no one who lived there would be likely to forget the eighteen-hour deluge that had dropped more rain in a single day than most of them would see for the rest of their lives.

"So we built a new, roofed storage area onto the garage," TJ went on, "and haven't used the old one since. Well, for a while it was a sort of dump for things, but not anymore."

"You know," Haddon said, "we really should clean the place out and knock it down. It's disgusting. Breeding area for rats and all sorts of disagreeable things. I had no idea."

TJ gritted her teeth and glared at him. How many times had she told that to Haddon in the last five years? Ten? Twenty?

"Dr. Haddon—" she began, but clamped her mouth shut. Not in front of strangers. Not in front of anybody. She had borne him all these years without ever once becoming really, thoroughly unglued, and she could make it through to the following September. In less than a year he would be retired, with any luck at all they would appoint her director, and it would be a bright new world.

Of course she'd be a nut case by then, but nobody but she was going to know it.

Once in the enclosure, the policemen led them to the skull, which had been turned from its upside-down position onto its right side. "Please examine it for yourself," Saleh said. He stood aside to give them room.

The two Egyptologists looked at the skull, TJ on one knee, Haddon leaning over from the waist. The policemen stood quietly, obviously waiting for a response.

"What are we supposed to be looking for?" TJ asked.

But Haddon was quicker than she was. He pointed indignantly at the skull. "What's this?"

With her eyes she followed the direction of his finger. There on the left side of the frontal bone, a line of letters in faded black ink barely showed against the brownish ivory of the bone. No, not letters, numbers. She leaned closer.

"F4360," she murmured. "I'll be damned."

"What does this mean?" Haddon demanded, addressing the major. "Who wrote this?"

"Yes, this needs knowing," Saleh agreed.

"It's one of ours," TJ said and sat back on her heels, barely able to keep from laughing. "The damn thing is from our own collection."

The two officers exchanged a look.

Haddon stood up angrily, brushing off his knees although he had never been on them. "Do you mean to say the cursed thing is an archaeological specimen—one of *our* archaeological specimens?"

"F4360 is Fuqani 4360," TJ told Saleh. "It's from el-Fuqani, the Old Kingdom cemetery that was dug up in the 1920s." And now she did laugh. "You've got yourself a tough nut to crack, Major. Give or take a few years, he's been dead since 2400 B.C."

Saleh's smile was perfunctory and reserved. He was large for an Egyptian, with a smooth, impassive face and a knack for making you feel that you were keeping him from *really* important duties.

And we are, TJ thought. There had been another "incident of unrest" yesterday, this time not far from Karnak, in which fundamentalist crackpots had shot at a tour bus. An Australian woman had been wounded.

Haddon was fuming. "If he's been dead for over four thousand years, perhaps someone would explain to me how he came to be wearing modern dress." He pointed to the shoulder and arm bones protruding from a snarl of twisted *galabiya*; the cloth was clearly from the present day, a cheap, everyday material patterned with gray stripes, more filthy than rotted.

"Ah, but he wasn't," Saleh said. "These bones were not *inside* the garment, they were merely caught up in the cloth. These remains have been gnawed on by small animals, and dragged here and there across the ground. Is it surprising they became trapped in the cloth? Show them the numbers, Gabra."

The sergeant, some ten years older than his superior, squat-ted at the tangle of bones and cloth and gently turned the bones over. In the same faded ink, in the same precise, spidery, old-fashioned hand, F4360 had been written on the humerus and on the back of the scapula.

"It's on all the bones?" Haddon asked.

"Yes, sir, all bones with big sizes," said Gabra. "I think this lady's conclusion must be so. See how brown and dry are the bones? From olden times, assuredly." His English was less orthodox than the major's, but livelier.

Haddon turned grimly to TJ. "I think we'd better see what your husband has to say about this."

TJ nodded, but she didn't hold out any hope that Jerry would be able to shed much light on things. They had both come to Horizon House seven years earlier, hired as a team; TJ as a staff archaeologist and Jerry as administrator of the extensive library. It had taken four months before he'd hap-pened to notice that his official title was librarian/registrar, and when he'd asked Haddon what that meant, he'd learned that he was also in charge of the old collection of artifacts and skeletal remains—at least to the extent that anyone was in charge. In reality, neither Haddon nor anyone else (including Jerry) gave much of a damn about it.

Even TJ didn't. The fact was, it wasn't much of a collec-tion. Ninety percent of it had been excavated in the 1920s by the famous—to some, the infamous—Cordell Lambert. Those had been the days when most Egyptologists were still glorified grave-robbers, and Lambert, an Arizona copper magnate turned ardent archaeologist in his fifties, was even less well-trained than most. Objects had been torn out of the ground with no concern for stratigraphy or relationships. The few really extraordinary pieces had found their way into mu-seums and private collections outside of the country; the best of the rest had been commandeered by the Egyptian govern-ment; and whatever was left had been exhibited in Lambert's "museum" for a few years and then gone into storage to be forgotten.

The el-Fuqani skeletal collection was squarely in the last category. Crudely dug up and primitively processed, it had been placed in storage in 1927 and lain there ever since, exciting no interest, scholarly or otherwise. Why anyone would take the trouble to remove one of them and toss it into the junk pile was anybody's guess.

They found Jerry in his office off the library reading room. When he was told that the mysterious remains were apparently those of a Bronze Age man from the time of Userkaf, first pharaoh of the Fifth Dynasty, he too burst out laughing, which didn't appear to improve Saleh's mood any, or Haddon's either. But a discreet gleam of amusement appeared to play about Sergeant Gabra's dark eyes.

"And how did they get there?" the director asked crossly.

Jerry shook his head blankly. "Don't ask me."

"Perhaps we could now go and see where this collection is kept?" Saleh said, civil but manifestly impatient.

"Sure," Jerry said, "you bet, good idea." He unfolded his skinny frame from behind the desk. "Right this way."

He took them across a path to the modest but roomy structure known as the annex. It had been constructed by Lambert as his museum, but it had been decades since it had served as anything but a workspace and a repository for bones and artifacts.

As they entered Jerry grasped TJ's wrist and spoke in a whisper. "Where is this stuff, exactly?"

She laughed. "Are you serious? You don't know where the el-Fuqani material is? You're supposed to be the registrar."

"Listen, I'm lucky I know *what* it is."

"Back of the storeroom off Workroom A," she told him.

As they crossed the workroom with its pottery fragments in open trays and its containers of glue and preservatives, Saleh sniffed the air appraisingly. "I smell . . . what is it?"

Gabra knit his brow. "Pizza?"

"Must be the glue," Jerry said, straight-faced. He led them confidently through the storeroom to a floor-to-ceiling set of open metal racks on the end of which was taped a flyblown, typewritten placard: "El-Fuqani, 1921–23, C. Lambert." The three-shelf racks were loaded with heavy cardboard boxes stacked two high. Jerry moved down the racks, forefinger extended, scanning the numbers on the front of the boxes. A few stacks in, he stopped.

"Here we go, 4360."

He pulled out the box, set it on an empty rack, and, with a flourish, swept off the lid.

Except for a crumbly accumulation of bone dust, it was empty.

"So," Saleh said with his cool smile, "the mystery is solved. Nothing very serious, it seems."

Haddon's bearded jaw had stiffened. "I consider it quite serious enough," he said, looking directly at Jerry. "These specimens are housed here on the assumption that they be given proper care and protection. They have received that protection for some seventy years, but now it seems that some rather slipshod practices have been allowed to take hold."

"I'll look into the matter, sir," Jerry said with that serenity that sometimes infuriated TJ, sometimes filled her with admiration, and never stopped amazing her. Even after living with him for twelve years. How did he do it? And he wasn't even nursing an ulcer from suppressed emotions; he just didn't give a damn. In his place, she thought, flames would be shooting out of her nose.

"I think we'd better look into it right now," Haddon snapped, "while we still have the services of these good gentlemen."

"I don't know what—"

"How many more of our specimens have been made off with? Are *any* of them still in their boxes?"

The same question had occurred to TJ, but she had hoped to examine the rest of the collection with Jerry later on, without anybody—especially and above all others, Clifford Haddon—watching balefully over their shoulders, waiting to pounce.

"Well, let's just see," Jerry said amiably, and took the lid from 4370, the box that had been beneath 4360. It was full of old brown bones. So was 4340, 4350, and 4370. So were the other fifty-two boxes. Everything was as it should have been; only 4360 was not peacefully resting where it was supposed to be.

Gabra, who had opened cartons with the others—Saleh had stood watching, glancing occasionally at his watch—rubbed dust from his hands. "Very good. Merely an error of some untrue sort."

"Gentlemen," Haddon said ardently, "you have my sincere apologies for wasting so much of your time."

"I assure you, it was no trouble," Saleh said formally. "I am only happy that it was not a more serious matter requiring continued police attention."

"No, no, I take full responsibility for the actions and oversights of my staff."

TJ silently ground her teeth again. What an unfailingly petty sonofabitch the man was. In his spiteful, self-centered way he managed to see all this as some kind of personal loss of face, which meant, from his point of view, that somebody—anybody but him—had to be blamed.

"Please, please," said Gabra, who seemed like a nice guy. "It was a most interesting morning with no apologies being necessary."

This elicited a few curt, unintelligible syllables in Arabic from Saleh, and a moment later the policemen had gone, leaving Haddon, Jerry, and TJ staring at one another over the empty box.

"I hope you understand," Haddon said, "how deeply displeased I am, and that I am forced to consider the two of you responsible for the lapse in proper procedure that allowed this ludicrous incident to take place. As the major said, we're fortunate it wasn't more serious. This entire collection might well have been walked off with."

"Dr. Haddon, let's look at this reasonably for a minute," TJ said. She didn't feel like being reasonable, she felt like bashing him with the Seventeenth Dynasty stone jug on the rack behind him. Seven years she'd been there, and never once until now had she heard him express the slightest interest in the skeletal collection. If he'd ever been in this room before, it was news to her. So why all this goddamn fuss now? He was blowing a trivial, silly incident all out of proportion. It was odd, yes, but hardly earth-shattering.

"Only one set of bones was missing," she said calmly, doing her best to emulate Jerry. "Whoever threw it out, and whatever reason he did it, we now have it back. In very short order, 4360 will be back in his snug little box again, as good as new."

"Except for a gnawed bone here and there, and whatever

was carried off by the rats," Haddon said, "but what's that among friends?"

TJ eked out a smile. "Well, actually, I think the rats got to him back in the Fifth Dynasty. They usually don't find 4,400-year-old bones very appetizing."

"I don't find any of this very appetizing."

"Sir," Jerry put in, "you can rest assured that nothing like this will ever happen again. I'll go over the security arrangements with a fine-tooth comb—"

What security arrangements would those be, TJ wondered.

"—and make whatever changes are necessary. I'll clear them with you first."

"Do," Haddon said aridly, and to TJ: "Shall we return to the scene of the crime, Doctor?"

"Sure," said TJ, but wasn't this the scene of the crime?

Haddon picked up a femur and rubbed the dirt off with the heel of his hand. "Forty-three sixty," he read aloud, shaking his head. "Do you have any idea what a laughingstock we'll be if this gets out?"

TJ studied her toes.

Haddon dropped the bone back in the dust and wiped his hands on a handkerchief. "First," he said, "I want this area scoured for every bit of bone that can be found. *You* do it; your husband wouldn't know a metacarpal from a marshmallow. Then I want them cleaned and put back where they belong. And then I want this horrible enclosure torn down and its contents thrown away. I want it done immediately, is that understood? Have Mrs. Ebeid see to it."

"Getting the garbage people to come out anytime soon is going to be a problem," TJ said. "They're—"

"Bury it, then. Dig a hole, shovel it in, and cover it over. Use the whatever-it's-called."

"Backhoe," said TJ. "There's a lot of stuff in here. It'd have to be a pretty big hole."

"Well, put it—where was it Arlo suggested?—in the northeast corner, where Lambert's people used to bury their trash. That's appropriate enough; some of this rubbish has been around at least since then." He kicked disgustedly at an old-fashioned kerosene space heater, dented and rusty, and gestured with both arms. "What a pigsty. We should have had it cleaned out—" He stopped, frowning and uncertain, his eyes focused on something in his mind. "Wait a minute. Wasn't there . . ."

He turned to look at a corner of the enclosure, against which an old bed frame was propped. He pointed at the base of the bed frame. "There was a head there."

"No, sir," TJ said after a second, "the skull was over here, by the—"

"Not a skull, a head."

"A—head?"

"The head of a statue," he said irritably. "A statuette. What the devil did you think I meant?" He prowled around the enclosure, edging around bones and junk, his eyes searching the ground. "Yellow jasper, or possibly quartzite—about half-life-size, I think. It's not here." He peered at her. "You didn't see it?"

"No, sir," she said respectfully.

"Don't take that tone with me, young woman. I was neither overtired nor intoxicated." But he seemed uncharacteristically indecisive on this point himself. He chewed at his lower lip. "Of course it was dark, and there was a great deal of excitement, what with Arlo hopping about, and the light flashing everywhere. It's possible that I may have been . . . didn't I point it out?"

TJ shook her head. "I don't think so."

"I didn't?" He grew more unsure still. "That's odd, I'm sure I remember . . ." He poked randomly at piles of trash with his foot. "Well, it's not here now, at any rate."

"No, it doesn't seem to be," TJ said.

"Could someone have taken it?"

"Taken it?" TJ said. "You mean, *taken* it? Between then and now?"

"I mean—never mind." He continued to worry his lip. "Now that I think of it, I suppose it could have been an illusion caused by the flashlight beams. All those moving shadows . . ."

"I can ask the others if they saw it."

"Yes, do. No, don't. We'll keep this between ourselves. I shouldn't want anyone to think . . ." He cleared his throat and drew himself up, recovering some of his firmness. "And need I point out that nothing about this outlandish affair need be repeated to our visitors? There is no reason in the world for Bruno Gustafson or anyone else connected with the foundation to know anything about—"

"Um," said Tiffany. She was trying to decide how—or whether—to break it to Haddon that Bruno already knew about the finding of the skeleton. He and Bea had provided the pizza and joined in its eating the previous night, and the discovery in the enclosure had naturally become the main topic of conversation once she, Arlo, and Jerry had arrived.

"Um," she said again. "There's a slight problem—"

"Hi!" Bruno himself said brightly, appearing magically at the entry to the enclosure. "What's going on in here?"

Haddon blinked and walked toward him, blocking his view. "Why, good morning, my dear Mr. Gustafson. I understood that you were flying to Abu Simbel today."

"Nope, just Bea. I've been there before and it's just—Hey, looka here—TJ, is that the skull you were talking about?"

Haddon glowered murderously at her.

TJ cleared her throat. "Uh, well, actually, Mr. Gustafson, it's, uh—"

Haddon flung up his hands. "Never mind!" he shouted skyward. "We at Horizon House have no secrets. We are an open book. Tell all, tell all!" And he stamped off, his tuft of beard stiffly leading the way.

A momentarily crestfallen Bruno watched him go. "What did I say?"

TJ smiled. "Nothing, he's been under a little strain, that's all. It's nothing personal."

"Glad to hear it. Hope he's okay." He looked happily down at the skull. "So tell me, what's the story?"

"It's a long one, Mr. Gustafson," TJ said.

Chapter Six

Gideon was not at his most scintillating. He was, in fact, having trouble keeping awake. It had been a long couple of days.

He and Julie had left Port Angeles before dawn the previous morning, starting with a three-hour trip by car and ferry to the airport. Then a long wait at SeaTac, followed by sixteen grubby hours and ten increasingly debilitating time-zone changes to Cairo International Airport. This was followed by a hair-whitening forty-five-minute taxi ride into the city to clear up a problem with their visas, and then back to the airport by means of a taxi journey that was marginally less bloodcurdling than the first one (or were they already getting used to it?). They'd missed their flight to Luxor and had had to wait for two hours in the grungy, noisy airport, fidgety and disoriented, until the next one left.

They had arrived at Horizon House in time for a shower, a dazed tour of the facility and a round of introductions, followed by cocktails that they hardly needed but accepted anyway, and a heavy "roast beef" dinner that Gideon was fairly certain had been water buffalo, not that his taste buds were at their most discriminating.

Afterward, as he did most evenings, Haddon had invited a few people to his study for after-dinner drinks and a little anthropological chitchat. Julie had wisely declined, going off to bed instead, but Gideon had accepted for courtesy's sake. Grainy-eyed and dopey, he was doing his best to participate, but it was a losing battle. And the subject matter wasn't helping things. Since halfway through dinner they had been mired in a lexicological discussion, or rather a lexicological lecture by Clifford Haddon, on the vagaries of Middle Egyptian script.

But then Clifford Haddon was famously more at home in the remote past than in the present. Gideon had never met him before, but had heard it said of him that while teaching in the classics department at Yale in the 1950s, he would stand at the blackboard drawing wonderfully detailed street maps of ancient Alexandria, or Herculaneum, or fifth-century Athens ("This was where Socrates lived, this would have been the house of Alcibiades . . .") but would have to rely on the kindness of colleagues to drive him to and from campus because he could never get the hang of downtown New Haven. In the same way, he knew most of the many versions and derivatives of hieroglyphic script, along with ancient Greek, Latin, Sumerian, and Coptic—but, even after eighteen years in Egypt, had never bothered learning more than a few catchphrases of modern Arabic.

Gideon had found the stories amusing, but the man in the flesh considerably less so. And Middle Egyptian was heavy going, particularly on thirty hours without sleep.

"And so, despite the predilections of contemporary scholarship," Haddon was saying, brandy in hand, his slight body at ease in the old leather chair, "I continue to adhere to my original view that the splitting of the determined infinitive in Middle Egyptian was far more widespread than is commonly understood, even today." He had been in full pedantic flight for some time.

"Fascinating," Gideon said, not above borrowing a leaf from Rupert LeMoyne's book in a time of need.

Still, he had to admit that there was a certain fusty charm to Haddon's speech, a Victorian cast that went well with their surroundings. They were in Haddon's two-story study, a big, headmasterish room straight out of *Goodbye, Mr. Chips* and dating back to the days of Cordell Lambert, the first director of what was then known as the American Institute of Egyptian Studies. Along one wall was a dark sideboard with cut-crystal flasks and glasses from which Haddon had offered port and cognac (no takers except Haddon himself and Bruno Gustafson). Next to it was a black iron staircase that spiraled up to the narrow, railed mezzanine that gave access to the room's chief glory, the Lambert Egyptological Library, housed in section after section of finely made, glass-fronted cabinetry.

In the main part of the room, on a threadbare rug over a red tile floor, were a chunky Victorian two-seater and two worn, deeply buttoned, burgundy leather armchairs arranged to face a formidable, homely old desk with scalloped edges and a glass plate on top.

In books on the history of Egyptology there was usually an old photograph of a stiffly posed Cordell Lambert, chin in hand, sitting at this very desk, in this very room—only the walls were different; flowered wallpaper instead of today's off-white paint—and it was behind the same desk that the current director, Clifford Haddon, now sat so comfortably. Gideon was in one of the armchairs, Bruno Gustafson was in the other (Bea had gone off to bed), and, side by side on the uncomfortable-looking two-seater were Tiffany Jane ("Call me TJ. Or else.") Baroff, Horizon's assistant director and supervisor of field activities, and Arlo Gerber, the head of epigraphy.

TJ Baroff was an outspoken, strapping woman in her mid-thirties, leggy and casual. When they'd arrived she'd been wearing wrinkled tan shorts, an oversized man's work shirt, and dirty Converses. Now, in a clean T-shirt and wraparound skirt, barelegged and sandaled, she still looked like what she was: a field archaeologist at her happiest grubbing in the dirt for a crumbling fragment of a clay cooking pot. Her roughly pulled-back hair was sun-streaked, her arms and legs chapped and sunburnt, her knees scuffed.

Gideon had liked her right off. During dinner she had helped keep his chin from settling into his soup with a hearty denunciation of the fossilized, old-style Egyptologists—if she included Haddon she didn't say so—who had ruled Egyptology for so long and were more like dilettantish linguists and classicists than real anthropologists, more interested in quibbling over verb-form distinctions and royal family trees than in using the techniques of modern archaeology to reconstruct the lives and institutions of the ancient Egyptian people. Not her; she'd ten times rather discover a peasant's hut full of everyday tools and utensils that said something about real, daily life than be the one to find the legendary sun temple of Nefertiti.

Gideon felt the same way and said so.

Arlo Gerber, who had sat next to Gideon at dinner, was another sort, a defeated, indoorsy kind of man with an ashy pallor that was common enough in Seattle, but must have been no mean trick to maintain living year-round in Luxor. In his early forties, he could hardly be called a fossil yet, but it wasn't going to take long. Hunched, narrow-shouldered, and restrained—well, stuffy—with graying temples and a sorry little cat's-whiskers mustache, Arlo was a classically trained Egyptologist whose job it was to supervise the intricate, exacting process of Horizon's epigraphic unit. There, weathered and broken stone texts and scenes were reconstructed, interpreted, and recorded through a complex technique involving photography, line drawings, blueprints, and—above all—the scholarship of men like Arlo.

To be honest, five years of it was enough, he had told Gideon. But what he *was* excited about, and he knew Gideon would be interested in this, was the book he was working on, *Personal Ornamentation from the Time of Akhenaten*. Saying the title did for him what saying "Shazam" did for Billy Batson. Behind that modest brow, mental muscles of steel had suddenly flexed and rippled. His pale eyes had gleamed. He had pulled his chair a few inches closer to Gideon's, the better to talk about it. Wasn't it extraordinary how little had been done on Amarna Period jewelry? There was some material in Aldred, of course, but that was about it as far as anything of breadth and substance went. Wasn't it high time that this sad situation was rectified?

Gideon, working hard to keep his chin out of the mashed potatoes, had said that it certainly was.

That had been an hour ago. Now he glanced up at the

pendulum clock on the wall. Nine-forty. They'd been in Haddon's study only fifteen minutes. He would give it another twenty to be polite, and then call it quits. Any more than that and they'd have to carry him to his room.

Haddon was sipping brandy and staring at the ceiling, apparently gathering further thoughts on the determined infinitive in Middle Egyptian.

"Any promising fieldwork going on these days, TJ?" Gideon asked, in hopes of heading him off.

TJ came out of her own reverie. "What? Well, yes, as a matter of fact. We're in our fifth season of a dig right across the river, in the Western Valley. It's a workers' community—something like Deir el-Medinah, but not as big. Lambert originally excavated most of it in the 1920s, but in those days they didn't have the techniques to do the kind of job we can do today, and we're doing it right this time. We're learning a lot about New Kingdom daily life—ordinary people, I mean, not the royal court."

"It sounds interesting," Gideon said. "Maybe I could get out to see it sometime this week?"

TJ's teeth flashed. "Sure! Just tell me when—"

"You know," Haddon said airily, his eyes still on the ceiling, his hands clasped behind his neck, "I was just thinking: these questions pertaining to the split infinitive bring naturally to mind the controversy over the supposed use of the independent pronoun to express a relation of possession. In that matter, I must respectfully take issue with Gardiner's views. I believe I can do so persuasively. Ahem."

Gideon steeled himself, but the courageous Bruno took advantage of Haddon's cogitative pause to change the subject.

"Say, did you ever find out any more about those bones?" he asked the director.

Gideon perked up a little. Bones?

Haddon turned abruptly snappish. "There was nothing to find out. It's all been taken care of with no harm done."

"What do you mean, nothing to find out? What about what it was doing there?"

"Honestly, Mr. Gustafson, it was no more than—"

"Seemed to me like something for the Skeleton Detective,'' the impervious Bruno continued. He looked toward Gideon with a jocular wiggle of the eyebrows. ''The Case of the Body in the Dustbin.''

Haddon smiled thinly. ''I doubt very much if it would hold Dr. Oliver's interest.''

He was wrong, of course. Bones could always hold his interest. And compared to Middle Egyptian split infinitives, they were spellbinding. ''Actually—'' he began.

''And what about that head?'' Bruno asked. ''I heard—''

Haddon yawned delicately, tapping his mouth with his fingers. ''I do beg your pardon,'' he said. ''Obviously, it's past my bedtime. And Dr. Oliver must be positively exhausted. How thoughtless of me to keep you up. Tomorrow's another day.''

After that there wasn't much to say other than good night.

The living quarters at Horizon House—twelve bunk-bed cubicles for graduate students and seasonal staff, eleven roomier but no less Spartan rooms for permanent staff and visitors, and the director's two-room apartment—all opened off the handsome courtyard-patio with its arched portico, its fig and mango trees, and its tinkling, tiled Moorish fountain. Gideon and Julie's room was in the north wing where the accommodations for visiting VIPs were located along with two rooms for married staff. Bruno, who was a visiting VIP if there ever was one, had chosen instead to stay at the New Winter Palace Hotel (or rather Bea had; if she was going to go traipsing around the Third World, she'd declared, she was damn well going to do it first-class). He headed for the front gate of the compound, where the guard would call him a taxi, leaving Gideon, TJ, and a yawning Arlo to walk across the tiled patio to their quarters.

Jerry Baroff, whom Gideon had met at dinner, was sprawled in one of the rattan garden chairs in the dark, feet up on a low table and placidly smoking his pipe.

''Hi,'' he said, ''how'd the seminar on Middle Egyptian go?''

Gideon smiled. ''You mean the subject's always the same?''

"Uh-uh, lucky guess. Sometimes it's the Co-regency. I don't know, tonight just felt like Middle Egyptian." He pointed the bit of his pipe at them. "Verb forms, am I right?"

"Right on," TJ said, laughing. "Right up until Bruno brought up the bones, and then it was 'Good night, ladies.' "

"What was that all about?" Gideon said. "I didn't have a chance to ask."

"Good God, it'd take all night to tell," Arlo said. "You must be falling off your feet."

"Not really," he said truthfully. "I'm dragging, all right, but I'm not sleepy."

Jerry hooked a skinny ankle around another chair and pulled it toward Gideon. "Have a seat, then." He got up in loosely coordinated segments and brought another one for TJ. Arlo, who seemed torn between staying and leaving, finally sat down too, but on the edge of the chair, prepared to leave at any moment.

Gideon was happy to stay outdoors for a while longer. Their room was on the musty side, and Julie would be profoundly, unwakeably asleep anyway. Out here the night air was fragrant with flower blossoms and pipe tobacco, the breeze soft, the purling of the fountain timeless and serene. The thick stucco walls surrounding the patio softened the steady traffic noises.

TJ flopped into her chair and swung a knee over the armrest. "Okay, we've got this Fifth Dynasty skeletal collection that we keep in the museum . . ."

Ten minutes later, with occasional help from Arlo and Jerry, she'd finished.

"That's strange, all right," Gideon said. "But you know, people are always stealing stuff from skeletal collections. They make good souvenirs, I guess."

"And dumping them in the trash fifty yards away?" she asked.

"Well, that part's funny," he agreed. After a moment he said: "Was there anything special about this particular skeleton?"

TJ shrugged. "Not that I could see. I think it's a male, but that's about all I could . . . I don't suppose you'd like to take a look, would you? You could do it now. It'd only take a minute.''

Gideon smiled, more wide awake than he'd been for hours. "Let's go."

"I'll come too," Jerry said. "What do you say, Arlo?"

Arlo raised his hands. "Spare me," he said with feeling. "I've done all the looking at bones I care to for some time to come, thank you. They're all yours.''

Chapter Seven

In roughly anatomical position, under ferociously bright fluorescent lights, on a scarred, rimmed, metal table, they lay where Gideon had placed them: a skull, both femurs, both tibias, one fibula, three vertebrae, four ribs, a right scapula and humerus, and the bones of the pelvic girdle. Some, according to TJ and Jerry, had been attached when discovered, but handling since then had disarticulated them. A handful of smaller bones had been pushed to a corner of the table as being from rodents; all except a couple of metacarpals and the first phalanx of the right index finger, which were anatomically placed with the others.

These, Gideon thought, looking down at them, are my kind of bones: ancient, brown, desiccated. Archaeological, not forensic. Nothing wet, nothing smelly, nothing nasty. And from a man so remote in time that it would have been affectation to talk with sadness or solemnity about his death. But not so remote that the bones didn't form a link back to him. Gideon ran a hand down the smooth, flat surface of a tibia and thought, with a feeling that would have been hard to describe, although he'd had it often enough: I am touching a man who ate, and walked, and laughed, and made love in the Bronze Age, a thousand years before King Solomon, two thousand years and more before Julius Caesar and Jesus Christ.

"You said he's from about 2400 B.C.?" he asked.

"That's right," TJ said, "Fifth Dynasty. Four thousand, four hundred years ago."

"Four thousand, four hundred and seven, if you want to be exact," Jerry said.

TJ looked at him. "Now how in the world would you know that?"

"Because," Jerry said, "I remember you telling me when we first started here that the el-Fuqani material was 4,400 years old. And that was seven years ago. So . . ."

They all laughed. "Well," Gideon said, "then we know that 4,407 years ago, our friend here got himself done in by a nasty crack on the head." He patted a narrow, four-inch-long fracture in the right parietal, running diagonally forward and down to the coronal suture.

The others craned forward. "This little crack killed him?" Jerry asked.

"That's the way it can be with brain injuries and subdural hematomas."

"Subdural whats?"

"Hematomas. Internal effusions of blood. Leading cause of death in head injuries. Sometimes there's no visible damage to the skull at all."

"Yeah, but you can't *know* that that's what killed him, can you?" Jerry asked "I mean, other people get skull fractures and live. I had one myself when I was a kid, bigger than this, and I'm doing just fine, thanks." He scratched the corner of his mouth with his pipe. "Well, fairly well."

Gideon smiled. "Sure, but I think we can assume that yours has healed, Jerry. This guy's hasn't. That means he died before it had a chance to start mending. Which means the chances are very good that it's what killed him. Of course, it's possible that something else might have done it, so if we want to stay within the realm of certainty, all we can say is that he received a severe head injury very shortly before his death."

"Well, yeah, I guess I can accept that," Jerry said, getting out his tobacco again.

TJ gave him a brisk double-tap on the shoulder. "Good of

you, old chap. So, Gideon, aside from that, is there anything special about him?''

"Give me a minute and we'll see," Gideon said.

Using the usual criteria on the skull and pelvis, he had already established that it was a "him," and probably middle-aged. There was some arthritic lipping on the vertebrae, but not much, which meant that he'd probably made it into his forties, but not out of his sixties. The sutures on the skull, not the most reliable of indicators, were mostly sealed, but parts of the later-closing ones—the sphenotemporal, the parietomastoid, the squamous—were still open, suggesting an age in the forties, maybe the fifties. Except for the oddly worn-down incisors (what in the world had this guy been *gnawing* on?), tooth wear was about right for a man in his middle years too. Taken all together, he estimated the age at forty to sixty-five.

Anything finer than that was difficult because the ends of the long bones had been pretty well chewed away, and so had the pubic symphyses. Those were where the best indicators of age were to be found, but, unfortunately, they were also the softest bone, and the scavengers went for them first and most thoroughly.

The excavation records were no help at all. The yellowing card titled *4360* said *Male, probably tall. No distinguishing characteristics*. That was all. Such brevity was par for the course in 1920s Egyptology, especially for an excavation headed by a rich amateur, at a run-of-the-mill site at which there had surely been no trained physical anthropologist. There wasn't even a list of the individual bones, which meant that there was no way of knowing if animals had carried anything off while they were lying in the enclosure.

So at least Gideon could say he had contributed a little to the knowledge of the el-Fuqani population by coming up with an age estimate, however approximate. He added a little more: the bones were dainty and slight—"gracile" was the anthropological term—indicating that 4360 had been a man of modest muscularity. And Lambert had been right about the "tall." Gideon guessed he'd been about five foot eight

which was big for an ancient Egyptian. He might have confirmed the height by taking some measurements of the long
bones and applying a formula, but what did it matter?

Now he lifted the skull again. Rodents had gnawed through
the zygomatics on both sides, two teeth had come out at least
a year before death, and two any time in the four-thousand-
plus years since. Beyond that, there wasn't much to say about
it. He turned it gently in his hands. "How long did you say
it's been lying out there?"

"Nobody knows," Jerry said. "Anytime up to five
years. Or it could have been just since last week, for all
we know."

Gideon shook his head. "No, two or three years, anyway."
He picked at a chalky fleck on the curvature of the frontal
bone, just above the faded, old-fashioned *F4360*. "This scaly
stuff all over the crown. That's spalling, exfoliation. It comes
from weathering, and it doesn't happen in a week. Neither
does this dappling here, these lighter areas. That's sun-bleach-
ing."

"But how do you know that didn't happen before?" Jerry
asked. "Like during the Fifth Dynasty."

Tiffany laughed. "Jerry, how would his *bones* have gotten
sun-bleached before he went into the ground?"

Jerry weighed this, then pointed his unlit pipe soberly at
TJ. "Good point, Dr. B."

Gideon went slowly over the pelvic bones with his hands
and eyes, not really looking for, or expecting to find, anything
notable. It had been half an hour since he had taken the
remains one by one from the carton and laid them out, and
the grinding, mind-numbing fatigue was creeping back. He
had begun to wonder why he hadn't gone to bed and left this
for another time. Why, really, was he bothering at all? What
difference—

He halted with his hands on the underside of the left hip
bone. His eyes closed. His fingertips continued to explore.

"Progress?" asked TJ.

Gideon didn't answer. He was alert again, and interested,
his fingers playing over the bone as delicately, as sensitively,
as a blind man's on braille. He traced the rough, irregular

surface of a large oval eminence at the base of the ischium, the lower rear section of the hip bone—the innominate to an anthropologist.

He opened his eyes, turned the bone over and examined it. He looked briefly at the right innominate and nodded to himself. "What do you know," he murmured.

"Progress," TJ decided.

Gideon picked up the fibula—the long thin bone that, together with the more robust tibia, forms the skeleton of the lower leg, and held it out at arm's length, squinting. Then he placed the solitary finger bone in his palm, lightly ran his fingertips down it, and put it down. "Well, well."

"Gideon," TJ said, "are you planning to let us in on this anytime soon?"

He looked up, smiling. "I guess I can tell you one thing special about him, after all. I can tell you his occupation."

"His *occupation*?" They both said it at once. Jerry's match had stopped on the way to the pipe.

Gideon spread his hands in a flourish that encompassed all the bones on the table. "The gentleman we have before us," he announced, "earned his living as a scribe."

All right, he was showboating. Skeletal work was fascinating in and of itself, but there were things every now and then that also made it good, plain fun, and one of them was pulling magical rabbits out of the hat for the amazement of one and all. He rarely passed up the chance to do it. Julie had once told him it was the ham in him that made him such a successful teacher. He had chosen to take it as a compliment.

"A *scribe*?" TJ echoed. Her right hand caressed the humerus gently, almost reverently.

"Of course I can't be sure," Gideon said in a brief attack of modesty, "but that's what it looks like."

How, they wanted to know, could he tell something like that? Gideon told them, demonstrating as he went. The craggy, oval area on the bottom of each innominate bone was the ischial tuberosity. It was the site of attachment for several powerful ligaments and muscles. It was also, he explained, the part you sat on, and when you spent a great deal of time sitting, especially sitting on a hard surface like the ground, a chronic osteitis developed, resulting in an appearance even more craggy than the norm.

"And this is more craggy than the norm?" TJ was holding the bone in her hand, thoughtfully feeling the tuberosity.

"Much," Gideon said. "So—"

"But isn't this also called a squatting facet?" she asked. "And scribes didn't squat, you know."

"No, squatting facets are different. They're on the femur or the tibia, and our man here doesn't have any. But he does have something else." He held up the fibula for them. "Can you see that it's laterally bowed?"

Jerry had finally gotten his pipe going. He looked at the slender bone through wreaths of smoke. "Nope."

"I can," TJ said. "Just a slight curve."

"Right. It comes from sitting cross-legged, which puts a tremendous amount of sideways pressure on the feet, which in turn—"

"And that's the way scribes sat," TJ said, beginning to see the picture. "On the floor, legs crossed, linen skirt stretched stiffly across the thighs as a writing surface . . ."

"Exactly," Gideon said. "And here's the clincher: this ridge along the finger bone." He held it so that they could see it clearly, although he knew they were unlikely to make anything of it. Even his students had a hard time with the individual phalanges of the fingers. Too many of them—twenty-eight, counting both hands—and too much alike.

"This is the first joint of the right index finger, and the ridge we're looking at is on the palmar surface. It's where the flexor ligament attaches. Ordinarily you can barely see it—"

"I can barely see it now," Jerry said.

"—but it can get enlarged like this from grasping something between finger and thumb, firmly and for long periods of time."

"A stylus," TJ said under her breath. "Well, how about that."

"There's no way to be sure," Gideon said, "but it all adds up to a scribe. Put all these skeletal things together, throw in the fact that we're talking about a Fifth Dynasty Theban, and that's what you come up with. At least, it's what I come up with.''

He brushed bone crumbs from his hands, well content. ''Not that it gets us any closer to what he was doing in the junk heap.''

''Who cares?'' TJ said, beginning to put the bones back in the carton. ''This has been really neat. Maybe I should have been a physical anthropologist.''

They were saying good night in the patio, at the foot of the stairs that led to Gideon's upper-floor room, when he said: ''I suppose I ought to mention this to Dr. Haddon. I'd feel a little funny not saying anything.''

''Up to you,'' Jerry said, ''but if it was me, I wouldn't. Personally, I don't think he'd be real thrilled to find out we got you involved in this.''

''Thrilled?'' TJ said with a laugh. ''He'd have a fit . . .'' She frowned. ''That reminds me. There was something funny this morning—I forgot to mention it to you, Jerry. Something Dr. H said.''

Her husband looked leery. ''Do I want to know this?''

''Oh, it's nothing bad. It just makes me wonder about his—well, he asked me what happened to the head that was there last night.''

Jerry frowned. ''The what?''

''In the enclosure. He seems to think he saw a yellow jasper head in there, near the bones, or maybe it was quartzite. Look, keep this to yourselves, will you? I wasn't supposed to talk about it. Not that it matters. Bruno already knows.''

Jerry stood leaning on the railing, silent and contemplative, pulling on his pipe.

''You mean he said it was there last night, but not this morning?'' Gideon asked.

''Right. And it worried me, because—look, Gideon, this is not for public consumption either, but he got a little tiddly last night, which he tends to do most nights, no big deal, never during working hours, but this is the first time that he ever—well, hallucinated, I guess you'd have to call it. He even thought he remembered pointing it out.''

"He did," Jerry said quietly.

TJ swung to face him. "Did what?"

"Point it out."

She stared at him. "Jerry, I was right there. If he—"

"He didn't say it was a head. He said . . . I don't remember his exact words . . . he was flashing his light around, and he said, 'What's that piece over there,' or, 'See that thing over there,' or something like that. Don't you remember?"

"No!"

"Well," Jerry said, "there was a lot of excitement, you were arguing with him—"

"What was he pointing at? How do you know it was a head? Did you actually see anything?"

"No, I wasn't really paying attention. But maybe Ragheb saw it, or Arlo."

TJ shook her head. "No. I asked them, even though Dr. H told me not to."

"Huh? Why would he tell you not to?"

"I think he thinks he was dreaming himself." She hunched her shoulders. "He was pretty well potted, Jerry."

"Yeah, he was that." Jerry banged his pipe on his palm to knock out the dottle, pulled the pipe apart, and blew wetly through the stem. "Tiff," he said slowly, "you don't suppose that maybe there *was* something, and Ragheb came back during the night, and, well . . ."

"Stole it?" TJ said indignantly. "Of course not. And even if he'd wanted to, all he had to do was take it in the first place, before he ever came in to call us."

"Maybe he didn't see it until Dr. H pointed it out."

"Jerry, I can't believe you're saying this. How can you believe Ragheb is a liar and a thief? He's been here almost as long as we have, he's the nicest, gentlest—"

"I'm just trying to look at all the angles, Tiff," Jerry said peaceably. "Why would Dr. H imagine he saw a quartzite head?"

"Why would Ragheb steal it?" TJ countered.

They turned to Gideon as if they expected him to resolve the dispute, but Gideon had reached the end of his rope. He was beyond overtiredness now, finally ready for sleep, wondering only where he was going to find the energy to climb the stairs to the room. He tried unsuccessfully to smother a prodigious yawn.

TJ laughed. "Let's get this poor guy upstairs before he collapses on us. He's got a long day tomorrow; six-bit tour in the morning, and then off to Amarna in the afternoon."

"Amarna?" Gideon said fuzzily. "I thought that wasn't in the schedule anymore."

"It wasn't, but Forrest decided that artistic integrity demanded its inclusion after all. Even if we have to rush like hell through everything else."

Gideon yawned again. "Good. I'd hate to miss it."

"We really ought to get up," Julie said.

"Mm," replied Gideon.

Neither of them stirred. After a while Gideon gently brushed the backs of his fingers over her cheek, pleased as always by the softness of her skin, pleased as always with himself for having her beside him morning after morning, night after night.

"I mean," said Julie, "we can't very well lie in bed all day like a couple of slugs. Not that this wasn't a nice way to start the day."

Gideon smiled. "I'd hardly say like a couple of slugs."

"No," she said, laughing. She turned on her side to face him, cradling his hand between her cheek and the pillow. Her eyes, glossy and ink-black, were a foot from his. "But we're going to have to get going sometime. I hear they have a full day planned for us."

"Whatever it is, it's going to be downhill from here."

He had awakened earlier than he'd wanted to, at 6:00, and silently gone to the dining room to bring back coffee from the twenty-four-hour urn. Julie had downed the first cup without quite waking up, which was normal even when she wasn't suffering from jet lag. She had grunted something and held out the empty cardboard cup, and he had gone for refills. As always, the second one got her blood moving and her nerves functioning, and by the time she had finished it, she was not only speaking in intelligible words, she was feeling playful and affectionate.

He had wound up back in the bed, the time had flown by, and now, somehow, it was 7:30.

"Gideon," she said when another five minutes had passed and they had yet to move, "do we really have to follow Dr. Haddon's schedule? What's the chance of our playing hooky and going out and seeing Luxor Temple? Just us?"

"I wish I could," he said sincerely, "but I have to take the obligatory tour here at the House. But you don't. Why don't you go ahead on your own?"

She wrinkled her nose, the only person in the world on whom it looked absolutely stunning. "I don't want to go ahead on my own. I want to go with you."

It warmed him to hear her say it, but thought it only right to say otherwise. "But I can't, Julie, and I wouldn't want you to miss—"

"*Why* do you have to take the obligatory tour?"

"Professional courtesy, for one thing. Haddon expects me to, and I *am* his guest."

"You're not Haddon's guest," she said sensibly. "You're the Horizon Foundation's guest. You're here to narrate a film, that's all. You're not an Egyptologist and don't pretend to be one, you're not a board member like Bruno, or the power behind a board member like Bea, and this may be our one and only free morning in Luxor. Unless you'd rather spend it learning more about Middle Egyptian hieroglyphs and epigraphic techniques, of course."

He raised the eyebrow that wasn't pressed against the pillow. "Are you kidding? But how do I get out of it? What do I tell Haddon?"

"Tell him that your wife insists on going into Luxor, and she greatly desires your company, and her every wish is your command."

Gideon considered this for a few moments. Then he kissed her a final time, on the spot on her nose where the wrinkle had been, rolled out of bed, and began getting back into his clothes.

"I will," he said, and did.

Chapter Eight

The distance from the front gate of the Horizon House compound to Luxor Temple was well under a mile, all of it along the avenue referred to as Shari el-Bahr on maps, but invariably called the Corniche by locals and tourists alike—as the riverfront street in every Nile town and city is called the Corniche, whatever its designated name. Remnants of the French influence die hard in Egypt. Luxor's Corniche was a particularly handsome, tree-shaded boulevard that ran beside the Nile for the length of the city, with tourist shops and fine hotels and high-walled gardens on one side, and posh, white cruise ships moored along the quays on the other.

At 8:45 A.M. the sun was not yet oppressive, the smog not yet risen, and the Corniche relatively quiet, the trucks and tour buses having yet to come out in force. The roadway was almost free of traffic, and what there was, was picturesque: bicycles, robed men on slow-moving donkeys or in donkey-pulled carts, and the ubiquitous, garishly pretty horse-drawn taxis called caleches (another tag-end of Napoleon's occupation). Cars passed not once in two minutes. Instead of blaring horns, diesel engines, and screamed curses, there was only a muted clip-clopping, lazy and affable.

On the face of it, then, the walk from Horizon House to

the great pharaonic temple of Amenhotep III should have been a relaxing and agreeable way to launch their stay in Egypt, a peaceful, fifteen-minute stroll through the middle of an exotic picture postcard.

Exotic it certainly was; relaxing and quiet, by no means. In six years, Gideon had almost forgotten what it was like for foreigners, especially reasonably well-dressed foreigners, to walk down a street in an Egyptian tourist center. Anytime they stopped for even a few seconds to admire the view of the Nile, or to tie a shoelace, or to wonder what lay behind some ornately gated high wall, men and boys, all with goods or services to sell, appeared from nowhere to descend enterprisingly upon them.

"Welcome in Egypt!"

"Hello, English? Where you from?"

"Caleche?"

"Taxi?"

"Felucca ride, Banana Island?"

"Just look, not buy!"

"Hello, Karnak, yes? I take for nothing."

"Come on, at least say hello. What it can hurt?"

Sometimes laughing young men would hurl a barrage of English—probably their total arsenal—at them, seemingly just for the fun of it: "Hello! Thank you! Good evening! Bye-bye! Michael Jackson!"

By the time they were halfway to the temple, they had learned, as all visitors sooner or later did, that in order to make any progress they had to avoid the eyes of strangers and ignore the frequent questions and greetings that came their way. For New Yorkers, thought Gideon, this would probably be nothing new, but for a couple of people accustomed to the neighborly, easygoing rhythms of the Pacific Northwest it was going to take some getting used to.

"I feel like the original Ugly American," Julie said to him as they quickened their pace past a caleche driver ecstatically welcoming them to Egypt. "How cold they must think we are. But if you say something polite you end up feeling like a—like a slab of meat in the middle of a swarm of flies. And I can't quite tell when they're poking fun at us."

"I know," Gideon said sympathetically, "but it can't be helped. I know one Egyptologist who says it's the worst part of being here. You can't walk three steps—at least in a place like Luxor—without being made to feel like either a sonofabitch or a sucker. He says it'd drive him crazy if he let it."

"So what does he do?"

Gideon shrugged. "He tries not to go out in the street."

From a distance of two blocks, the Temple of Luxor was a letdown. They had come eager to be overwhelmed, but the famed monument had next to nothing in common with the evocative nineteenth-century paintings and drawings of a great, ruined, enigmatic temple half-buried in shifting dunes, with no signs of human habitation in sight, and only the occasional artfully posed Bedouin to give it scale. They had known, of course, that it had been largely—but not altogether—dug out of the sand, but they had failed to realize how fully in the heart of downtown Luxor it now sat, looking forlorn and not so very monumental, surrounded by wide pavements, modern buildings, and passersby who didn't bother to give it a second glance.

But once they'd paid their admissions and entered the grounds, actually walking through the tumbled, eroded masonry, the modern city receded and the magic enveloped them. How could it not? They were in the very heart of ancient Egypt's capital city, the ceremonial center of what had been called at various times, by various peoples, the City of Amen-Ra, the Biblical city of No, the great city of Thebes (so named by the Greeks of Homer's time, long after its heyday).

For almost two hours they prowled over the grounds at will, drawing envious looks from groups of glazed-eyed tourists being herded by umbrella-toting guides. Mostly, they walked in silence, without even a guidebook, content to take in the grandeur and history without fussing about the details. They walked reverently through the great Colonnade of Amenhotep and along the Avenue of Sphinxes; they gawked up at the First Pylon and the colossal paired statues of Ramses II. They stood before the famous rose granite obelisk, also once part of a pair, but solitary since its twin had been shipped off to Paris's Place de la Concorde in the 1830s.

Across the river, framed by the temple's columns and only slightly obscured by the brown haze that had materialized over the city with the daily appearance of exhaust-belching trucks and buses, was a bleak moonscape of low, corrugated hills and arid canyons. In one of those wan, scorched canyons, Gideon knew, was the most famous, most fabulous burial complex in the history of the world.

"The Valley of the Kings," he said. "The carefully hidden tombs of Ramses after Ramses, the grand celestial chambers of Seti I and Amenhotep, the golden treasures of Tutankhamun. Sixty-four pharaohs were buried there, Julie. The Place of Truth, they called it, the City of the Dead—"

"The Forest Lawn of Egypt," Julie said.

He blinked.

"That's what your friend at the Smithsonian calls it," Julie said. "If you ask me, he has a point."

Gideon laughed. "Was I getting a little lyrical there?"

"Just a little."

"I think maybe we've done enough sightseeing for a while?"

"Could be."

"And it just occurred to me—we haven't had anything to eat. Could you stand a little breakfast?"

She grinned up at him. "Good gosh, I thought you'd never ask."

A few blocks back up the Corniche, the Savoy Hotel advertised a full English breakfast on its signboard, and delivered on its promise. Julie and Gideon sat in its outdoor café, among neat trees and potted plants, protected from the sun by a tentlike canopy, and wolfed down scrambled eggs, bacon, toast, and tea. The bacon wasn't really bacon, and the eggs had been scrambled in something that wasn't butter, but the tea was good, strong English tea, the marmalade was straight from Edinburgh, and all in all they had no complaints.

With every bite they could feel their strength picking up, their normally positive outlooks surging back.

"All right, I have a theory for you," Julie said, laying marmalade on her second piece of toast.

This was announced without preface, after a long, satisfying stint of dedicated eating, but Gideon knew what she was referring to. Earlier, when he'd told her about the discovery of the el-Fuqani skeleton in the old storage enclosure, she had said little, but he could tell that she was filing the data away, and it wouldn't be long before a hypothesis emerged.

"All right, let's hear it," he said.

He enjoyed her ideas. They were always inventive, frequently entertaining, and sometimes extremely helpful. He often discussed his forensic cases with her, and more than once—many times more than once—she had come up with an insight or observation that would never have occurred to him. Once she had solved a case for him by wondering aloud if the "polish" he'd been describing on the right first metacarpal and multangular (the bones at the base of the thumb) of a set of unidentified remains might not have been due to the repeated movement of striking a keyboard space bar. Indeed they had, and the remains had quickly been identified as those of a woman who had worked at a computer keyboard for ten years.

He had split his consulting fee with her.

"You said he was a scribe, right?" she said.

"Yes, apparently."

"Okay, I was thinking: what if there was some kind of valuable papyrus in the box with him?"

"I don't follow you."

"What if, among the things that he was buried with, there was a papyrus that he'd written, or scribed, or whatever they did? What if it was the papyrus that someone was after, not the skeleton? And so they just got rid of the bones in the nearest convenient place and ran off with the papyrus?"

Gideon shook his head. "No, the el-Fuqani collection is just a bunch of remains from an ordinary, middle-class cemetery. No fancy tombs, no mummification process, no objects buried with them. Just a hole in the ground, and in they went. Besides, even if there was something in the box with him, why bother taking the bones at all, why not just the papyrus?''

"Maybe someone had to move fast, and couldn't afford to poke around looking for it in the box, and just grabbed everything in it and ran.''

"Then why not take the whole box? It's not that big.''

"What if someone saw him running off with it?''

"What if someone saw him running off with bones falling out of his arms?''

"Well, yes,'' Julie said, "I see your point.'' She poured them both more tea. "What's your theory, then?''

"Hypothesis,'' he corrected, "or conjecture, if you prefer.'' The breakfast had relaxed him and made him feel more expansive. "Theory implies a reliable inference based on at least some supporting evidence.''

"Ah,'' she said, lifting her eyes skyward, "the joys of being married to a professor.'' She picked up the teapot. "Want some more?''

He nodded and held out his cup. "Whereas a hypothesis is little more than one of many possible tentative explanations based on incomplete—or in this case, nonexistent—evidence of any kind.''

"Keep it up,'' she said, pouring for both of them, "and you're going to get this in your lap.'' She slid the milk across to him. "What's your conjecture, then?''

"My conjecture is that one of the students who are always spending a few weeks or months at Horizon House decided that he wanted to take a knock-'em-dead souvenir back to his room at State U, and one of the unguarded, ignored el-Fuqani skeletons made easy pickings.''

"So what was it doing in the garbage heap?''

"Cold feet, probably. Maybe it'd been taken after a few too many beers, and in the stark, clear light of the next morning, he—or she—realized that there was going to be big trouble ahead when those bones went through Customs. So they got tossed. Safer than trying to get them back into their box.'' He swallowed a last forkful of eggs. "Seems like the simplest explanation to me.''

"Maybe," she said doubtfully, "but it seems to me you have to conjecture up a pretty ghoulish student to make it work."

"Not at all. They do things like that all the time."

"They do?"

"They do. And not only students. Did you ever hear of the Neiman-Marcus skull fragment?"

She shook her head wearily. "Do I want to?"

"The Neiman-Marcus fragment was a piece of John Kennedy's skull, so-called because, after disappearing from the street, it turned up in a respectable Dallas doctor's little collection of memorabilia, swathed in cotton in a Neiman-Marcus box."

"Ugh."

"Not only that, but after it was retrieved it disappeared again, and so have some of the other fragments. And where do you think Einstein's brain is?"

She began to shake her head again, then grimaced and burst out laughing at the same time.

He looked at her curiously.

"I was only thinking," she said, "how dull my breakfast conversations would be if I'd married that electrical engineer from Des Moines." She shook her head wonderingly. "My God, what a question. Anyway, the answer is that I have no idea where Einstein's brain is."

"Neither does anybody else, because, you see, somebody walked off with it, also apparently for a souvenir. And that's just for starters. There's Emanuel Swedenborg's skull, Josef Haydn's—"

She held up her hand. "Thank, you, starters will be sufficient. Tell me, how does the disappearing head that Haddon saw—"

"—or says he saw."

"—fit into this? Or don't you have a conjecture?"

"On that," said Gideon, "I don't even have a surmise. My guess—"

"Is that above or below a surmise?"

"Below. My guess is he imagined it. Nobody else saw it." He glanced at his watch. "Maybe we ought to be getting back. We're flying to el-Amarna in a few hours."

"We have time to finish our tea. Let's relax for a few more minutes. It's lovely here."

"It is that."

"Come to think of it," Julie said, "why are we going to el-Amarna anyway? What's at el-Amarna?"

"El-Amarna, or rather Tel el-Amarna, is the modern name for Akhetaten, the city built by Akhenaten as his new capital when he decided to move the court out of Thebes—"

"Yes, I know all that. A new center of worship to his beloved god Aten, rather than Amon."

"That's right."

"Well, you don't have to sound so amazed. I do have an education, you know. But my question is: why are they filming there? What does Amarna have to do with Horizon House?"

"Not a lot, really, but Cordell Lambert's old Institute of Egyptian Studies apparently started out up there. They did a season's digging before moving to Luxor, so in a sense that's where Horizon House began. The other thing is that later on, in the 1930s and 1940s, the University of Bern was one of the outfits that ran excavations there, and one of the graduate students who worked on them and took graduate classes on the side was the young Clifford Haddon. He learned his hieroglyphs in the expedition headquarters building—which is now the Amarna Museum."

"Ah," Julie said, nodding. "Human interest."

They sat in companionable silence, sipping the cooling tea, digesting their breakfasts, and soaking up atmosphere. The Savoy's café was about as international as a restaurant could be. At the tables around them were Arabs, black Africans, Europeans, Americans, and Asians laughing and chattering away in a happy babble of languages. At their feet a slate-gray cat worked the crowd, moving from table to table, eyeing the clients, and then, depending on its appraisal, either waiting for a handout or moving contemptuously on. From Julie and Gideon it got offers of the baconlike mystery meat (reservedly accepted) and marmaladed toast (scornfully declined).

"We'd better go," Gideon said after a while. "They'll start thinking we've gone over the hill altogether."

Leaving the café they passed close by the table of two thin, elderly Englishmen who looked like brothers, sharing a pot of tea and a basket of pastries.

"Smog in Luxor," said one of them, sighing deeply. "Who would have thought?"

The other shook his head. "There wasn't any in '49, I can tell you that. Think what it's doing to the monuments."

"Think," said the first, "what it's doing to the people."

The other tore a piece of baklava in two and licked his slender fingers. "That too," he agreed languidly.

Two hours later, in the heat of the afternoon, both of the Horizon House vans drove up the Shari el-Matar to the small airport outside Luxor, arriving with twenty minutes to spare before the chartered ZAS flight to el-Minya at 2:00. In the vehicles were the participants, direct and indirect, in the making of *Reclaiming History: The Story of Horizon House*. In all, twelve people piled out of the vans and into the concrete-block terminal.

Besides Julie and Gideon, there were Bea and Bruno Gustafson, representing the Horizon Foundation, and Haddon, Arlo, TJ, and Jerry from Horizon House. The ninth, tenth, and eleventh members of the group were Forrest Freeman, who was directing the documentary, and his bare-bones staff: Cy, an aging, placid, child of the sixties who wore his much-thinned hair in a graying ponytail; and Patsy, a rail-thin, sinewy woman of forty-five who smoked little black cigars and might have been mute for all she said. Cy was the cameraman. Patsy seemed to do everything else, a combination soundperson, gaffer, grip, and gofer. The third member of the crew—Kermit Feiffer, the assistant director—was being left behind in Luxor to make copies of the tapes that had already been made and do arcane things with them at the local MisrFilm studio.

Their leader, Forrest Freeman, was a burly man of forty with the body of a wrestler and the soul of a worrywart. Forrest was a fretter, a man who expected the worst and expected it to be worse than he expected. Gideon had spoken with him for no more than five minutes at dinner the evening before, and another five in the van, but he had already heard about problems with the shooting schedule, with lighting, with transportation, with weather, and with the equipment. Actually, none of these had yet come to pass, but from Forrest's point of view, it was only a matter of time. The Fates, he seemed convinced, had it in for him personally.

To be fair, he'd already had his share of woe. One of his crew, he told Gideon, had been arrested at the Cairo airport for bringing in half a kilo of hashish inside a camera. ("Can you believe it? Smuggling hash *into* the Middle East? Where do I get these guys?") Forrest had been lucky they'd let him and the rest of the crew in, but he was left with only three people instead of four, and one camera instead of two. On top of that, the authorities had gotten sticky about work permits, requiring him to finish up in Egypt and move on to his next production in Turkey five days sooner than planned. Did Gideon have any idea of the pressures that created on this job? Everything was going to have to go like clockwork.

Only of course, Forrest had said, staring moodily out the window of the van, it wouldn't. That went without saying. But what the hell, the sooner he got to Turkey and to bribing the local officials for the permits and concessions he needed to begin work on *Hunting the Anatolian Boar*, the happier he would be. Five extra days in Turkey would mean, with any luck, that he would have time for some avocational hunting of his own. You could still shoot wolves, and fox, and mountain goats in the Anatolian mountains, did Gideon know that? Now there was life at its best: it was—well, splendid. Up in the morning with the sun to the smell of coffee being brewed by your guide . . . and Turkey! Turkey was a civilized country compared to Egypt.

Forrest had accepted the assignment to make *The Story of Horizon House* in a weak moment, because it was so easy to tack onto the Turkish trip, and, frankly, the money wasn't bad, but it had been sheer misery from the beginning. In the first place, as he should have remembered, he couldn't stand Egypt; he'd made five documentaries here in the last seven years, and you'd think he'd know by now. In the second, Clifford Haddon, as he also should have remembered, was the most self-centered, fault-finding, aggravating old fart anyone ever had to deal with. And third, the project itself was the most excruciatingly dull, pedestrian thing he'd worked on since *The Joy of Spring Bulbs*. He didn't mind exacerbating his ulcer, he'd said, as long as it was in a meaningful cause, but this . . . ! He was a maker of serious films, after all, not just another hack for hire.

And so he was. Despite his twittering air of impending doom, Forrest had built a respectable reputation as a maker of archaeological documentaries. A few years ago Gideon had seen and admired the one that had made his name, *The End of Eternity*, a four-part PBS special on the destruction of Upper Egypt's greatest monuments by erosion, pollution, and the crush of tourists. That had been a six-month project, produced as well as directed by Forrest, and he had done most of his on-site research at the Horizon House library, getting to know the institution and its people.

All of which made *The Story of Horizon House* a natural for him, at least from the foundation's point of view.

The last of the twelve was Gideon and Julie's old friend, Phil Boyajian, free spirit. Divorced (amicably), a few years older than Gideon, and also an ex-student of Abe Goldstein's, he now lived in Bellingham, a couple of hours north of Seattle. Of all the anthropologists Gideon knew, Phil had had perhaps the most peculiar career. Armed with a Ph.D. in cultural anthropology and Middle Eastern studies, he had begun with fieldwork in Jordan and Tunisia, but claimed it made him feel like a voyeur. So he'd taken an assistant professorship at the University of Washington, only to find university politics more than he could stand. He'd then tried teaching at a Seattle junior college, but couldn't bear the committee assignments. And finally, completing this resolutely backward progression, he'd wound up teaching at a high school in Olympia, which had kept him contented for almost five years—a long time for Phil.

Then, seven or eight years ago, he'd spent a summer vacation doing travel research for a new guidebook called *Egypt on the Cheap*, geared primarily to students and backpackers. The book had been a great success, and Phil was now firmly and happily ensconced as a contributing editor to the flourishing *On the Cheap* series, which helped travelers get around in developing countries with a minimum of stress and confusion. In addition, two or three times a year he accompanied alumni tours to North Africa or the Middle East, acting as a sort of cultural liaison to ensure that their existence was as untroubled as possible. Whenever he came back from such a trip, Gideon and Julie could be assured of an evening's good stories, but this time they wouldn't have to wait for them. It was Phil who had arranged the flight to el-Amarna, and the Nile cruise, and he was along to head off whatever problems might arise.

Gideon understood the need for him. Egypt wasn't an easy country to get around in. There were frustrations at every turn: bureaucratic muddles, "rules" that didn't exist yesterday and wouldn't exist tomorrow, unexpected demands for fees or for permits that could only be gotten in Cairo on the first day of the second week of alternate months. There were confusions and noisy fracases over matters whose import—whose very sense—eluded foreigners. And, especially, there was an utter unconcern for time—nobody in Egypt was ever in a hurry—and a disinclination to interfere with the not-always-transparent manifestations of God's will that had driven more than one harried Westerner around the bend.

It was to spare the group these adversities that Phil was there. With his excellent Arabic (his father had been a petroleum engineer, and Phil had spent much of his first twelve years in Riyadh and Cairo), with his scruffy, eager, friendly manner, with a perpetually sunny disposition and a willingness to see the best in people, with an insider's perspective on the Egyptian view of life, and with a resilient, take-things-as-they-come approach to the inevitable hard knocks of travel, he was just the person to smooth over whatever vagaries lay ahead.

Vagaries were not long in coming. The ZAS plane that he had chartered was not ready and waiting when they arrived. Worse, no one was able to tell them why it wasn't there, where it was, or when, precisely, it was expected. *Shortly*, *very shortly*, they were told by an eager-to-please clerk in a trim, Sadat-style blue suit.

Phil was turned to for counsel. "Go, as they say, with the flow," was his cheerful advice, delivered in the faint but crisp British accent that was a remnant of his Saudi Arabian school days. "Speaking for myself, I intend to sit down and have a Coke."

"Third World travel," said Bea philosophically. "How I love it. Well, I'll have a Coke too, Bruno."

At 3:00 there was still no sign—or word—of the plane. A testy Haddon, having gone with the flow as long as he could, stamped up to the counter. "I'm not going to wait here all day," he snapped, his beard jutting aggressively. "Is it or is it not expected? Answer truthfully, please."

"Oh, yes, sir, to be sure," the clerk told him with an encouraging smile. *"Inshallah."*

God willing. The others looked at each other. It didn't look good.

"This is your fault, Forrest," Haddon said crossly.

Forrest Freeman, who had been sitting glumly in a corner and not bothering anyone, surfaced from whatever worries he had been chewing over.

"What? My fault?"

"I maintain, as I have from the beginning, that there is simply no good reason for us to be making this trek, given our ridiculously compressed schedule." *Shedyule*, Haddon said. "Tel el-Amarna hardly represents a critical milestone in the history of Horizon House."

Forrest sighed, a man who had been through this before. "Sorry, but I have to disagree with you there. And as long as I have—"

But at that point ZAS Airlines was heard from, and twenty minutes later the plane rolled up outside the window. The party shouldered their carry-on luggage and prepared to leave the terminal.

"One moment, please, ladies and gentlemen, there seems to be an additional small problem," the clerk told them jovially, "a very small problem indeed."

"Imagine that," Bea said.

"Hardly any problem to speak of," the clerk went on. "No, not really a problem at all. It seems that the baggage hold of this airplane is already filled with baggages from an earlier trip which was unfortunately misrouted, through no fault of the airline or this airport. These baggages are on the way eventually to Cairo, and therefore there is no room for your own baggages on this airplane at this moment."

"Yikes," Julie said.

Next to her, Phil tapped the backpack that was slung over one shoulder of his T-shirt—his standard Middle Eastern apparel along with a long-billed "On the Cheap" baseball cap, rumpled beige shorts that came down to his skinny knees, and sockless canvas running shoes. "First rule: never travel with more than you can carry."

"Now he tells us," Gideon said.

Forrest, who had continued to sit in his corner quietly gnawing his lip, suddenly took to gibbering. "I knew this would happen! I knew this would happen! What about our equipment? We only have four miserable days, we don't have any spare time, we, we—" He switched suddenly to a long string of loud and impressively fluent-sounding Arabic. Other passengers turned to observe with interest and respect.

The clerk shouted back no less loudly, waving his hands and thumping the counter. Gideon had no trouble with the gist of it but understood not a word. Ordinarily he took pride in being able to get along in the language of whatever country he was in, but this time he simply hadn't had the time to learn. He could handle *hello-goodbye*, *yes-no*, and *please-thank you*, and that was it.

After a few seconds, Phil came to the rescue, edging Forrest out of the way and taking up the yelling match in his stead, his voice well up to the challenge. It went on for a good five minutes with, if anything, an increase in fervor; several times the clerk raised his face to the ceiling, apparently to address his thoughts to a higher authority. Phil, clearly having a good time, finally bent over the narrow counter and wrapped his arm around the clerk's shoulder. They leaned together, talking more quietly, until there was a sudden spate of good-natured laughter, a spirited shaking of hands, and an obviously amicable conclusion.

Phil turned to Forrest. "All right, your equipment comes with us."

"Whew," Forrest said, spent. "Gad. I knew this would happen." He appealed to his crew of two, slouched on a bench. "Did I or did I not say this was going to happen?"

"You said it was going to happen, man," Cy agreed.

Julie looked at Phil. "How in the world did you do that?"

"You don't want to know," he said.

"You bribed him, you gave him him some what-do-you-call-it, *bakshish*, didn't you?"

Phil grinned. "I showed him the error of his ways. I revealed to him a better path."

"You gave him money."

"I did not give him money. No such thing. Not a single piaster. And anyway, I'll be reimbursed."

Julie shook her head. "Is this what it's always like?"

"Yes," Phil said happily.

"Fortunately," the smiling clerk now said, "we will be able to place all of your baggages on the very next flight to Cairo. A special intermediate stop at el-Minya shall soon be arranged, I am happy to say."

"Oh, yes? And when would that be?" Haddon asked. "Any time this week?"

"To be sure," the clerk said earnestly. "Of course. You will have it in no time at all."

Haddon was unimpressed. "*Bukhra*, you mean?" he said sourly.

The clerk threw back his head and laughed. "*Bukhra*, yes, without fail! And now, you may be boarding, please, gentlemen and ladies?" He shook Phil's hand again and bowed them through the door to the tarmac.

"What's *bukhra*?" Julie asked Gideon as the group walked toward the mid-sized plane. "I'm afraid to ask."

"Phil, what's *bukhra*?" Gideon said over his shoulder.

"*Bukhra*? Literally, it means tomorrow. But—put it this way. When someone in Egypt tells you *bukhra*, treat it in the same manner as when someone in Mexico tells you *mañana*."

"Great," Gideon said.

"Except, of course, without the same sense of urgency," Phil finished.

"Rats," Julie said. "And us without a change of clothes."

"I wouldn't worry about it," Gideon said with more assurance than he felt. "He said the very next flight. We'll probably get it before the night's out."

Julie, who took logistical problems in her stride better than he did, laughed.

"*Inshallah*," she said.

Chapter Nine

Ninety minutes later they deplaned at el-Minya, a drab, sprawling city chiefly known for processing sugar and making cheap soaps and perfumes. There, as directed by Phil, they went to a waiting area where transportation to el-Amarna was to be waiting for them. There was nothing there. Passersby looked curiously at the stranded-looking knot of Americans surrounded by videotaping gear in dented metal trunks and valises.

Forrest turned apprehensively to Phil. "I thought there was supposed to be a van to meet us."

Phil nodded. "Sort of."

Forrest twitched slightly. "What do you mean, sort of?"

"Sort of a van," Phil explained.

"Well, where is it? We're almost two hours late, why isn't it waiting?"

"They probably went for tea when they heard we'd be late. They'll be along."

A tic beside Forrest's right eye started jumping. "Now, but—look, Phil, we're on a very tight schedule, we, we need our transportation to be right bang on time, right on the minute."

"Then my advice is to shoot this thing in Switzerland,"

Phil said pleasantly. "Cheer up, Forrest, you know the way things work here. You ought to be used to it by now."

"Oh, God, do I know the way they work," Forrest said, "but I'll never get used to it. Not in a million years will I get used to it."

Phil smiled encouragingly at him. "Everything will work out; you can trust me."

Forrest heaved a great, pathetic sigh, and sank down onto a metal bench. "Why do I keep doing this to myself? Why don't I ever learn?"

But at that moment, the "sort of a van" came coughing and chugging up to meet them, with two smiling Egyptians in the front seat. It was a doddering old flatbed truck with benches bolted to the bed and a canopy rigged on top, probably used for hauling local workmen to and from their jobs.

"Christ," said Forrest, but he wasted no time getting his equipment aboard, and within a few minutes they were on their way. They boarded the ferry to cross the Nile, then drove in the deepening twilight past dilapidated tenements, falling-down houses, and beautifully, meticulously cared-for garden plots of tomatoes, onions, wheat, and potatoes, then into the desert, and finally to their lonely destination on the east bank of the Nile. To everyone's astonishment, and even Phil's mild surprise, the ship was there waiting for them; a white, modern, two-level affair tied up beside a dusty, rubble-strewn embankment, boxy and welcoming in the uneven glare of a couple of wavery, generator-powered spotlights set up on the shore. On its side, in gleaming metal lettering was its name: *Menshiya*.

They boarded by means of a gangplank, under the engrossed, unswerving gaze of a row of Arab men from the nearby village of el-Till. A pack of giggling, *bakshish*-demanding, sociable children ("Hello, mister! What's you name?") were kept ineffectually at bay by an unshaven, patently unmenacing local policeman in a frayed, untidy black uniform with a private's stripe safety-pinned to one sleeve.

The Americans ran this lively gauntlet and reported to the dining room, where the boat's manager, Mr. Murad Wahab, formally introduced the ship's captain, *Reis* Ali, a ferocious-looking, weathered old man who seemed to be wondering how he'd gotten mixed up with all these infidels, and the lined-up staff, ten dark, shy, friendly men, half of whom would work on the upper deck as servers and room attendants, and the rest of them out of sight as cooks and boat crew on the lower.

Mr. Wahab then gave a short speech of welcome on behalf of the Happy Nomad Navigation Company, cordial in tone, but consisting mainly of admonitions to report to the dining room at the stated times if they wished to eat. Breakfasts would be from seven to eight o'clock, lunches from one to two, dinners from seven to eight-thirty. Exceptions would be made in cases of illness only. Tea, coffee, and biscuits would be served on the poolside terrace at ten-thirty in the morning and four in the afternoon for forty-five minutes. Guests were strongly advised not to drink or brush their teeth with water from the taps. Ample bottled water would be provided to each room daily. Women guests were asked to refrain from using the swimming pool or wearing immodest clothing when the ship was close to land, as when going through the locks at Asyut the following day.

Mr. Wahab, himself an amiable man, moderated the severity of this presentation with the announcement that this evening's special meal would be a typical American dinner in honor of the guests and their recent national holiday of Thanksgiving.

Whereupon the four servers who had gone back into the kitchen returned with happy smiles, wearing white jackets and black ties, and bearing trays of roast turkey, cranberry sauce, and Yorkshire pudding.

It made a pretty good combination, Gideon thought.

The staterooms were forward on either side of a lushly carpeted corridor. Gideon and Julie's surprised them with its roominess, and with the small but sparkling bathroom and shower. Heavy curtains covered two big rectangular windows. There was a table, three chairs, an ottoman, a TV set, a knee-high refrigerator, an ample chest of drawers. The air-conditioning was quiet and effective. The only important deficiency was readily repaired by their moving a night table aside and pushing the two single beds together.

"Posh is right," Julie said appreciatively. "I don't think I'm going to have any trouble living here for a few days. As long as our luggage catches up with us pretty soon."

"*Bukhra*," said Gideon.

"That's what worries me." She took a hairbrush out of her bag, put it on the chest, and lined it up neatly with the edge. "Well, it certainly makes unpacking a snap." She held up a plastic container. "At least we have toothbrushes."

She kicked off her shoes, plumped up the pillow and sat on the bed. "Is there anything cold to drink in here?"

In the little refrigerator he found miniature soft-drink bottles, water, and a stack of plastic glasses. He poured them each a glass of mandarin-flavored *Schweppes*. "Did you happen to notice the name of the ship?"

"The *Menshiya*?"

"Right. Phil probably lined it up on account of the name. Do you happen to know what the original *Menshiya* was?"

She shook her head.

"Have you ever heard of the Deir el-Bahri cache?"

She sighed. "Gideon, dear, have I ever pointed out to you that you have a slightly annoying habit of starting your stories by asking me if I've heard of something that hardly anybody has ever heard of? The Deir el-Bahri cache, the *Menshiya*, the Neiman-Marcus fragment—"

"Many times," he said, flopping into one of the beige armchairs, putting his feet up on the ottoman, and stretching comfortably out on his lower spine. "It's just a pedagogical stratagem, well known to ensure listener participation in the communication process."

"Well, sometimes it just ensures listener teeth-gnashing. What's the Deir el-Bahri cache? Just tell me, don't worry about my participation in the communication process."

Deir el-Bahri, he explained, was the name of one of the rocky burial canyons near the Valley of the Kings. In it, at the beginning of the Twenty-first Dynasty in about 1000 B.C., the authorities took action to protect the great pharaohs' mummies from the profanations of the thief-families that had been robbing the nearby royal tombs for five hundred years. They had gathered up the desecrated mummies from their plundered tombs and put them all in a single place—the tomb of Queen Inhapy, behind the more famous, more showy temple of Hatshepsut, and there, stripped long ago of anything worth stealing, they were to lie undisturbed and eventually be forgotten.

Centuries passed. Millennia passed. Then, in 1891, a thief named Ahmed er-Rassul, a member of one of the local families that still made their living by systematically looting the same tombs—a piece here, a piece there, so that the market was never flooded—had a falling-out with his brothers. Out of spite he led officials into the unremembered mass tomb, which only the er-Rassul family knew about. There the officials were stunned to see, stacked on top of one another like so many logs, something that scholars thought no longer existed: the actual, preserved bodies of most of the legendary pharaohs of the Eighteenth, Nineteenth, and Twentieth Dynasties: Thutmose III, Seti I, Ramses II—''

"And where does the *Menshiya* come into it?" Julie said, finishing her drink and stretching. "I don't mean to rush you, but we have to be up early tomorrow morning."

"They couldn't leave the bodies where they were," Gideon said, "so they shipped them to Cairo for safekeeping. The boat that took them was called the *Menshiya*. Can you imagine? The ancient kings of Thebes on their last journey after three thousand years. The news got out and people lined the shore all the way from Luxor to Cairo. Women tearing their hair, men firing guns into the air . . .''

"Can I ask you something? Did you actually know all this before, or did you learn it from boning up these last few weeks?"

"Don't ask rude questions. Anyway, there's more. I haven't gotten to the best part. When they arrived, these old mummies had to be assessed for duties, like anything else coming into Cairo. The problem was, there wasn't any classification they fit into. They weren't stone, they weren't cloth, they weren't wood. So the tax collector and the officials got their heads together, came up with a compromise solution . . . and the greatest rulers of the ancient world made their triumphal entry into modern Cairo classified as dried fish.''

Julie spluttered with laughter. "Not that far off, when you think about it. You know, there's got to be a moral there somewhere."

"There sure does. Maybe some day I'll figure out what it is."

The morning began on a happy note. The baggage had arrived at el-Minya at 12:30 A.M., and Phil had somehow gotten it delivered to the ship in (and on) two rickety taxis. So as individuals began emerging from their staterooms a little before 7 A.M., they found their luggage stacked neatly in the corridor beside their doors. There were yips of joy as people were reunited with their underwear and toiletries. Even Haddon went out of his way to shake Phil's hand.

It was all mildly amazing and a bit amusing to Gideon. At home Phil's life was an exercise in planned disorganization. Constantly behind in his schedule, constantly overlooking things like bills and appointments, perpetually late ("Sorry, I remembered I had to do the laundry." "Sorry, the rubber plant needed repotting."), he bumbled along from one day to another, happily enough, to be sure, but always seemingly on the edge of chaos. Here, in his professional capacity, he was a man of infinite capacity, his fingers on the strings of every available resource.

During breakfast, a bright buffet of melons, figs, dates, tangerines, and warm loaves of sweet bread, Forrest went over the shooting schedule. All of the morning's interviews would take place in or around the Tel el-Amarna Museum not far from the ship. At 8:00, Haddon would talk about his early experiences there. At 9:30, it would be Gideon's turn; he would discuss Pharaoh Akhenaten and his times. And Arlo would display and discuss some of the old finds from Lambert's day at 11:00. TJ had an off-day.

"But which finds?" Arlo asked. "What do you want me to talk about?"

"Anything," Forrest said. "Talk about jewelry."

"Well . . . there *is* some jewelry here that I'm quite interested in myself, but I don't know—"

"Fine, perfect."

In his own way, Arlo looked pleased.

"So long as it's visual," Forrest said.

"Well, of course it's visual."

"Fine, perfect."

As Forrest went on, Arlo leaned worriedly toward Gideon. "What does he mean by visual?"

"You've got me, Arlo."

"Isn't jewelry visual? I mean, by definition?"

"You'd sure think so."

"I'm really not very good at this sort of thing," Arlo said.

"Okay," Forrest said, "anybody who's not involved in the shooting, you're free to spend the morning wherever you want. But remember, the boat has to leave at one o'clock sharp, so *please*—give my ulcer a break and be back in plenty of time. We're on a tight schedule and I wouldn't even want to *try* to extend our time in Egypt."

And miss even a single, splendid day of Anatolian boar-hunting, Gideon thought.

Chapter Ten

The Tel el-Amarna Museum stood at the desert's edge a few hundred yards from the river, a little more than a mile south of the huddled brown village of el-Till and hard against the scant remains of what had once been the King's Street in the great city of Akhetaten. No more than a utilitarian structure when constructed in 1913 as headquarters for Lambert's first excavation, the plain, one-story stucco building had been going downhill ever since. For twenty years after 1913 it had gone unused. In the 1930s, the University of Bern had taken it over for two decades. Then, in the 1950s, it had been turned over to the Egyptian government for use as a museum, but the money had never come through to properly maintain or staff it, and its finer pieces had gone one by one to more prestigious institutions. Now its undistinguished and slowly deteriorating collection was open to the public only a few afternoons a week, and irregularly at that.

It was nobody's fault, Gideon knew. Egypt, possessor of the greatest accumulation of archaeological material in the world, also happened to be one of its poorest countries. If there wasn't enough money to shore up the Great Sphinx against the groundwater that was eating it away, or to safeguard Luxor Temple against the corrosive salts in its soil, what chance was there to turn the dowdy Tel el-Amarna

Museum into anything special? And if they did, how many
people would come to visit it? Why would anyone, given the
mind-numbing wealth available in the rest of the country?

Those members of the Horizon expedition who had the
choice went elsewhere this morning. TJ took Julie on a tour
of the ruined estates and houses that had made up the northern
"suburbs" of Akhetaten, Bruno and Jerry trudged up the
long incline to the famous painted cliff tombs on the ridge
behind the city, Phil wandered around the village of el-Till
making new friends, and Bea got a book and a pitcher of tea
and went up to the *Menshiya*'s sun deck.

Gideon, Arlo, Haddon, and the film crew had the museum
to themselves except for Dr. Afifi, the cadaverous, understandably hangdog museum director, who hovered, apolo-
getic and solicitous, in the background.

Shooting began in the workroom, formerly a classroom
in which a bright and single-minded twenty-year-old named
Clifford Henry Haddon had been among those who had succeeded in penetrating the mysteries of hieroglyphic symbols
at the feet of the celebrated Professor Heinrich Wiedermeister
of the University of Bern.

But this morning's interview, with Gideon watching from
the back of the room, got off to a poor start. Haddon, standing
in front of some racks of inscribed stone fragments and looking slightly ridiculous in an oversized bush jacket with enough
shotgun-cartridge loops to satisfy the most bloodthirsty White
Hunter, was stiff and fussy, squinting under the hot pole-
lights. Patsy, cigarillo dangling from the corner of her mouth,
was sweating grouchily over a tangle of wires while Cy,
looking as if he might topple over asleep at any second,
manned a videocamera set up on a tripod. Forrest, who had
the ability to look bored and desperate at the same time, was
alongside the camera, keeping his eyes mostly on a monitor
a few feet away and prompting Haddon with edgy questions.

"And so after you got your master's degree at Yale, you
came directly here to work on the dig and study with Wiedermeister, is that right?" He was maintaining the singsong,
doggedly cheerful tone employed by the edgy young when
dealing with the recalcitrant elderly.

"Well—"

"Cut," Forrest said. "Please, Dr. Haddon, look, I don't mean to keep interrupting, but would you try not to start every sentence with 'well'?" It was only 8:10 in the morning and already his smile was tight and glassy. "Okay? All right?"

Haddon compressed his lips and nodded. His beard stuck out straighter.

"All right, do you want to start again? Try to make it sound interesting now."

"I will try," Haddon said, "difficult as it may prove."

Things, Gideon thought, were not improving.

Haddon waited for the signal to begin again, and peered frankly into the lens. "In the fall of 1944, with my master's degree in hand, I leaped at the chance to come—"

"Cut," Forrest said. He smiled harder. "This is just great, really great, but it would be even better if you didn't look into the camera. It makes it a little severe. You know, like Uncle Sam saying 'I want you'? We can't have that, can we?"

He laughed. Haddon glowered.

Forrest's massive face arranged itself into a merry smile. "So. Just speak right to me, not to the camera. "Okay? All right?"

Haddon gritted his teeth, nodded, and started when Forrest dropped his chin. "Well—"

"*Please.*" Forrest's voice was a little strangled. "No 'well's. Okay? All—"

"Young man, I will make a bargain with you," Haddon said. "If you stop saying 'Okay? All right?', I'll stop saying 'well.' How does that suit you?"

Gideon winced. Tempers were already simmering, and it was just the first hour of the first morning of taping. Making a movie, a retired Port Angeles neighbor who had worked in Hollywood had once told him, was like making sausage. The finished product might be terrific, but you didn't necessarily want to watch the process.

He made an unobtrusive exit and wandered for twenty minutes or so through the ill-lit, poorly labeled museum, but there wasn't much to hold his attention: broken stelae, fragmentary statues, a few shabby, anonymous mummies and mummy cases. All in all, watching the rest of Haddon's interview promised to be more uplifting.

On the way back he passed a small library in which Arlo and Dr. Afifi stood at a table, arranging five or six shoebox-sized containers. When Gideon entered, Dr. Afifi excused himself and humbly backed out, leaving the room to the two Americans as if he had been the intruder.

"Oh. Thank you, Doctor," Arlo called absently after him, staring dejectedly into the boxes. "Just look at this," he said to Gideon. "Nobody but an anthropologist would know this was anything but a pile of junk."

"Mm," said Gideon. He was an anthropologist, and it looked like a pile of junk to him.

In the boxes, arranged without apparent design, were blackened, kinked strands of metal—probably low-quality gold—squashed into shapeless clumps; dull pebbles that on closer examination were drilled beads of faience, carnelian, and jasper, the remains of necklaces or collars that had fallen apart millennia before; flattened, crumpled, copper armlets and anklets; bent, broken amulets in the forms of fish and flowers; various gewgaws of faience, the ubiquitous glass paste of ancient Egypt. There were gobs of unrecognizable stuff with tags attached to them by red string—like toe tags in a mortuary, Gideon thought, and there was something appropriate in the parallel.

It was material that had been in storage for fifty years, Arlo told him, ever since Lambert had excavated it; never written up in the literature, never even properly catalogued. Apparently it had been dug up out of the ground, brushed off, stuck in its boxes, and then utterly forgotten. If there had been any attempt at repair or restoration, there was no sign of it.

It was Egyptian archaeology's old, familiar story, Gideon thought. There was simply too much, that was the problem. Too much material, too many eager excavators over too many decades, and not enough patient, expert people to make something of what came out of the ground. Even the great Cairo

Museum was reputed to have an attic and two basements full of crates from the 1890s that they hadn't yet gotten around to opening.

"They're no help to you in your book?" Gideon asked.

Arlo uttered a rueful laugh. "Not in this condition. And half these things aren't jewelry anyway, despite the labels."

He fingered a clump of dull metal strands in one of the boxes. Bits of black flecked off to join the layer of similar debris in the bottom. He picked up a small almond-shaped eye of black and white faience, rimmed with metal, and turned it disgustedly over. "The eye shows up frequently enough as an amulet motif in the Amarna Period," he said in a dusty, disheartened voice, "but never in its naturalistic form. Only as the Eye of Horus."

Gideon nodded. The Eye of Horus, or *udjat*, with its characteristic, curling ornamentation, was familiar to anyone who had ever opened a book on Egyptian art. "What are they then?"

"What?" Arlo shrugged and put it down. "Bits of toys, funerary objects, what difference does it make? No doubt they'd be of interest to others, but not to me." He flicked some of the other things with his fingers. "Very possibly there are some things here that might amount to something, but it would take someone months of restoration even to begin to know."

"And you don't want to do it?"

"Me? I wouldn't know how. I've spent my whole life as an epigrapher. I'm not like you, you know. I don't know how to *do* anything."

Well, what was there to say to that? Arlo's doughy, woeful face and subdued little mustache, combined with the depressing state of the Tel el-Amarna Museum, was getting to him. His spirits, which had started the day blithely enough, were sinking fast. "I guess I'd better get back to the workroom, Arlo," he said. "I'm up next after Haddon, and Forrest will get nervous if I'm not around. He wants to shoot before the sun gets too bad."

"Yes, do that." Arlo's eyes were still on the boxes of

blackened metal. "Do you suppose I really ought to talk about this on camera, or find something else?"

"I'd say something else," Gideon said gently. "Whatever 'visual' is, I don't think this is it."

When he peeked gingerly back into the workroom, Gideon found things much improved. Haddon, perhaps more relaxed now that he was used to the lights and the equipment, was being charming. In front of a broken tablet that had been mounted on the wall, he was bent sharply at the waist and had his head tipped ludicrously, as if he were trying to read the inscriptions upside down.

Indeed, he explained for the camera (but looking at Forrest), he *was* reading them upside down because it was the only way he could translate them. That was the way he'd learned because in 1944, with the war going on, books were hard to come by. The class had been held—in this very room, sitting right at this very table—with only one copy of the text for old Professor Wiedermeister and his three students. The professor, a better scholar than he was a teacher, had mumbled his lectures with the book on the table in front of him, turned toward himself most of the time.

"And I," Haddon said with a comical grimace, "had the misfortune to have the seat directly across from him."

Forrest urged him on with a rolling wave of his hand. *"Great,"* he mouthed. Gideon, smiling, thought so too. Haddon could be charming when he wanted to.

"And let me assure you," Haddon added, twinkling away, "that was far from the worst aspect of sitting opposite him, in his line of fire, so to speak. Old Wiedermeister, you see, had the habit of chewing raw garlic cloves." He rolled his eyes. "The man had breath that could knock over an Apis bull at fifty yards."

"Cut, that'll do it right there," said Forrest. "That was wonderful, Dr. Haddon, just outstanding." He was patently pleased but already glancing at his watch and worrying about the time. "Don't go anywhere, Gideon," he called over his shoulder. "We'll set up outside on the King's Street, in front of the palace."

* * *

King's Street. Palace. The words seemed overblown now,
even ironic, Gideon mused aloud, trusting that the tiny lava-
liere mike that Patsy had clipped onto his windbreaker was
picking it up. His hand rested on a leaning, rusted stake that
was part of the single-strand, barbed-wire fence surrounding
what had once been the house of the pharaoh. The royal
boulevard of Akhetaten was now the desolate, sandy track
stretching away into the distance behind him, the remains of
the royal palace all of two feet high. The gracious villas and
open temples, the elegant pools and gardens, were desert
once again. In the whole of this vast, once-glorious capital
city, virtually nothing remained that was higher than the waist
of a man.

It had all been built of mud-brick that began to deteriorate
the day it was made. In ancient Egypt, stone had been saved
for the afterlife: for the tombs of the dead and the temples
to the gods. Living people, from humble laborers to great
pharaohs, had settled for sun-baked mud. In all of Egypt,
with its hundreds of temples and thousands of tombs, not a
single standing building remained to tell us how the ancients
actually lived. What we knew, we knew from the clay models
sometimes left in the tombs and—here Gideon waved an arm
to encompass the acres of crumbling, desert-colored foundations glaring in the sun—excavations such as this one.

"Very nice, very nice," Forrest said, nodding, as Gideon
went on in this vein, "but could we get to the city itself now?
And just stick to the main points, okay? All right?"

Gideon had thought he was doing rather well but was
willing to trust to Forrest as the director. "The royal city of
Akhetaten—" he began accommodatingly.

"And could you make it a little punchier? You know, just
the main points? We're not looking for 'Ozymandias' here.
No offense, but we have a boat to catch and I still have Arlo
to do."

Gideon took no offense, or hardly any. It was probably
good for him to have somebody like Forrest around. His
students were hardly in a position to tell him when he was
getting windy, and he had recently noticed, as most professors

did after a while, that his lectures mysteriously seemed to be getting longer with time.

And he was glad now that he'd taken Julie's advice and decided not to start with a quotation from "Ozymandias" after all.

Sticking closely to the main points, he told of how Akhenaten and his beautiful queen, Nefertiti, had decided in 1348 B.C. that the mighty priests and pantheon of Thebes had had their day. They had built this completely new capital city far to the north, and almost overnight the cult of Amon, supreme until then, had been stripped of its power. The new supreme deity—the only deity—was the god Aten, until then very small-fry indeed. The political and social ramifications were terrific.

The Amarna Age it is called now, and its religious and artistic upheavals were tremendous. In religion, it was the beginning of the great tide of monotheism. In art, a revolutionary new style, naturalistic, varied, and no longer unquestioningly reverential, burst on the scene. The famous head of Nefertiti, possibly the best-known piece of art in the world, had been sculpted in a studio in the workmen's village a few hundred yards from where Gideon was standing.

Society, in short, had been stood on its ear—for a while. After Akhenaten's death, the supporters of Amon had their revenge. The city was razed. The court and all the people were moved back to Thebes. The subversive art style was purged. Images of Aten were obliterated. The name of Akhenaten was chipped out of inscriptions and struck from the historical roll of kings.

The grand experiment had lasted fourteen years.

"That's a wrap," Forrest said jubilantly. "Just great, Gideon. Nice and lively."

Nice and short was what he meant, Gideon thought. Under half an hour in all. There would be plenty of time for Arlo's segment before they had to get back to the ship.

Arlo's search had turned up a few modestly presentable items—part of an inscribed boundary stela, a bit of painted pavement, some fragmentary inscriptions dealing with Akhenaten's eldest daughter, Meritaten—and Forrest had agreed that they were sufficiently visual. It took a while to get the lights set up in the main exhibition room so that they didn't reflect off the glass cases, but finally everything was ready.

Forrest pointed one finger at Arlo, who swallowed, and the other one at Cy, behind the camera. "All right, Arlo, tell us what's so interesting about that stela," he said, and to Cy: "Roll tape."

Arlo peered woodenly and somewhat dazedly into the lens, like a frog gazing down the throat of a snake.

"Well—" he began.

Gideon quietly made his escape.

Chapter Eleven

"This could be a hundred years ago," Julie said dreamily.

"Hm?" Gideon wasn't sure where his own thoughts had been, but he brought them back and turned toward the eastern shore, in the direction she was looking.

He nodded. "It could be a thousand years ago."

It could have been five thousand. Along a waterside path, perhaps a hundred yards from where they sat, walked a family group and its animals, slowly returning from its maize or bean plot to their village a quarter of a mile downstream The *galabiya*ed father, head down, led a water buffalo on which a young boy sat. Behind it came a veiled woman on a donkey and a little girl on foot, holding on to its tail. Against a near background of date palms and tamarisks and a distant horizon of tawny desert hills, moving at the lolling, rhythmic pace of the animals, they made a picture that would have been familiar in the time of Abraham.

And even then, thought Gideon, even then as it was now, the tomb complex at Saqqara, not far to the north along this same river, would have been the oldest man-made structure in the world.

It had been like this all afternoon, ever since the crew had let loose the *Menshiya*'s mooring lines and the big white ship had drifted to the middle of the river and begun to pull against the slow, steady Nile current, heading upstream toward Abydos, Dendera, and Luxor. Gideon and Julie had found an awninged, isolated corner of the upper deck, and there, a stack of untouched novels and guidebooks on the table beside them, they did what boatloads of Nile cruise passengers had been lazily and contentedly doing for centuries: they sat and watched the Nile slide by.

Flocks of white egrets drowsed in brown, foam-flecked shallows and rose in great, wing-beating clouds when the boat came too near. Children shouted "Hello-hello!" from the banks and responded with glee to any hint of a friendly response while their more reserved mothers and sisters washed clothes in the river. They saw mud-brick village after mud-brick village, the next one coming into sight before the previous one was gone. Since el-Amarna, the only reminders that they were in the twentieth century had been the clattering, ramshackle diesel engines that pumped water up the low banks and into the fields every few hundred yards, replacing in a single generation the primitive, counterbalanced *shadufs* that had served since the time of the pharaohs.

Whether the local inhabitants were pleased with the simplicity of their lives was open to question, but to a couple of tourists—and for the time being Gideon and Julie were working at being tourists—it was Egypt as Egypt was supposed to be. For over four hours they sat at the railing, hardly moving, speaking little except to point things out to each other. And even then they were sorry when it came time to leave.

But at five o'clock everyone had been asked to gather in the Isis Lounge, a handsome, vaguely nautical room outfitted with polished brass and old, oiled teak. There, a slender, softly smiling Nubian, as black as obsidian, stood behind the bar in white jacket and black tie, serving cocktails, sherry and soft drinks, all courtesy of the Gustafsons, while excerpts from the day's takes were viewed on a television monitor set up on an overhead rack.

"Posh is right," Gideon said to Julie, returning to a corner banquette with two glasses of single-malt Scotch on the rocks. He sank down into the chamois-soft leather and sipped gratefully. "You know, I could get used to this kind of life."

"Don't," Julie said. "Not unless you're expecting the next edition of *A Structuro-Functional Approach to Pleistocene Hominid Phylogeny* to make the best-seller lists."

"You never know. I've been talking to my editor about retitling it. What do you think of *Forbidden Lusts of the Cave People*?"

As Gideon had expected, Haddon's taped segment, shown last, was the hit of the cocktail hour, bringing great belly laughs from Bruno and Phil, and a smile or two even from TJ.

Ensconced in a big wing chair, still in his White Hunter's bush jacket, Haddon preened happily. "So the old man still has it when he needs it, eh? Not *quite* ready to go tottering off to his well-earned rest, after all."

He swirled his Manhattan while people smiled and murmured politely, and went on. "Oh, yes, that reminds me. I should also like to take this opportunity to reassure you, without qualification, that Clifford H. Haddon is not, after all, suffering from *dementia praecox*."

"Do you know what he's talking about?" Gideon heard Jerry, sitting on Julie's other side, ask Arlo.

"I never know what he's talking about," Arlo said.

"Or *non praecox* either," Haddon continued from his seat. "I am quite aware that the prime topic of conversation at Horizon House for the last two days has been the existence or nonexistence of a certain statue head. Was it there or was it not there? Was the esteemed director imagining things, or was he not?" He paused for some further complacent swirling and another sip.

People exchanged frowns and curious glances. TJ, who was drinking her third sherry and showed it in the red blotches on her cheeks, rolled her eyes but said nothing.

"Well," Haddon continued, "I am happy to report that with the exception of one or two minor aspects, the enigma has been solved. The solution is quite simple. The fragment *was* there . . . and then it was *not* there." He smiled.

People fidgeted some more. Gideon looked more closely at Haddon. How many Manhattans had he drunk?

"The fragment in question," Haddon told his audience,

"is from our own collection, a small, Amarna-style head of a young girl made of yellow jasper, approximately five inches from top of head to base of neck, attractive but not particularly distinguished—"

"Clifford," Bea Gustafson interrupted with something like regal annoyance from the opposite corner of the room, "if you're under the impression that all of us know what you're talking about, you're dead wrong."

"Really? That surprises me," Haddon said. "I would have thought people had been talking of nothing else."

"Amazing," Jerry murmured to Arlo with something like wonder in his voice. "He really, truly thinks people spend all their time thinking about nothing but him. I mean, 'the *prime* topic of conversation'? Give me a break."

"The nub of the matter is this," Haddon said. "The other night, when a skeleton appeared so unexpectedly in our storage enclosure—you do know about that amusing little contretemps, Mrs. Gustafson?"

"Yes," Bea said patiently, "I know about that."

"Very good. As it happened, I also observed, half-hidden by a rusting bed frame, a small Amarna head. Strangely enough, although there were four other people in the enclosure with me, no one else seemed to take notice of it."

Out of the corner of his eye, Gideon saw TJ muttering into her sherry.

"The fragment, as I say, is from our own collection," Haddon went smoothly on. "To be more precise, from the 1924 Western Valley excavations of Cordell Lambert. Apparently—"

"How do you know that?" TJ blurted. "Do you mean you've *found* it?"

"Oh, yes, I found it." Haddon finished his Manhattan and smiled at her.

"But we looked all over the enclosure," TJ said. "It wasn't there."

"No, Tiffany, it was not there. Why was it not there? It was not there because by then it was back where it belonged, back from whence it had been removed—presumably at the same time as our friend F4360 was so cruelly torn from his own humble abode."

Gideon shifted his legs restlessly. He was starting to see what it was about Haddon that got on people's nerves.

TJ put her sherry on a cocktail table and leaned forward over bony knees and gigantic sneakers. "You're telling us you found it back inside—in the annex?"

"Exactly. The possibility of its being there occurred to me yesterday, belatedly, to be sure, and I went in search of it. And, lo, I did find it, reposing comfortably in a drawer, precisely where it belonged among its fellow sculptural oddments of the Amarna Period."

It was sad, really. Haddon's manner, his scholarship, his interests, were all relics of another age. He was a man who had overstayed his welcome, who hadn't been perceptive enough or brave enough to get out when it was time, when his reputation was still intact. Don't let it happen to me, Gideon thought. When the handwriting's on the wall, let me recognize it.

TJ sank back in her chair, patently doubtful. "That I'd like to see," she said under her breath, but in an otherwise silent moment it dropped into the void and Haddon picked it up.

"And so you shall," he told her without apparent offense. "You and anyone else who cares to." He raised his arms. "All are invited."

Gideon was starting to get uncomfortable. Haddon was tight. TJ was getting there. The evening was unlikely to improve and it was only 6:30.

"Clifford," said Bea, who wasn't the least bit tight, "I'm still not sure I'm following you. Are you telling us that this fragment you saw outside with the bones the other night wasn't there the next morning because someone took it away and put it back in a drawer? During the night? Secretly?"

"In a word," said Haddon, "yes."

Julie leaned toward Gideon. "The plot thickens."

"Thickens?" he said. "It's practically coagulated."

"But—but who?" a frowning Arlo asked Haddon. "To what end?"

Haddon smiled brilliantly at him. "And there, my dear Arlo, with your usual ready acumen—"

Arlo's vague mustache twitched. His expression turned opaque. He looked at the floor.

"—you have put your metaphorical finger on those *res gestae* of the case that are so extraordinarily intriguing." He swirled his glass absently and drank down melted ice. "In fact, I do have some thoughts on the matter, some rather obvious thoughts, really, but I suspect it would be a bit premature to discuss them."

At which convenient point one of the staff entered, smilingly raised a miniature xylophone to shoulder height, and beat a tattoo that made up in enthusiasm for what it lacked in musicality.

Dinner was served.

Bruno and Bea caught up with them on the way to the dining room. "Are things getting interesting or what?" Bruno asked. "What do you think is going on? I know the way I figure it—" He glanced around. Behind them, TJ and Jerry were deep in their own conversation, but he lowered his voice anyway.

"The way I figure it, only four people besides Haddon could have known that head was sitting there, right? Arlo, Jerry, TJ, and the Arab guy. So one of them must have snuck back and put it in the drawer. It has to be. The question is, why?"

"No, I don't think that's necessarily right," Julie said. "Any of them could have told other people about it. So could Dr. Haddon, for that matter."

Bruno considered this briefly. "True. But the question still remains: why? I mean, I could see if somebody came back and stole it, but what's the point of putting it back in the drawer? That's where it would have wound up the next morning anyway, right?"

"Actually—" said Gideon.

"Wrong," Bea said. "Bruno, I will never in my life figure out how a meathead like you ever managed to make three separate fortunes."

The way he beamed at her, it might have been a compliment. "Don't forget, I managed to blow two of 'em too."

The small, tidy Nefertiti Restaurant had been set with places for four at each table: three glasses, multitudinous silverware, thick, spotless linen. They went to a table near a window. Outside, here and there in the growing dusk, the neon signs atop minarets began to flicker on in red and green.

"Now," Bea said to Bruno once they'd sat down, "how many years have we been coming to Horizon House? Don't you know Clifford Haddon yet? He thinks all we've been doing for the last three days is wondering if he's cuckoo or not, and it's been driving him bonkers."

Julie smiled. "You don't like him very much."

Bea seemed surprised. "I don't dislike him. I admire him very much. But I also know the way the man's mind works. He can't stand to look foolish, and the fact that he saw something that wasn't there, and that everybody knows it— or so he thought—has been preying on his mind. So, being Clifford, he has to make up this fairy story that's supposed to prove it was really there, only some tricky devil came skulking back in the dead of night and put it back where it belongs. It's ridiculous, but how can anyone prove it didn't happen?"

Bruno looked doubtful. "I don't know, hon . . ."

"Gideon agrees with me. I can tell from that pensive, furrowed brow. That's what I like about Gideon. The man's an open book."

"Well, I'm not sure about it." Gideon looked up from the water goblet he'd been turning in slow circles. "What doesn't quite ring true to me is his recognizing the head when he saw it in the drawer. As I understand it, he only got a glimpse of it the night before, in the dark, with all that commotion over the bones. And he said himself it wasn't that distinctive—"

"So how can he be so positive it was the very same one he saw the night before in the enclosure?" Bea finished for him. "You're absolutely right."

Gideon himself was less sure. "Maybe."

The waiter approached to pour glasses of red wine for them, then set the bottle on the table: Omar Khayyám Grand Vin Rouge. "Most good wine of Egypt," he told them. "Very tasty."

Julie pointed out that they now had a chance to fulfill the

promise they'd made to themselves to share a bottle of wine while watching the sun set over the Nile, and wouldn't it be nice to find a more pleasant subject?

This idea was endorsed by all parties, and they spent a congenial hour and a half over several more glasses of Egypt's finest and a praiseworthy meal of *chiche kabab à la broche* and *riz au sauce de tomates*.

While Bruno related to them the startling experience of G. Patrick Flanagan of California, whose dog converted permanently to vegetarianism after exposure to the healthful rays of pyramid power.

It was, said Bruno, a known fact.

Chapter Twelve

"Gideon!"

He started, deep in some queer, muddled dream about working on an assembly line, trying to nail something together to the beat of tom-toms. The tom-toms were keeping time, like drums on a slave galley, but he couldn't quite find the beat and his hammer kept going soft on him. And somewhere in the distance someone was calling his name—

"Gideon!"

His eyes opened. The room was black and silent. Beneath him the bed vibrated with the steady throbbing of the ship's engines. The tom-toms started again.

"Someone's at the door," Julie murmured beside him.

"Right," Gideon said, more or less coming awake. "Door."

"Gideon, wake up, will you?" It was Phil. "There's been an accident. It's Haddon."

God. Not the kind of words to bring one gently from sleep. Gideon pressed his fingers to his eyes, rolled out of bed, and stumbled to the door, barking his shin on a corner of the refrigerator in the unfamiliar room. He edged the door open and squinted into the bright light of the corridor.

"Phil—what happened? What time is it?"

"It's five-thirty. He fell overboard. Last night. He must have been wandering around by himself—"

"Last *night*? You don't mean he's—"

"As a doornail. They found his body half an hour ago, and Wahab's tearing his hair out."

"Wahab."

"The boat manager. Come *on*, wake up. We've already called the police, but Wahab's screaming for a doctor at the scene and you're the closest thing we've got, so let's get going." He pushed the door open further. Oh, Lord, you don't even have any clothes on. Get dressed, will you?"

"Okay, all right, I'll be right out." He closed the door, leaving Phil in the hallway, and flicked on the lights.

"You heard?" he said to Julie as he slipped quickly into a shirt and trousers.

She nodded thoughtfully, sitting up in bed under the covering sheet, her arms around her knees. "Gideon, you don't suppose . . ." She stopped, looking hard at him.

He glanced up from tying the laces on his deck moccasins. "Suppose what?"

"You don't suppose that . . . that someone . . ."

But he did suppose. Haddon had tracked down the "missing" head, or so he'd said. He'd made a public fuss about it, he'd offered to show it to one and all, he'd brayed about having "thoughts" on who had done it and why. That had all been less than twelve hours ago, and now he was dead. As a result of falling overboard. In the middle of the night. With no witnesses.

Wasn't it just a little too convenient, too timely, too . . . tidy? Wasn't it possible that he'd touched on something that someone wanted to keep secret so badly that—

No, this wasn't even conjecture, not even surmise. It was no more than a mechanical reaction, a kind of conditioned paranoia. There were a thousand other possible explanations, why leap to this one? Damn it, this was what came of taking on more forensic cases than were good for him. He was starting to see murder behind every door, under every freshly spaded garden plot.

And now he even had Julie doing it. "No, I don't suppose," he said gruffly. "You know what? You think about murder too much."

Her lips curved in the palest of smiles. "Gee, why do you suppose that is?"

Apparently, Haddon had fallen from a rear corner of the upper deck, Phil told him as they hurried down the corridor and went below by way of a musty, enclosed stairway that was ordinarily used only by the crew. He had not, as Gideon had supposed, fallen directly into the water, but had struck a one-by-two-foot wooden platform, or step, that projected from the side of the lower deck near the stern to make boarding easier for the men who delivered food and supplies in heavy sacks and boxes. He had evidently landed on his head, then toppled into the water, but one of the epaulets from his jacket had caught on a metal rod that was part of the platform's support, and he had been dragged along beside the ship since a little after midnight.

"How do you know the time?" Gideon asked.

"One of the crewmen was taking soundings and he heard a thump in the rear, and then a splash. He had a look but didn't see anything. But then he didn't think to look straight down almost under the platform; he was looking behind the ship, in the wake. Then this morning one of the cooks saw him while he was dumping garbage overboard. They came and got me. I went and had a look and turned right around and came and got you."

He pushed open a dented metal door. "Here we are, ground floor."

The *Menshiya* was a sort of floating "Upstairs, Downstairs." Above, on the passenger deck, all was comfortable chairs, lounges, picture-windowed staterooms, and sparkling cleanliness. It was like a roomy, floating palace, seemingly self-maintaining except for the pleasant, cordial Mr. Wahab, and an occasional silent, smartly groomed waiter to bring drinks or serve food. But here at water level, it was a different world, dingy, scuffed, smelly, and cramped. Passengers did not come down here. Crew members, except for the waiters and stewards, never left.

The space into which they emerged from the stairwell had sacks of rice, or beans, or flour stacked in one corner, clean towels and linens in open boxes in another, and some hammocks and bedclothes thrown carelessly into yet another. Other hammocks, still strung on hooks attached to walls and posts, were being pulled down by excited crew members. It was only with an effort that Gideon recognized one of the young men, in jeans and age-grayed white undershirt, as the smiling, white-jacketed boy who had played the xylophone at dinner.

Phil led him quickly from this dormitory—storage room with its single naked light bulb through a galley that stank of cooking oil and engine exhaust. There was a chef's sink, two big food lockers on opposite walls, and an enormous 1930s cooking range in the center with all four legs in kerosene-filled tuna cans to keep the roaches at bay. An aproned old man sitting on a stool, apparently annoyed at having his work schedule disrupted, grumbled at them as they went by, a half-inch cigarette stub jiggling on his lip.

The back door of the galley led to a small deck at the stern, where there was a deeply worn butcher-block table at which the kitchen staff chopped everything from sides of beef to bunches of scallions. Here too was where food deliveries were made from shore, and where the crew came for their breaks, to sit on the deck, and talk, and smoke, their backs against the gunwale.

There were two crew members there now, but they weren't sitting and they weren't smoking. They stood, frightened and anemic-looking in the mix of light from a single yellow bulb beside the door and a washed-out dawn just cracking the sky over the eastern mountains. Phil said a few words, at which they nodded apprehensively and tried to cram themselves still further into the niche on the other side of the table as far as possible from the figure on the deck.

"Well, there he is," Phil said unnecessarily.

Haddon lay on his back, spreadeagled across the rough decking, still oozing water from hair and clothes. He'd died with his eyes slightly open, so that *tache noire*, as the pathologists called it, had already stained the whites to a muddy tobacco-brown. That would have taken a few hours, Gideon knew, and suggested that the *thump* heard some six hours earlier had indeed been him. And, yes, he'd certainly landed on his head; that was all too clear. Medically speaking, he'd sustained a twelve- or fifteen-centimeter depressed fracture involving both parietals just anterior to lambda. In layman's terms, a saucer-sized disc of bone—almost the entire crown of skull—had been driven into his head. In effect, there wasn't any more crown.

Gideon knew this because a good part of the cracked, splintered bone was visible. Haddon's scalp had split open from the impact, which also must have meant a tremendous and immediate loss of blood—no other surface of the body was so well supplied with blood vessels, and when it was ruptured you could always count on a terrific mess. The massively broken skull had meant more mess, of even a worse sort. But Haddon's body and clothing were unsullied by blood, or brains, or anything else. Six hours of being hauled along in the wake of a fast-moving cruise ship had taken care of that.

Thank the Lord for small mercies, Gideon thought. He had never claimed to be among the most strong-stomached of forensic scientists, and this was six o'clock in the morning.

He knelt gingerly beside the body and ran his eyes over it. Haddon was wearing the ridiculous, oversized bush jacket he'd had on all day yesterday, still buttoned but rucked up around his chest. If he'd been wearing shoes they were lost to the Nile, as was one of his socks. The combination of death and water had diminished him terribly. Beneath his soaked and clinging clothing he was as scrawny and pathetic as a drenched monkey. Even the proud tuft of beard was plastered down into sodden lumps below an open, gray-lipped mouth.

After a few minutes Gideon sat back on his heels with a sigh.

"Shouldn't we close his eyes?" Phil asked uneasily. "They're terrible to look at."

"I'm not going to touch him," Gideon said.

Phil looked at him curiously but said nothing.

Some of Gideon's reluctance was constitutional, an old story. Despite repeated exposure, he had never learned to feel easy around recent, violent death. He leaned back on his haunches and turned his face away from Haddon, up to the soft, thick breath of the Nile for a moment. How was it, he wondered, as he did a lot these days, that he kept finding himself in situations like this? And would he ever get used to them? No, he didn't want to get used to them. At least he was well past the stage of throwing up, which he'd done into a stainless steel sink in San Francisco's Hall of Justice on his first or second homicide, admittedly a lot more awful-looking than Haddon was. He'd thrown up, and then rolled up his eyeballs and keeled over onto the tiled floor, plop.

Old Wilkie, the coroner, had been scandalized at the time, but he'd been dining out on the story ever since. Even now, Gideon heard it back every once in a while from somebody who'd newly heard it from Wilkie.

But there was more to his reluctance to handle the body than simple aversion. The striking timing and peculiar conditions of Haddon's death had never stopped playing on his mind, despite what he'd said to Julie. Over the railing and into the river in the dead of night. If he hadn't happened to hit the little projecting platform, and if his jacket hadn't gotten hung up on the little metal post, he'd be many miles behind them by now, at the bottom of the Nile. It would have been days before the gases of decomposition brought him to the surface, and then the current would have kept him headed in the opposite direction, downstream toward Cairo, the Delta, and the Mediterranean.

With all of the refuse floating in the Nile, the chances of ever finding him again would have been slim at best. In the single afternoon of their cruise so far, Gideon had seen a water buffalo and a dog bobbing slowly by, and several big clumps of organic material that he'd chosen not too look at too closely. And if Haddon's body had gotten caught in or under the choked masses of water hyacinth that appeared now and then, clotted with thick, yeasty froth, no one would ever have seen him again.

But he *had* hit the platform, and he *had* gotten hung up on the post, and now he was lying on the deck in plain sight, and there was something about him—about his body—that puzzled Gideon.

He stood up, realizing that full daylight had come. The overhead light had been turned off without his noticing. And the *Menshiya* was passing under a bridge, pulling toward a sizable city. He walked to the side of the ship and looked down at the waterswept wooden platform about a foot above the river's surface.

"This is what he was caught on?"

"That's right," Phil said.

Gideon examined it closely, not only the surface of the wood but the projecting ends of the steel supports. He looked at the outer surface of the gunwale too, and leaned out to look up along the side of the ship, then down to as much of it as he could see beneath the surface of the water. Then he pulled his head back and stood thinking.

"Phil, do you know who it was that heard that thump last night?"

"Yes, Mahmoud here." He gestured at one of the two men; a boy, rather, of seventeen or eighteen, who longed transparently to be anyplace in the world other than right there. "The same lucky guy who found him this morning and pulled him out of the water with his friend here."

"I'd like to ask him a few questions. Could you translate?"

"Of course." Phil addressed a few friendly words to him, and the boy, in grease-stained, canary-yellow trousers and a sleeveless, faded blue Atlanta Braves sweatshirt, came forward a couple of hesitant steps, trying to smile but not quite managing it.

"I'd like to know exactly what he heard."

Phil asked, then listened to the answer. "A bump and a splash," he said. Mahmoud added a few sentences. "Even at the time, his first thought was that somebody had fallen overboard."

"And he's positive it came from here?"

Phil's question received a vigorous nod and a long, excited recitation.

"He says he ran back here and looked for a long time. He had his pole ready to drag someone back in, but he couldn't see Haddon because he was hooked on the post at the *front* of the platform, so he was being dragged along underneath it, where there wasn't a chance of seeing him in the dark.

Besides, it never occurred to him that anything was caught on the ship itself. He was searching the water behind it. The poor kid's afraid he's going to lose his job over this."

"No, he didn't do anything wrong. We can speak up to the captain for him if need be."

Mahmoud looked only marginally heartened when this was passed along in Phil's reassuring fashion.

"When he found him this morning," Gideon said, "how was Haddon in the water? Face up? Face down? On his side?"

"On his side," Phil said after getting an answer, "with his back against the ship. The epaulet was caught from behind."

"When he pulled him up onto the deck, did he possibly bump Haddon's face against anything?"

"If he did, I assure you he's not going to say so."

"Probably not, but ask him anyway. Tell him he's not going to get in any trouble."

Mahmoud's answer was earnest and involved, with the other crewman chiming in too. There was much ardent chest-pounding.

"They say they couldn't have been more careful. They handled him like a baby. They swear on Allah's name that his head was broken before they ever touched him."

Gideon almost smiled.

"What's up, Gideon?" Phil asked. "Why all the questions? Is there a problem?"

"I think so, Phil."

He got back down on one knee, beside the dead man's ashen face, to look again at two relatively inconspicuous sets of marks in the skin, one on the prominence of Haddon's left cheek, the other on the rounded part of his forehead above the half-closed left eye. Compared to the wound at the top of his head, of course, anything would have been relatively inconspicuous, but these really were nothing very striking, nothing very serious. The ones on the cheek were a couple of straight, half-inch-long scratches or indentations, parallel to each other, an inch apart, and offset by about half an inch. The ones on the forehead were similar, but instead of being parallel, the two lines intersected to form a perfect little *X*. These too were superficial. There had been no bruising, and probably not much bleeding.

"These marks on his face," Gideon said. "Do you remember seeing them yesterday?"

Phil leaned close to Haddon for a better look. As a man who had put in a lot of time in the back alleys of Cairo and Istanbul, squeamishness wasn't one of his problems.

"No," he said, straightening up. "They weren't there yesterday, not at dinner."

"So when did he get them?" Gideon asked as he got to his feet. "That's the problem."

"Are you serious? The man falls from the upper deck onto his face, cracks open his head, is then dragged alongside a boat for five hours, and you're wondering why he's *scratched*?"

"He didn't fall onto his face, he fell onto the top of his head."

"All right, he scraped it on the way down, against the side of the ship."

"They're not scrapes, they're clean, sharp impact abrasions—well, I think they are. What you get from being hit straight on."

"Well, then, why couldn't he have bumped his head on the railing before he toppled over? He was pretty thoroughly potted, remember."

"He hit his head on the railing and then fell *over* it? That's a little hard to imagine, no matter how potted he was."

"All right, then, perhaps you're wrong about his landing strictly on his head. Perhaps he fell in such a way as to strike both his face and . . . no?"

Gideon was shaking his head. He brought Phil over to the side to look at the small outboard platform.

Phil looked. "What am I supposed to see?"

"What did he hit his face *on*? What is there to make those parallel lines, that *X*?"

"Well . . ." Phil cocked his head and rubbed his hand over his short brown hair. "You know, you're right," he said. And where there had been a tolerant skepticism before, there was something else now: a thoughtfulness, a quickening interest.

"I see where it is you're heading, Gideon. Let me make sure I have it straight. Are you saying that someone killed him? Someone hit him in the face with something, maybe knocked him unconscious? And then threw him overboard? Because of . . . what? That affair with the statue head? Is that what you're thinking?''

Yes, it was what he was thinking, it was precisely what he was thinking. But hearing it laid out as baldly as that, he found himself backing off. This wouldn't be the first time he'd let himself get carried away on ambiguous little forensic clues—on hunches, really. Sometimes there turned out to be something to them; more often there didn't.

"Well, I'm not ready to go as far as that, Phil."

But now he'd gotten Phil going. "Baloney, I know you, Gideon. That's what you think, all right. And I think you're right."

"Not necessarily. How do we know he didn't hurt his face after dinner last night, two or three hours before he went overboard?"

Phil laughed. "Do I have to convince you now?"

"Maybe he walked into his door or something, or slipped in his cabin. It's possible. He *was* pretty potted."

"Good point. Let's go and check." Although three inches the shorter of the two, he tried to turn Gideon around by the shoulders and aim him toward the door.

Gideon dug in his heels. "What do you mean, check?"

"Let's go and look at Haddon's cabin and see what we can find." He administered an encouraging little shove. "Come on, come on."

Gideon held his ground. "Phil, you know we can't do that."

"Why not? We can get the key from Wahab."

Gideon laughed. Phil's attitude toward bothersome trivia like rules, regulations, and minor laws was unabashedly pragmatic. Action over talk, that was his motto, with a plan to suit every occasion. In its way it was one of the most appealing things about him, and it was one of the things that made him so successful at what he did, having gotten him and his charges out of tight spots around the world. But it had also gotten him into jams in places where getting into jams wasn't a good idea. Once he had spent two nights in a Damascus jail because, in an effort to get better treatment for his tour group, he had claimed to be a distant cousin of Hafez Assad. Another time he had pretended to be a drug enforcement agent in Jordan, with similar results.

"Never mind the key," Gideon said. "Just calm down now. The point is, we've got a violent death here, and the police are on their way to investigate it, and one of the things I'm not about to do is go poking around in the victim's belongings and messing up possible evidence before they even get started."

Gideon expected an argument but Phil's wiry shoulders rose in an amiable shrug. "If you say so."

"Believe me, they'll spot those marks on his face for themselves. They'll know what to do."

"Mm."

"What does 'Mm' mean?"

But the ship had reversed its engines and was shuddering to a halt beside a cracked, concrete-and-rubble mooring dock at the foot of a dusty, awakening city.

"Beautiful downtown Sohag," Phil said.

They went to the side to watch the sailors throw out and secure the lines—ragged young bystanders on shore lent eager hands—and swing out the gangplank. Two men were waiting to board, one of them erect and natty in a military-style uniform, the other a stooped old man in a decades-old black suit without a tie, holding an ancient, cracked, doctor's black bag to his chest with both arms.

Once the gangplank was in place, Mr. Wahab came hurrying down to greet them, and a few minutes later the newcomers appeared on the stern deck, with Mr. Wahab flitting anxiously behind them.

"I have the honor," he sang out nervously from behind the officer's right shoulder, screwing his eyes to the side in an effort to avoid looking at Haddon's body, "to present Mr. Hamsa el-Basset, Commanding General of River and Tourist Police, Governate of Sohag."

Chapter Thirteen

The man was every inch a general: ruggedly handsome, assured, authoritative. A person of consequence. He was meticulously turned out in a simple but perfectly tailored uniform with glossy Sam Browne belt, holstered pistol, and creamy, creaking boots redolent of leather polish. His cap was under his arm, revealing thick, black, oiled hair brushed straight back (with silver-backed military brushes, no doubt) from a face that was narrower at the graying temples than at the muscular, cleanly shaven jaw.

His hopelessly outdone companion, by comparison, looked like Gabby Hayes on a bad morning at the cookstove. A wrinkled, bent, dour man—"No English" had been his curt, muttered greeting on being introduced—he seemed to have come directly from bed and didn't look any too pleased about it. He was close to eighty, with sleep-mussed white hair, a week-old stubble of beard, and a drooping mustache that covered his mouth like a filter of tobacco-stained baleen. In the open neck of his misbuttoned shirt could be seen what looked like the top of a pair of grimy longjohns. This, el-Basset said in barely accented English, was Dr. Dowidar, consulting physician to the Ministry of Public Security, who would be conducting the official examination of the body.

On second thought Gideon decided that it might be a good idea to point out those abrasions after all.

"General," he began, as Dowidar put his case on the deck and leaned grumbling over the body, "I'm a physical anthropologist, and I do a lot of work with the police in my country. I'd—"

El-Basset examined him closely for the first time, not hostilely, but not cordially either. "Oh, yes?"

Police, thought Gideon, were the same everywhere, at least in one regard: they did not appreciate unsolicited incursions onto their turf. Sometimes not even solicited ones.

"As you know, I've just looked at Dr. Haddon, and I thought I should call to your attention—"

"Thank you, but for now I wish to examine these matters for myself. And I wish first to speak with this boy, who was first at the scene of the accident."

Mahmoud, seeing himself indicated, responded instantaneously with a toothy, accommodating grin. Either that, Gideon thought, or he was having a psychomotor disturbance induced by extreme terror. It was probably the first time he'd had direct intercourse with a police official as grand as the Commanding General of River and Tourist Police. Most of the policemen to be seen in Egypt were ragged recruits like the sleepy young man with the safety-pinned private's stripe who'd been guarding the boat at el-Amarna. He'd been wearing laceless blue sneakers, not soft, gleaming boots, with his old woolen uniform.

"You will excuse me for the time being?" el-Basset said, already turning away.

"General," Gideon said, "I'm not sure it *was* an accident."

El-Basset paused to look at him again with a tolerant smile. "Not an accident? What then?" He might have been speaking to a precocious twelve-year-old.

Don't get touchy, Gideon told himself. It's just the guy's manner. "There are some indications of trauma that suggest—"

"No, no," el-Basset said, waving the rest away, "I'm extremely sorry but we must get on with our procedure now."

"But—"

"Please." El-Basset raised a peremptory hand. "Everything in good time."

"Look, General," Gideon said, openly bridling now, "what—"

"Um—" Phil touched Gideon's elbow. "Time to go, I think."

On the stairs Gideon was fuming. "Did you see that? He didn't hear anything I said. He barely knew I was there."

" 'The barking of a dog does not disturb the man on a camel.' " Phil said. "Old Egyptian proverb."

"Great, just what I need."

When they got back upstairs, Phil laid a hand on Gideon's arm. "Would you like a word of advice?"

"Sure."

"I wouldn't go around telling the Egyptian police how to do their job."

Gideon nodded. "Or any police," he said.

Julie shook her head doubtfully. "But how can you be so sure he didn't get those scratches when the sailors pulled him up? It would have been a struggle getting him into the boat."

"No," Gideon said, stripping the peel from a finger-sized Nile banana, "I think Mahmoud and his pal were telling the truth."

"Even if they were, they might have hit his face against something without knowing it."

"I don't think so. Postmortem abrasions have a funny look to them—yellow, almost translucent. If they happen before death, they're sort of rust-colored, pretty much the way they are on living people—and that's what these were."

"I'm impressed. I didn't know you knew so much about that kind of thing."

"I guess I've seen enough of it by now," Gideon said. "Unfortunately."

He looked at the banana and decided he didn't want it after all. Instead, he poured himself some more coffee.

A simple buffet breakfast had been laid in the dining room. Gideon and Julie had taken a pitcher of coffee and a plate of fruit, pastries, and hardboiled eggs up to the swimming pool area, preferring the outdoors to the grim atmosphere of the dining room and the subdued but glittery-eyed discussions of Haddon's demise. Julie had started on some date bread while Gideon told her about what had happened, but she soon lost her appetite. Gideon had never had any.

"So the question is," she said, "what would make marks like that?"

"Right. I keep trying to come up with a simple, innocent explanation. Sometimes if a person is hit with the flat side of something hard and narrow—a board, say—you get those parallel lines, because the edges dig into the skin. But a lot of bruising usually goes along with that because the flat part crushes blood vessels underneath. And there isn't any bruising on Haddon."

"So what would be a simple, innocent explanation?"

"That he accidentally hurt his face sometime between dinner and the time he fell over. I'd just feel more comfortable if I could figure out on what. It's that X that's so peculiar. What would do that? A tool of some kind? A . . . Hi, Phil."

Phil had slipped into a vacant chair at their table with a self-satisfied expression on his face and a tray with a cup of tea and a couple of gooey, stringy cakes drenched in honey in his hands. "You two are looking mightily puzzled."

"We were talking about those marks on Haddon. I still can't—"

"Well, it wasn't anything in his room, I can tell you that." He lifted one of the dripping cakes above his head, lowered it carefully to his mouth, end first, and bit half of it neatly off. Not a driblet of honey made it to his chin.

"You went to his room?" Gideon said.

Phil nodded, chewing. "Certainly I went to his room. Of course I went to his room."

Gideon leaned back. "Why am I not surprised?"

"As I remember it," Phil said, "you said *you* couldn't go in there. That's fine. I didn't say *I* couldn't go in there. Don't worry, I didn't step on any clues."

"Phil—"

"What did you find?" Julie asked.

"Nothing that could have made those marks. No convenient mirror, or picture frame, or table, or box with sharp corners that he might have cut his face on, no projecting cupboard doors, no convenient X-shaped rivets on the walls. Nothing.''

''Well, that's something to know,'' Gideon said.

''So I thought I'd walk around the deck and see what I could find.'' In went the other half of the pastry, to be followed by a swig of tea.

''And?'' Gideon said.

''And I did,'' Phil said around the mass of food, then set himself to serious chewing.

Gideon looked at Julie. ''Do you suppose he's planning to tell us what he found anytime soon?''

''Not just something,'' Phil said, getting most of it down. ''I found what we're looking for.''

Abruptly, he was out of his chair. ''Come along, Skeleton Detective, I'll explain the whole thing to you.'' He led them rapidly around the swimming pool to the port railing.

''There you are,'' he said, pointing straight down, toward their feet.

They were standing near the center of the ship at a gate in the railing that was now closed and locked, but was used for boarding from the port side. At those times the gangplank was hooked to a grating in the deck, a two-by-three-foot rectangle fitted into a space that had been cut in the flooring for it, and on which they were now standing. There was an identical arrangement on the starboard side, to which the gangplank was now attached.

Looking through the open grillwork of the grate, Gideon could see a section of the lower deck twenty feet below them.

''What do you think?'' Phil asked. ''Is that what did it or not?''

He was pointing at something below, but Gideon couldn't make out what. The life-ring holder? The bench alongside the crew's cabin? ''Is *what* what did it, damn it?''

''No, not down there, here.'' He tapped his foot. ''This, you dummy. The grating.''

''The grating?'' Gideon echoed, and then he understood. ''The *grating*!''

He dropped to one knee beside it. It was a latticework of sturdy, edge-up metal strips that crossed each other to form diamond-shaped spaces. The sides of the diamonds were about an inch apart, and because a diamond was a rhombus the parallel lines were slightly offset, precisely like the parallel marks on Haddon's cheeks.

And each intersection was, of course, a perfect little *X*.

"Well?" Phil demanded.

Gideon got to his feet. "You're right," he said softly. "He fell. Here, on his face."

Julie let out a sigh. "What a relief. That is," she said quickly, "it's a relief to know nobody *hit* him in the face, nobody threw him overboard. There's no murderer in our midst. An innocent slip by a tipsy man on a dark night, that's all."

Phil scratched his cheek. "Too bad, in a way. I mean to say, as long as he's dead in any case, a murder would have made it more interesting, if you know what I mean." He frowned. "I didn't put that very well, but it was exciting while it lasted, wasn't it?"

Gideon was looking down at the grating, his arms folded. "Don't write it off too soon."

"Uh-oh," Julie murmured, "here comes a new theory. Pardon, hypothesis."

"Whenever you find facial impact abrasions from a fall," Gideon said, almost to himself, "it's almost certainly a sign that the person wasn't conscious at the time that he went down. Nobody, tipsy or not, lands flat on his face like that. You turn your head, you throw up your hand to break the fall. It's instinctive."

Julie frowned at him. "All right, so he lost consciousness and fell. Maybe he had more to drink in his room. What's so suspicious about it?"

"It's not suspicious that he fell, it's suspicious that he got up again."

"I don't understand," Julie said.

"I don't understand either," Phil said.

"How did he get over the side?" Gideon asked them.

"How?" Julie said. "He got to his feet, he staggered to the railing, he lost his balance again—"

Gideon shook his head. "When you pass out from drinking it's because your central nervous system has essentially collapsed on you. And your blood alcohol level doesn't start going down just because you've stopped drinking, it keeps on rising because the alcohol is still being absorbed. An hour into unconsciousness you're drunker than you were when you passed out; a lot of times that's when people die. Believe me, nobody who passes out drunk is going to be getting up on his own steam anytime soon.''

Phil leaned his arms on the railing, gazing across the river. "So you're implying . . ."

"I'm implying Haddon was unconscious—maybe dead—when he fell here on the deck. I'm saying it took somebody else to get him over the side."

"We're back to murder?" Julie said. "Oh gosh, what now?"

"Now," Gideon said, "I think I better go take on the Commanding General of River and Tourist Police, Governate of Sohag." He pushed himself away from the railing. "Not that I'm looking forward to it."

"Try not to make him mad," was Phil's helpful counsel.

General el-Basset was not to be found on the stern deck when Gideon got there a minute later. Neither was Dr. Dowidar or either of the sailors. And neither was Haddon. The decking where he'd lain had already been swabbed. Gideon was astonished. He'd been gone only an hour.

At the guest services desk upstairs Mr. Wahab told him that the general was in the guest library next to the dining room. He also informed him, with equal parts outraged dignity and nervous distress, that nothing such as this had ever happened before in the history of the Happy Nomad Navigation Company.

Gideon offered his apologies, which seemed to make him feel a little better.

He found el-Basset at the single table that almost filled the little room, a row of outdated *Country Life*s on the magazine rack behind him and an emptied Turkish coffee cup at his elbow. He was smoking a cigarette and making notes in Arabic in a pad, but looked up when he saw Gideon approaching, screwed the top on his fountain pen, and motioned him into a chair across from him. He appeared at peace with himself; relaxed and above it all.

"You wished to talk," he said. "I was about to come and find you."

"Ah," Gideon said. Permit me to doubt, he thought.

"Now. What may I do for you? Would you like me to call for something to drink? I can recommend the coffee."

Gideon wasn't interested in social amenities. "Where's Dr. Haddon?" he asked bluntly.

El-Basset eyed him levelly while he took a long pull on his cigarette. The remains, he explained, had been taken by ambulance to the hospital in Sohag, where they would be kept under refrigeration while the American embassy in Cairo was contacted. Then, in all probability—

He paused. "Is there something the matter? You're frowning."

Yes, something was the matter. What kind of fatal-accident investigation—an unwitnessed accident under ambiguous circumstances—could be wrapped up in an hour, including releasing the remains? Were there to be no lab tests? No interviews? What was going on?

Not that Gideon said this aloud. He wasn't intimidated by el-Basset—not exactly—but he was well aware that customs varied from one place to another, that he had no status in this, that he was far from his own turf in every sense of the word, and that there was only one driver's seat and the commanding general's well-tailored bottom was in it.

Even so, he didn't see how he could just drop it. "There were some things I wanted to mention about the body," he said mildly. "Did you happen to notice the marks on his face?"

"Certainly I noticed them, as did Dr. Dowidar. Everything will be contained in the report."

"You didn't find them unusual?"

El-Basset smiled, polished and confident. "When a man falls twenty feet onto his head, a few unusual marks are to be expected."

"He didn't get these when he fell."

Gideon explained about the grating. El-Basset heard him out.

"So it may very well be," he said. "Thank you, I'll see that it's put in the report."

Gideon stared at him. Put it in the report without checking for himself? "I think it raises some questions," he said. "General, it's been my experience that when you find facial impact abrasions from a fall, they indicate that the person wasn't conscious when he fell."

"Has it? In *my* experience, not necessarily," el-Basset said pleasantly. "But let's say you're right. Tell me, what are these questions that are raised?"

He lit a second cigarette from the first, settled back with his arms crossed, and gave Gideon his attention. It was hard to miss the point: el-Basset would listen, but Gideon had only one more cigarette's worth of time. There were other things on el-Basset's plate, other places to be.

"Questions as to just what happened," Gideon said. "How does a man who collapses unconscious on the upper deck end up over the side?"

"How? He arises, then collapses a second time. Dr. Haddon had had a great deal to drink. Dr. Haddon, like many elderly people, was also taking antidepressant medication for his chronic depression."

"He was?" Gideon said.

If it was true, it cleared up something that had been bothering him. Haddon had been drinking, but not recklessly; not to a fall-down-drunk-and-pass-out-cold degree. But even a couple of drinks combined, say, with one of the tricyclic antidepressants—

El-Basset smiled, pleased at having told Gideon something he hadn't known. "Oh, yes, I have been talking to people, you know. Our investigation has been quite thorough."

"Ah," Gideon said again. You must be an awfully fast talker, he thought.

"Alcohol and drugs," el-Basset said. "They don't go well together. What then is so questionable about his falling down while he walks the deck, then picking himself up and falling a second time, but this time, poof, over the side?"

"It doesn't strike you as unlikely that someone who collapses—goes into a coma—from a combination of drugs and alcohol is going to get up on his own and start walking around again anytime soon? By rights, he ought to still be lying up there."

Persuasive it may have been with Phil and Julie, but it missed the mark with el-Basset, who tipped his head back to laugh while he blew smoke at the ceiling.

"Yes, it strikes me as unlikely. So? I'm a policeman. If unlikely things didn't happen every day, what would I have to do? You may trust my judgment, Professor. There is nothing here to require a more serious investigation."

"I think there is, General."

El-Basset lifted his hands in mock surrender. "Go on."

Gideon told him about Haddon's extraordinary speech the previous evening. El-Basset smiled through it, a gentle, surely-you-can't-be-serious smile.

"What are you suggesting, my friend? That he was murdered because of something he knew about this Amarna head, something that would be revealed when he showed the head to others?"

"Well . . . yes. At least, I don't think the possibility ought to be excluded."

El-Basset shook his head. "I have noticed this before about you Americans. You have too much crime in America. It makes you suspicious over nothing. You don't mind my saying this?"

Gideon sighed. Yes, he minded it. "I don't see what—"

"Consider what you propose," el-Basset said, leaning over the table. "A statuary head of no great value is removed from its drawer and mysteriously placed in an abandoned enclosure, where it is seen by Dr. Haddon—" The cigarette, down to its last third, was jabbed at Gideon to emphasize the point. "—Dr. Haddon and no one else. During the night it again disappears, only to be found a day later, also by Dr. Haddon, back in its drawer. It has not been stolen. It has not been made off with. It is precisely where it belongs, precisely where it all along would have been if no one had disturbed it."

He took a final pull on the cigarette and ground it out, smoke purling from his nostrils. "Now, where is a motive to murder anyone in all this?"

Gideon wished he knew, but one was there all right. Somewhere.

"Look, General," he said, knowing that it was already

too late, that he had struck out before he'd gotten started, "I know you know your business. I just think it might be a good idea to look into things more fully."

"In what way, more fully?" But his attention was already elsewhere. Gideon had had his chance; the interview was over. El-Basset glanced at his notes before slipping the tablet into his tunic. He slipped his fountain pen into a breast pocket and buttoned the flap. He glanced over the table to see if he was forgetting anything.

"Talk to the people on the ship some more, run some lab tests on Haddon—"

"And delay the ship's progress? Delay the transfer of Dr. Haddon's remains?" He laughed at the impossibility of it. "Certainly not. I have seen these things before, many times, and to my eyes we have here a simple case of death by misadventure. However, I will review the matter in light of what you've told me." He stood up and held out his hand. "Thank you for your cooperation, Professor."

There wasn't much to do but stand up, shake the proffered hand, and leave.

Game, set, and match. Gideon hadn't broken serve.

Chapter Fourteen

It took Julie twenty minutes to get him even a little soothed down.

"It's just that I've never been in a situation like this, Julie," he said, striding back and forth in the deserted Isis Lounge. "I'm practically *sure* Haddon didn't die accidentally, and I can't do a damn thing about it. El-Basset just isn't interested, we're in a foreign country, there's no pathologist to speak of, and Haddon's body is gone anyway—"

"Gideon, you've done all you can," she said sensibly. "The police have been here, you've told them what you think, and they've come to their conclusions . . . Gideon, you're not thinking of pursuing this, are you? On your own, I mean?"

"Of course not."

"You have been known to do that."

"Not in Egypt, I haven't." He sighed and dropped defeatedly onto the banquette next to Julie. "I don't know, maybe I ought to try going over the guy's head."

Julie laughed. "Great. Except how do you go over the head of a commanding general?"

When they went upstairs at Bea's request a few minutes later they found everyone gathered on the swimming pool veranda. Bruno was standing with his back to the bar, solemn and ill at ease.

"I just thought you'd all want to know what's going on. Phil is over at the hospital making sure everything goes smoothly with Dr. Haddon. Apparently he has a sister in Iowa, and that's where his remains are going. Um, I've also been in touch with the board as to whether we ought to go ahead with the documentary or not—"

Gideon thought he saw a small gleam of hope kindle in Forrest's eye.

"—and the feeling is that we'd like to go ahead with it as planned, if that's all right with everybody?"

Other than the glow in Forrest's eye going out, there were no responses. Bruno took it as being all right with everybody.

"And of course," he went on, "Horizon House will continue its affairs and programs exactly as they were under Dr. Haddon, with TJ here—uh, Dr. Baroff—in charge until the board takes formal action on a replacement."

"I'll do my best," said a sober TJ.

Mr. Wahab, who had been waiting politely on the perimeter, caught Bruno's attention.

"Excuse me, please, Mr. Gustafson. The caleches are below, as you wished. The visit to the museum at Akhmim can start just now."

"Great!" Bruno said, his gravity readily departing. "Let's get everybody down there who wants to go. Let's get this show on the road."

"There's a visit to a museum?" a bemused Jerry said, looking up from cleaning his pipe. "Now?"

"Well, Phil said he's going to be tied up till eleven," Bruno explained, "so the boat's not going anywhere till then anyway, and I just thought people could stand to get off it and get their minds on other things for a while. It'll be fun. They're supposed to have a wonderful collection of mummies. Come on everyone, a change of scene will do us good."

Julie leaned toward Gideon as most of the others left in varying states of enthusiasm. "I hate mummies. I think I'll just stay up here and watch the feluccas."

"I'll stay with you," Gideon said. "I don't like mummies either."

Her eyes widened. "Are you serious?"

He nodded. "They're too naked, too defenseless. I feel embarrassed when I look at them."

"That's the way I feel, but isn't it a little odd coming from you? How can people get any more naked than being skeletons?"

"True, but Egyptian mummies were prepared and embalmed so that they'd last forever, and then put in six or seven layers of cloth and wood and stone, and hidden away so no human eyes would ever see them again. And now, there they are, these august dignitaries, moldering away in the open with their noses falling off, and anybody who wants to can walk in and gawk at them for as long as they want. It's not quite—well, decent."

Julie tilted her head to study him. "I've finally figured out what your problem is. In life, I mean."

Gideon laughed. "What's my problem?"

"You're too squeamish to be a forensic anthropologist."

He grinned. "Tell me about it."

When a subdued Phil came back from the hospital and joined them on the deck he was unsurprised by Gideon's recounting of el-Basset's refusal to look the facts in the eye.

The Egyptian police, he explained, were in a difficult position at the moment. The tourist trade that was so vital to the economy had fallen off since the fundamentalist unrest and especially the attacks on foreigners had begun. As a result, a worried government was putting a lot of pressure on the police to stay on good terms with foreign countries, particularly countries with thousands of tourists who might visit Egypt. Particularly, in other words, the United States.

"I don't get it," Gideon said. "They certainly weren't trying to stay on particularly good terms with me."

That wasn't the point, Phil said. From their point of view, it was bad enough to have a prominent American like Clifford Haddon die in an accident on a Nile steamer, but to turn it into a murder investigation was the last thing in the world they wanted.

"And on top of that to find themselves putting some *other* American on trial?" Phil shook his head while he sucked down iced tea. "To end up having to *execute* him, perhaps? You can forget that."

"So what are we supposed to do?" Gideon asked grouchily. "Go with the flow?"

Phil's thin shoulders lifted in a weary shrug. "I suppose so."

Phil had had a tough morning too. Unshaven and red-eyed, he looked so thoroughly wilted that Gideon didn't have the heart to pursue it. Besides, he didn't have any ideas either.

For the rest of the day an edgy, unsettled moodiness prevailed. The *Menshiya* left at 11:30 and made its slow way to Abydos, where there was an afternoon's taping among the dim, appropriately funereal sanctuaries of the Temple of Seti I. Gideon, backed by the splendid, brooding stone pillars of the Inner Hypostyle Hall, talked about the place of the afterlife in the daily lives of the ancient Egyptians, but his mind wasn't on it and it went poorly. So did the rest of the shooting, despite Forrest's desperate efforts to pump some energy into it.

Matters weren't helped by the arrival of a huge bilingual tourist group whose two guides nattered on unrelentingly in English and French and spurred their grumbling charges from one echoing sanctuary to another with the imperious *tlik-tlak* of hand-clickers. When Forrest finally lost what little patience he had left and screamed at them to be quiet, the frazzled guides screamed back, clicking their clickers in his face. It took two elderly tourist policemen half an hour to settle things down enough for the taping to proceed.

At one point, when Gideon went out into the forecourt to get some fresh air and natural light—and a little quiet—TJ trudged up to him.

"I don't suppose you've seen those stupid ornaments, have you?"

"Huh? What ornaments?"

He had been leaning against the building's wall, absorbed in looking out at the ramshackle village that sprawled around the temple site. Except for the thatch-roofed tourist compound directly across the dusty street—"Cafeteria Camp. Sandwich hot and cold drink. We sale perfums.''—it looked as if it had been there for millennia, as long as Abydos itself. But it had achieved its remarkably tired and dilapidated look all in this century. He knew because the early photos of Abydos showed the temples sitting all alone in the desert, half-buried in miles of drifting sand. Things aged quickly here.

"Those things Dr. Afifi got out for Arlo. You're the only one I haven't asked.''

"No, I haven't seen them. Why, are they missing?''

"Misplaced, more likely. I called Horizon House from Sohag to check in with Mrs. Ebeid and she told me he called to ask if we happened to take one of the boxes with us. I didn't even know what she was talking about. Arlo says they never left the room they were laid out in, as far as he knows. He also says they were junk.''

"That's what I'd say too. You know, a busload of school kids showed up about the time we were leaving. If the boxes were still right there on that table, it could be that one of them walked off with it.''

"Maybe. What would a kid want with stuff like that?''

Gideon shook his head. "What would anybody want with it?''

TJ sighed. "Well, thanks anyway. Hell, if this is the kind of thing the director spends her time on, I'm not so sure I want the damn job.''

They were silent for a few minutes, enjoying the shade of the thick, ancient wall at their back and watching the tour group get herded unwillingly into the Cafeteria Camp across the street.

"Can I say something?'' TJ said suddenly. "Forget trying to figure out which one of us killed Haddon.''

Now where had that come from? He'd said nothing to anyone else aboard the ship about those marks, and he was positive that Julie and Phil hadn't either.

"When did I ever say—''

"It's all over your face. You've been beady-eyeing everybody all day, thinking suspicious thoughts.''

Gideon smiled. That made twice in the last twenty-four hours that he'd been told his face was an open book. He was starting to think there might be something to it.

"It's not just you," TJ said as they began to walk along the temple wall. "Hell, it's only natural. Even I thought about it for a while there. I mean, it was just too weird. He makes all these bizarre statements about that dumb head and his theories and everything, and the next thing you know they find him with his brains bashed out. It's pretty suspicious. But there's nothing to it, Gideon."

"Why isn't there anything to it?"

"Because," she said firmly, "there is no head. There never was. He imagined it, that's all. The story about finding it in the collection later was just his way of saving face; classic Clifford Haddon."

"Maybe so," Gideon said.

"Definitely so." She stopped walking. "Look, the main reason I called Horizon House this morning was to have one of our best grad students go over to the annex and check out the Lambert collection."

Above them, in the chinks and crevices of a frieze that still had remnants of three-thousand-year-old red and green paint on it, agitated sparrows had begun to dart about and chatter at them. They moved on.

"And there *was* no yellow jasper head from 1924," TJ went on. "There were quartzite ones from 1919 and 1920, and some fragments, including yellow jasper ones, from a few different seasons, and most of a limestone head from 1925, I think. Three pretty much complete heads altogether, but none of them from 1924, and none of them yellow jasper. Stacey's positive."

"TJ, why would Haddon offer to show us a nonexistent head when we got back? Wouldn't that make him look like even more of a fool? If he was making it up last night, surely he'd have said it was one of the heads that *was* there."

TJ's smile was almost fond. "Trying to outfigure Clifford Haddon is the world's quickest way to go bananas. Trust me, I'm speaking from experience."

"I don't doubt it, TJ, but the fact that it isn't there now doesn't prove it wasn't there two days ago when he said he saw it."

"No way, Gideon." They stood at the head of the long, wide stone steps leading up to the temple mound for a moment, watching the two Arab men who swept it endlessly with endless patience.

"There's no yellow jasper head in the collection now," TJ said unequivocally, "and there never was. Stacey checked the records. Lambert was a lousy archaeologist, but he was a careful collector. Every artifact in that collection, every potsherd, got its own number and its own object card with all the pertinent information on it. And there is no record of a yellow jasper Amarna head. In 1924 or any other year. Stacey checked every card in the file, and if she says it isn't there, it isn't there. Talk to her yourself when we get back."

"I believe you," Gideon said truthfully.

"So there was no reason for anybody to kill him." She shrugged. "It was an accident, Gideon."

Strange. El-Basset said there wasn't any reason to murder Haddon over the head because it was in the collection. TJ said there wasn't any reason because it *wasn't* in the collection. The odd thing was, both of them made sense. Either way, there wasn't any reason for anyone to kill Haddon.

But somebody had. If not over the head, then over something else.

On the ship that evening dinner was a muted affair. Afterward, as previously arranged, Mr. Wahab showed *Death on the Nile* in the Isis Lounge, while they continued to sail upriver. It was not quite the hit it might have been twenty-four hours earlier.

On Friday, the long cruise to Dendera for a few more hours' shooting, with nothing to do but sit on the deck and watch the scenery slip by, began to have its effect. They fell into the rhythm of the Nile, the rhythm of Egypt, where man-made time partitions—this is play time, this is work time, this is rest time—fell away. For the Americans, the only things that shaped their day came from outside themselves, beyond their control: breakfast, teatime, lunch, teatime, cocktails, dinner. Brows cleared. Laughter and casual conversation came more easily. If anybody besides Phil, Julie, and Gideon was troubled by the circumstances of Haddon's death, it wasn't evident.

In the late afternoon, with the ship moored near Dendera,

people sat on the upper deck over their tea or coffee and watched half a dozen men fishing from brightly painted rowboats near the far shore. They worked two to a boat, with one man lustily beating the water with an oar and the other manipulating a long, narrow net that trailed behind.

"I've seen that before," Forrest said. "What's the point of all that splashing?"

"It's supposed to scare the fish into the net," Phil explained.

"They've been fishing like that for thousands of years," put in Arlo. "I've seen pictures from the Twelfth Dynasty of them doing it just that way."

"Well," said Bruno, "that proves something I've always said about fish."

Bea looked at him. "Which is?"

"Darned slow learners."

Late Saturday morning they finished shooting at Dendera, then continued upriver, reaching Luxor at 5:00. Mrs. Ebeid had the vans waiting for them, and they were back at Horizon House in time for dinner.

It was the first time in years that Clifford Haddon hadn't presided at the long table. His chair was left empty.

At 9:20 the next morning Gideon was back on camera and not enjoying himself at all. He was seated comfortably enough, in one of the old-fashioned wicker patio chairs, shaded by a backdrop of trellised oleander, but he didn't like the subject they had gotten him onto. It had begun, as scheduled, as a discussion of some of the recently developed ways of studying mummies without unwrapping them, such as CAT-scanning and various new image-processing techniques. But somewhere along the way, the topic had been diverted to the racial makeup of the ancient Egyptians.

"The best way to describe the people of dynastic Egypt," he said, making a third try at it, "is simply as Egyptians; a population derived from various Mediterranean and sub-Saharan roots."

"Oh, terrific. Now how about telling us what that's supposed to mean?"

Kermit Feiffer, Forrest's assistant director, was supervising the shooting while Forrest was editing earlier tapes. Kermit's directorial technique included frequent interruptions. The interviewee was supposed to respond, but take care not to make it sound as if he were answering questions. No *yes*es and no *no*s. And, needless to say, no *well*s. Later on he and Forrest would cut and edit as necessary, and record any needed voice-overs.

By now Gideon had gotten the hang of it and liked the informal tone it created—preferred it, in fact, to Forrest's heavy-handed fluttering—but every now and then Kermit got on his nerves. A golden-bearded, self-admiring man in his early thirties, Kermit seemed to take himself every bit as seriously as Forrest did, but with less apparent justification. Most of the time he seemed to find *Reclaiming History* tedious in the extreme, so that during the shooting he yawned and fidgeted, and closed his eyes despairingly, and wandered away in despondent circles, and even groaned in torment, which took some getting used to on the part of the interviewee. He had also taken it upon himself to inject controversy and tension into things wherever he could—not an easy task on a talking-heads documentary about ancient history, but Kermit appeared to consider it a personal challenge.

He was amply succeeding with Gideon.

"I *mean*," the assistant director went on, "for you to say that the Egyptians were Egyptians sort of begs the question, wouldn't you say? What race were they? White or black?" He placed his hands on his narrow hips. "What's the problem, afraid to take a position?"

Not afraid, disinclined. Gideon hated the whole subject, first because race, biologically speaking, was a very different and vastly more complex phenomenon than color, a point that anthropologists had done a lousy job of getting across to the public at large. Second, because he found this white-black question tiresome and anthropologically pointless. But mostly because what ought to have been studied in the spirit of scientific inquiry was being twisted into something where the answers came first and the questions came afterward, and when that happened, facts—data—got distorted and stretched, ignored or overemphasized.

Not that it was anything new. The first extensive anatomical study of mummies, made near the beginning of the century, had concluded unconditionally that they were Caucasian. That result had stood unchallenged for all of three years or so. Since then, subsequent investigators, generally reputable, had "proven" the ancient Egyptians to be descended from East Indians, American Indians, Blacks, Mongols, Bushmen, Libyans, Australian aborigines, and Pelasgians, to name only a few. Naturally, each new determination had provoked a fresh furor. And now they were at it again, hotter than ever.

"Asking if the ancient Egyptians were white or black isn't much different from asking if modern Egyptians are white or black," he said. "Some are white, some are black, and most are neither. Is Mubarak black? Was Sadat? Are they white? They're Egyptians; North Africans."

Kermit was circling back from one of his eye-rolling rambles, humming through his nose now. That meant he was pleased. Probably because Gideon sounded irritated.

"Were some of the rulers black?" Gideon continued. "Sure, the Hyksos rulers were Nubians, and there's no arguing that they were black. But most, in my opinion, were a type of their own, unique to their time and place."

"I don't know," Kermit said, "my sister's kid is taking anthropology in high school, and according to her teacher scientific studies now prove that Cleopatra was black, and the same goes for most of the pharaohs. Are you saying she's *wrong*?"

Gideon sighed. Maybe he preferred Forrest after all. He gritted his teeth. "I'm saying—"

But he was saved by the appearance of a dark, wiry Egyptian who had come up behind the camera and distracted his attention with a waggle of his fingers.

"Cut, damn it!" Kermit turned furiously on the man. "Who the hell are you? Can't you see we're shooting?"

The man tapped his chest. "Ragheb." He looked thoroughly pleased with himself, the bearer of important tidings.

"And what's so goddamn important, Ragheb?"

But Ragheb wasn't there to talk to a mere assistant director. He motioned to Gideon. "Come, please?"

"Come where?" Gideon said. "Is something wrong?"

The man's eyes gleamed.

"Moomy," he announced proudly.

This time it had been found in the most isolated part of the Horizon compound, a sandy area in the extreme northeast corner that had the lumpy, pitted look of an old garbage dump over which sand and soil had settled with time, and a few scrubby plants had taken tenuous hold. It was in fact an old garbage dump; it was where Cordell Lambert and his co-workers had buried their waste early in the century, when the only things to do with garbage in Luxor had been to bury it or to burn it.

It was also the area in which Haddon had more recently directed that the rubbish from the outdoor storage enclosure, along with the bulldozed wreckage of the enclosure itself, be plowed under. To that end, under Jerry's supervision, a sizable crater had been gouged in which most of the junk had already been buried. The original pit had not been large enough, however, and now a second, smaller hole had been scooped out by the backhoe. In so doing, it had unearthed trash no different from what might have been in an American landfill of the 1920s: bits of lumber and corrugated cardboard, deteriorating clothing, shoes (some with buttons), rusted tin cans and metal corset bones, and patent medicine containers—including six that were plainly recognizable as Milk of Magnesia bottles. Apparently American stomachs had not rested easily in foreign countries even then.

These had all been brushed off and placed in fiberboard boxes ready for stowing away, presumably for future graduate students desperate for thesis topics to sift through and theorize from.

But the newly found object that had caused Gideon to be summoned was set by itself on the ground at the feet of Jerry Baroff, who regarded it contemplatively, puffing on a pipe. "TJ's at the dig this morning so they called me. I thought I better call you."

It was a plain brown paper sack the size of a large grocery bag, crumpled and soil-stained, but not old. Protruding from it was the proximal end of a broken femur, unmistakably human. Inside was a jumble of other bones, no less certainly *Homo sapiens*.

Gideon looked at Jerry. "Another skeleton? This is getting to be old-hat around here."

"Not exactly," Jerry said. He leaned down to point with his pipe at a row of letters on the shaft of the femur.

Gideon bent to read them, then straightened up with a perplexed frown.

"I'll be damned."

It wasn't a row of letters, it was an identification number, written in a precise, spidery, old-fashioned hand.

F4360.

Chapter Fifteen

"Amazing, isn't it?" Jerry said. "All I can say is, somebody sure is bound and determined to get rid of the poor old guy."

"Except this isn't the same poor old guy," Gideon said.

Jerry peered at him. "But the numbers—"

"Look at this humerus," Gideon said, pulling it partway out of the bag. "The other one didn't have a left humerus, remember? It didn't have any cervical vertebrae either, and here's a C-5." He rummaged in the bag. "C-4 too."

"Easy for you to say," Jerry said.

Gideon probed gently through the bones. All of them were disarticulated, with only a shred or two of brown, dessicated soft tissue here and there. It seemed to be a more complete specimen than the one he'd examined the other night, and every bone seemed to have *F4360* on it, in careful, crisp, slightly faded, turn-of-the-century writing like the writing on the other set.

"Is it possible that the collection has two sets of remains with the same number?" he asked.

Jerry shrugged. "Who knows what's possible? I don't think anybody's gone through the el-Fuqani stuff in 50 years. And they made a lot of mistakes in those days."

Gideon nodded. They made mistakes these days too. And

not only at archaeological digs. Not long before, he'd been involved in a mixup at a medical examiner's lab when two sets of remains had inadvertently been assigned the same number. If it could happen there, in a state-of-the-art 1990s facility, then why not here?

But the numbers, the crisp, clean appearance of the numbers, had him thinking along different lines, trying to see again in his mind's eye just what all those 4360s had looked like on the previous Monday. He'd been ferociously jet-lagged then and hadn't paid much attention, but it seemed to him now that there had been a difference . . .

He hefted the humerus, eyes closed, then did the same with the sacrum. But it was hard to concentrate; forty feet away the backhoe reversed and moved forward, started and stopped, grumbled and snarled.

Gideon put the bones back into the bag and stood with his hands on his hips. "I think it'd be better to take these back to the lab where I can spread them out. Can I get into the annex?"

"Sure, there are some kids working in there, so the door's unlocked. I better stay with these guys a while. Who knows what kind of strange stuff they're going to turn up next?"

Whatever it was, Gideon thought, picking up the bag, it was going to have to go quite a ways to be any stranger than this.

The first thing he did was to go to the skeletal storage racks to assure himself that F4360 . . . the *first* F4360 . . . was still in its box.

It was.

All right, then. At least he wasn't letting his imagination run away with him. With the box under one arm and the bag under the other he went out into the workroom where five or six student interns were indifferently washing pottery fragments while they gossiped with morbid enthusiasm about Haddon's death and its repercussions for Horizon House. When they heard Gideon coming there was a switch to sober graduate-student-speak about horizons and time lines.

"Is there another workroom?" Gideon asked.

"Down the hall, second door on your right," he was told.

In the other room, a duplicate of the first, he closed the door behind him loudly so that they could get comfortably back to Haddon, and fifteen minutes later the two sets of remains were laid out on a library table, the largest surface in the room. The ones from the box were on his right, the ones from the sack on his left. He stepped back for a first visual comparison.

Except for a slight difference in color, they were superficially similar: dry, fragile, and crumbly, with the spidery F4360 neatly inscribed on almost every piece in very much the same Edwardian handwriting. Even the individual sets of bones came close to duplicating each other: skulls, pelvises, long bones, and a few odds and ends to round things out.

But that was only superficially. If what Gideon was thinking was true there was a hell of a difference between them.

He heard Phil Boyajian talking to the students in the other room and a few seconds later he appeared with two clinking glasses of iced tea. "Jerry told me you were working on yet another bag of bones. I thought you could use this."

"Thanks, Phil." He gulped the tea mechanically, too preoccupied to cringe at the usual three spoons of sugar, Middle Eastern style, that Phil had loaded it with. Phil, who was staying at Horizon House for a few more days while he gathered *On the Cheap* material, pulled over a high stool and sat down to watch.

"What's . . ." He blinked. "Two sets of bones with the same numbers? How can that be?"

In one hand Gideon was holding one of the femurs that had just been dug up; in the other a femur from the box. He sniffed at them alternately.

"Hm," he said.

"Really?" Phil said, ratcheting the English drawl up a notch. "How informative."

"Don't be impertinent," Gideon said. "Watch and learn." He touched both of the bones in turn to his tongue and considered.

Phil grimaced. "My God, what next? I shudder to think. Does Julie know that the man she kisses goes around doing that?"

Gideon held out the one from the bag. "Here, you try it."

Phil reared back. "You're out of your mind."

Gideon looked at him. "This from the man who never turns down a new experience? What would your readers think?"

Phil held up his hands. "You have to draw the line somewhere."

"All right, just smell it." Gideon extended the bone again.

Phil stood up, put down his tea, and sniffed, gingerly but gamely. He shook his head. "So?"

"What's it smell like?"

Phil was clearly at a loss. "Like a skeleton?"

"Like an *old* skeleton, right? Sort of musty, tomblike?"

Phil laughed. "Gideon, the only skeletons I've ever smelled have been old skeletons, and as I recall, this is what they smelled like. How would I know what a new skeleton smells like?"

"All right, what about this one?" Gideon held out the other femur. "This one's from the 4360 box. The first one was from the bag that just got turned up."

Phil took it from him doubtfully. "I hope I'm not being too inquisitive, but why are we standing here smelling bones, exactly?"

"Humor me."

Phil took another cautious sniff and shook his head again.

"Well?" Gideon said. "What's it smell like?"

"Like—I don't know. It doesn't have a smell."

"Not like a bone from a dig?"

"Well . . . I guess not. It doesn't smell like anything at all. Does that mean something?"

"I'd say it means it's a fake."

"A fake?" Phil laughed uncertainly. "A fake what?"

"A fake 4360."

He thought this over for a moment. "You mean an accidental duplication of identification numbers, an error in—"

Gideon shook his head. "I don't think so. Let's try something." He went to a steel sink along the wall, laid the femurs in it side by side, and set the rubber stopper in the drain. Then he ran a few inches of water into the tub, covering the two bones. "We'll let them sit for a minute."

He came back to the table with a magnifying glass from the shelf over the sink.

"A fake 4360," Phil was muttering, his skinny arms wrapped around himself. "Then this other set, the buried one, is the real one?"

"Seems that way." Gideon began using the magnifying glass to examine the numbers on the bones that had turned up that morning.

"And you know these mysterious and enigmatic things because the bones don't smell?"

Gideon laughed. "That and a few other things." He gave Phil the lens. "Compare the numbers on the two sets. Try the crania."

It took him only a few seconds. "The ones on this one—" He was holding the skull from the storage box. "—are fuzzier. These others—" He patted the skull unearthed by the backhoe. "—are crisper."

Gideon nodded. They were crisper, he suggested, because they'd been applied in the genuine 1920s manner: first, a patch of sealant (clear nail polish was as likely as anything else) would have been painted on the bone. Then the numbers would have gone onto this foundation in India ink, and then another layer of sealant would have been applied over them. The result was that the numbers were as clear seventy years later as they'd been the day they were put on.

But the numbers on the bones in the box had not been so painstakingly prepared. They had been written directly on the bone, and the ink had bled a little into the porous surface; not enough to notice if you weren't looking for it, but amply clear under the magnifying glass.

"Yes, I see," said Phil pensively.

"There's more," Gideon said.

The differences in color for example. Both sets of remains varied from individual bone to bone, as bones often did. But the ones from the bag—and not the ones from the box—had an amber, yellowish cast overall, and the pelvis and the two lumbar vertebrae were splotched with what looked like black lichen. The cloudy yellow sheen was the result of a gluey coat of shellac that had routinely been applied to skeletal material in the 1920s because it was thought to be the best way to preserve it. The black, lichenlike stains, on the other hand, went back quite a bit further. They were the residue of the asphaltlike substance that had been so copiously (and frustratingly, from the point of view of Egyptologists) smeared onto and inside mummies in ancient times.

"Now wait," Phil said. "Even I know that el-Fuqani was a commoners' cemetery. They wouldn't have been mummified."

"No, but even so they sometimes pumped a load of the stuff into the abdomen before they laid them in the ground, more or less for form's sake. That's why the stains are just on the pelvis and lower vertebrae."

Phil sipped his tea. "Ah, so."

None of these indicators, Gideon went on, were to be seen on the bones from the storage box. Hence, (a) they weren't from Lambert's dig, and (b) the chances were that they had never been on the inside of an ancient Egyptian at all.

"No offense, Gideon," Phil said at length, "but why didn't you mention any of this the other night when you looked at it?"

"I didn't mention it because I didn't notice it," Gideon said ruefully, "which is what I get for trying to show off when I'm half-asleep."

" 'He who plays with cats must bear the scratches,' " said Phil. "Another old Egyptian proverb, or maybe that one's Persian. Tell me, what was the business about tasting them?"

"Oh, I was thinking about all the trouble Luxor has with salts in the soil. I thought I might be able to taste them, assuming the bones spent a few millennia in the ground."

"And?"

"See for yourself," Gideon said. "Take your pick, any bone will do."

Phil smiled. "Why don't you just tell me?"

"The ones from the bag taste salty," Gideon said, "and the ones from the storage box don't."

"Which must mean you're right." Phil looked down at the bones. "The ones from the bag, the ones they just dug up, are the real McCoy. The ones they found the other night are fakes, new bones." He glanced up with a peculiar expression. "How new, I wonder."

"Ah, I almost forgot." Gideon went to the sink, got out the femurs, and patted them dry with paper towels from a roll on the wall. "Let's do some more smelling."

"Oh, good," Phil said.

Gideon sniffed at each of them.

"Strange," Phil murmured. "All those cases of yours that I've heard you talk about—I'm not sure what I pictured you doing, but I always imagined the basic tools were calipers and suchlike. I never realized the job was fundamentally nosework."

"More than you might think. Take another whiff yourself, will you?"

With a sigh of forbearance, Phil complied.

"Now it smells like *wet* old skeleton," he said. "Which one is this?"

"The real one, the one from the bag. Now try the other one."

Phil held it to his nose, sniffed, lifted his eyebrows, and sniffed again. "Now that's interesting. It's got a smell now. Like . . . like . . . what am I trying to . . . candles! It smells like wax."

"Exactly," Gideon said. "What you're smelling is the grease in the bone, the fat. It's what bones smell like for a few years after the flesh is gone. Sometimes, if the odor's started to fade, putting them in water brings it out. And it means the remains are recent."

"How recent?"

"Oh . . . under ten years, anyway. Two to five years would be my guess."

Phil picked up the skull that went with the femur. "This is only about five years old?"

"Maybe a year or two more."

Phil regarded him gravely, eyes narrowed. "So, Doctor, I take it you might be revising your earlier opinion?"

Gideon frowned. "My earlier opinion?"

Phil patted the skull. "About this gentleman having been a Fifth Dynasty scribe."

He cackled with laughter, and after a moment Gideon burst out laughing too. "I may have to rethink that, yes."

"Well, that's very reassuring to us poor mortals. To know

that even the great Skeleton Detective can screw up sometimes.''

"Royally," Gideon said.

"But you know," Phil said, "this is extremely weird. If you're right, think about what it means. Sometime in the last ten years someone takes the real 4360 from its box and buries it in the old dump—the *old* old dump. Then he substitutes a new skeleton for it—and where do you get a new skeleton, by the way?—and goes to the not inconsiderable trouble of writing all the numbers in this delicate, old-fashioned script to make it look authentic. And then he goes ahead and puts *that* one in the storage enclosure, where it was almost equally unlikely to be found. It doesn't—"

"Not exactly, Phil. I don't think anyone *put* those bones in the enclosure. I think they were there because somebody died there and never left. And I don't think the rest of it was done sometime in the last ten years, I think it was done sometime in the last ten days.''

The candle wax odor had seeped into the air from the damp bone now, faint but sickly. The students in the other room had gone. The musty building with its bits and pieces of five thousand years was silent and spooky.

Gideon leaned forward, palms on the table. "Last Sunday night, to be specific.''

"Last Sunday night?" Phil scowled at him. "But that's when they *found* it!''

"That's right. I think the numbers were put on after they found it, after they called the police. I think somebody came back in the middle of the night and did it.''

"You know, you're starting to sound like—"

"I know who I sound like.''

Clifford Haddon, on the last evening of his life, the evening before someone murdered him. Babbling about people sneaking back into the enclosure in the dark of the moon, sneaking furtively back to make off with a yellow jasper Amarna head that he and only he had seen. Well, maybe he *had* seen something—despite there being no evidence of such a head in the collection—and maybe whoever had skulked off with the head had first skulked around inside the enclosure long enough to write those numbers on the bones. And then maybe he'd skulked back to the annex to get rid of the real 4360 by putting the bones in a bag and going out to the old dump site with them—

"Help, wait, you're losing me," Phil said. "Why would he bury the real one?"

"Why? So that the next morning in the enclosure, when everybody saw those surprising numbers on the bones and ran back to the annex to check, they'd find, what do you know, that the box that they belonged in was really empty. So in went the supposedly traveling remains of 4360, and that was that. Everything accounted for, no more embarrassing questions about the skeleton in the enclosure, no loose ends, case closed."

"No, wait, that can't be. There must be an inventory of the individual bones that are supposed to be in each storage box, so they'd know if they didn't match . . . they wouldn't?"

"They wouldn't. No inventory. We're talking about the late, unlamented golden age of Egyptology here. Flinders Petrie's influence was yet to be felt at Horizon House."

Phil, wandering contemplatively around the room, found an old, wheeled office chair, sank into it, and shoved himself up against the wall with his feet. "Whew. Is this the kind of thing you usually do for a living?"

"No," Gideon said. "Thank God."

"Gideon, you realize what you're implying, don't you? If it really happened last Sunday—"

"It pretty much had to, Phil. Everything about this says it was a rush job. Whoever did it was under heavy time pressure. And he couldn't just come back during the night and get rid of those bones because they'd already been seen by Haddon and the others, right? It would raise all kinds of questions. So he came up with this wild scheme to thoroughly confuse the issue."

"Which he has, with enormous success."

"Whereas if he'd had some time at his disposal he wouldn't have had to go through this complicated rigmarole, he could have come back and gotten rid of the skeleton in the enclosure anytime, long before it was found. He could have carted it off and dumped it in the Nile or buried it fifty miles from here, out in the desert somewhere.''

"Why didn't he, then? If what you're saying is so, they'd been lying there for years."

It was a good question. "Beats me," Gideon said. He sat on a corner of the table, arms folded. "But obviously he didn't."

Phil was tipped back in the pivoting chair, hands behind his head, leaning against the wall. "Well, if you're right about it, it means it had to be one of the people who went out to look at them the night before: TJ, Jerry, or Arlo."

"Or Haddon himself, if we want to cover all the bases, or Ragheb—"

"True, but let's try to keep this reasonably realistic," Phil said. "Arlo, Jerry, and TJ—no, not Jerry. If he buried those bones he'd hardly have gone ahead and had them dug back up."

"But that digging was going on because Haddon ordered it," Gideon said. "Conceivably, Jerry figured the best thing to do was to let it go on so he didn't call attention to himself.''

"That could be," Phil agreed. "So: Arlo, TJ, and Jerry." He mulled this over.

"Yes, I guess so," Gideon said. He gave the matter some thought too, staring abstractedly out the windows. The room faced the back of the compound, away from the shaded paths, away from the city. He looked out at desert and the shimmer of heat. In the far corner of the compound the backhoe was still at work, with Jerry supervising from under a table umbrella. Beyond the compound fence, a few miles farther off, mirages shimmered like pools of quicksilver in the hollows of the brown hills.

"But right now," Gideon said at last, "what I'd love to know is who these bones belonged to. It has to be someone who disappeared in the time span we're talking about—the last three, four, five years. There have to be missing-persons records at the police department. I wonder if—"

"Why is it so important to know who it is? What's that going to tell you?"

"I was thinking it might provide a lead on who murdered him," Gideon said. "Which might provide a lead on who murdered Haddon."

Phil came away from the wall. "Hold on a minute. Now you're telling me *this* guy was murdered too?"

"It's starting to look like it."

"I thought you said he died from a fall," Phil said reproachfully. "Everybody seems to be under the impression that's what you said last week."

"That's what I still say. He's got exactly the kind of linear fracture you expect from a relatively low-velocity impact against pavement or tiles. Not a twenty-foot tumble like Haddon, just a simple, ground-level fall."

"So what's so sinister about a simple, ground-level fall? Why did someone have to kill him? People trip over things, you know."

"What's sinister is what happened later. If it was just an innocent fall, why did someone go to the rather extreme trouble—and extreme risk—of writing phony numbers on his bones to cover it up? Why did someone take the other skeleton out of the box and bury it?"

Phil nodded slowly. "Yes, I see what you mean." A flicker of excitement lit up his face. "You know, I could do some asking around about missing people at the city offices; a little *bakshish* goes a long way. If we could establish a connection between this character and—"

"If the *police* could establish a connection," Gideon said, heading him off before he got up a full head of steam. A moment later, a little doubtfully, he said: "Phil, when I tell the police about this they *will* have to act, won't they? It's got to be related to what happened to Haddon. They couldn't just ignore this thing too."

"Gideon, I'm sorry to be the one to keep telling you this, but they can do whatever they damn well please."

"But that's—"

"On the other hand," he admitted, "the Luxor police aren't the river and tourist police. These people are serious cops, more independent, so you might have better luck. Go ahead, give them a call; it can't hurt. Would you like me to do it for you?"

"Would you? Just ask them to send somebody over so I can show them. I'll be here for a while yet."

Phil nodded. He got up and took a last look at the bone-laden table.

"Well, what was he, then? If not a scribe."

Another good question, one that Gideon himself hadn't gotten around to thinking about yet. The first time he'd seen the remains he'd been misled because he had started with preconceptions about them. That was a lesson that never seemed to take no matter how many times he learned it, but the markers that had led him astray—that had let him lead himself astray—were real enough: the roughened ischial tuberosities of the pelvis, the pronounced ligament-attachment area on the finger bone, the bowed fibula.

In Fifth Dynasty Thebes they added up to *scribe*. But Thebes was long gone, and so the question was: what did they add up to in twentieth-century Luxor? What habitual, modern modes of behavior could mold the bone in these particular ways? And what other signs were there in the bumps and ridges and hollows of the bones that might provide clues as to how this mysterious man, so bizarrely misidentified in death, had lived his life? He didn't doubt that he had missed some during his brief, groggy examination the other night.

"I don't know," he said.

"Are you going to be able to tell?"

He shrugged. "Could be."

It was the kind of problem he loved, the essential question that was at the heart of every analysis of every paper sack or cardboard box or body bag of bones that had been made by every physical anthropologist since the field had begun: who and what was this person?

He had been getting a little tired, but now he could feel the energy begin to flow again. He was ready for another hour or two with the bones, but on his own. He needed to go at things at his own pace and in his own uneven, doubling-back way, without having to explain every step and every partial conclusion. He wanted time, solitary and leisurely . . .

Phil was still standing at the table, showing no signs of leaving.

"Phil . . ."

"I know, I know. I'm going. I've seen that look before."
He headed for the door. "If you don't show up at lunch I'll
bring over a sandwich."

Gideon was already bent over the bones, fingering, hefting,
comparing. "Hm?"

"Bye," said Phil.

Chapter Sixteen

He had no formulas or tables to work from, but he did find a pair of spreading calipers and a steel tape measure in the other workroom, and those would get him by. For an hour he made steady progress, interrupted only by the return of Phil at noon with two chicken-salad sandwiches and a bottle of Thumbs-Up Cola. The Luxor police had been contacted and had promised to respond with dispatch, he said. They had even sounded as if they meant it.

At 1:30, still hunched over the worktable, he had just gotten to the sandwiches when Mrs. Ebeid, Horizon House's administrative assistant, appeared. A meticulous woman of earnest propriety, she had commandeered Gideon and Julie for half an hour almost the moment they'd arrived to impress on them the sacrosanct and inviolable rules of Horizon House residence: towel allotments, linens, eating times, no food in the rooms, make your own bed, no air conditioner unless the temperature reached a hundred degrees.

"You didn't hear the telephone ring?"

Gideon, caught in mid-thought and mid-bite, looked up. "What?"

She eyed him. "You didn't hear the telephone ring?"

"No. Yes, maybe. It was in another room. I didn't think it was for me."

Mrs. Ebeid's nose quivered. She had picked up the smell of the still-moist femur. She looked down at what he was doing and took a step backward, apparently unused to seeing someone with a human fibula in one hand and a chicken-salad sandwich in the other.

Possibly it was against the Horizon House rules. "*Was* it for me?" he asked. Delicately, he placed the fibula on the table.

Mrs. Ebeid remained at her new distance, which made him twist to look at her. "It was. Major Saleh of the police. He is most anxious to speak with you."

"Well, I'm anxious to speak with him. How do I get hold of him?"

She handed him a slip of paper with the telephone number, leveled one more unappreciative glance at his work and/or his lunch, and made her exit.

Gideon had heard war stories from Phil about the misdirected calls, long waits, and generally horrible state of the Egyptian telephone system, but apparently they didn't apply to lines that went to the police department because he had gotten through to Saleh with satisfactory speed—on the second try, in fact—and the phone had been picked up on the first ring.

But the major's attitude proved to be less satisfactory. He began with condolences on Haddon's death, but Gideon had barely gotten to the skeletons when Saleh interrupted with an indulgent laugh.

"Let us go back a few days and look at this from the beginning, Professor. A human skeleton is discovered at Horizon House. How sinister! To the American mind, what can it be but murder? The police are called. An investigation is launched. And the result? Not murder at all, but an innocent museum piece many thousands of years old that had strayed a few feet from its place. The police file is closed."

It wasn't looking good. Saleh sounded just like el-Basset: important, dismissive, preoccupied, and wholly disinclined to take him seriously.

"Major—"

"An eminent American professor appears on the scene,"

Saleh continued over Gideon's voice, "and deduces that the bones are those of an ancient scribe." He paused to let this sink in. "That is correct, is it not?"

Yes, damn it, it was correct. How did Saleh know about it? "I made a mistake," Gideon grumbled.

"A few days later," Saleh went on, "another skeleton is discovered. The professor rethinks his earlier conclusions. The *new* skeleton is the migrating museum piece; the other one is not ancient after all, but that of a modern—"

"Major, it's not a matter of rethinking. There's evidence." He explained—briefly; he could sense Saleh's attention wandering—about the writing on the bones, about the coloring, about the smell, the taste—

"But all these things," Saleh interrupted again, "are, forgive me, matters of opinion? With no way to prove?"

"No, that's not so. Bones can be tested for age: fluorine level, nitrogen content, pH level—"

"And you can do these tests here?"

"Well, no."

"Well, neither can I."

Clunk.

Gideon tried again. "I think we have something more important here than how old the bones are, Major. I think we have a murder."

"Murder in the reign of Userkaf or murder now?" Saleh said pleasantly.

Gideon didn't like it, but he swallowed it. As calmly as he could, he explained, but he could hear Saleh engaged, *sotto voce*, in another conversation.

"Yes, well," Saleh said, interrupting him yet again, "we will certainly look into this."

Gideon was not cheered. "And there's something else," he said rapidly, trying to keep Saleh from hanging up. "I think Dr. Haddon's death may not have been an accident."

"Yes, I spoke to General el-Basset yesterday. He was quite impressed with your theories."

Gideon gritted his teeth and plowed ahead against the odds. "Those antemortem abrasions on his face—"

"Professor Oliver? Perhaps it would be better to consider one murder at a time?"

"Look, Major," Gideon snapped, "as far as I'm concerned, if you don't care about letting murderers run around loose, then the hell with it, do what you want. It's your country."

It was hardly the way to bring Saleh around, but by now Gideon was feeling patronized and thoroughly surly. It did him good to let off some steam.

Saleh let a moment pass, then surprised him. "Would it be possible for you to put your findings into a report?" As if Gideon hadn't just finished jumping down his throat.

It took him a moment to shift gears. "You want me to write them up?"

"If it would cause no difficulty."

"I'd be glad to." Was this progress? Had he shamed Saleh into action?

"And if I sent someone to pick it up at, say, four o'clock, it might be ready?"

"It'll be ready."

After he hung up Gideon took a walk to get his blood going again—he'd been cooped up with the bones for three hours—but was driven back by the sun into the relative coolness of the high-ceilinged annex. From the main house buffet he brought back a glass of blessedly sugarless iced coffee to sip while he stared moodily at the bones of the unknown man who'd breathed his last in the enclosure perhaps five years ago. He wasn't sure whether he'd gotten a brush-off from Saleh or not, but the major would get his report. And that would have to be that, however Gideon felt about it. He didn't see any way to fight the entire Egyptian bureaucracy, and solving crimes without the police was Phil's approach to things, not his.

The basic skeletal work had been done: sexing, aging, racing, stature estimation (that had taken a call to a Cambridge colleague for the Trotter-Gleser multiple regression formulas), and so on. And, of course, the probable cause of death. All in all, he'd pulled a fair amount of information from this chewed-up cluster of scraps, but he had yet to come up with what he wanted most: an alternative explanation for the assemblage of traits that so perfectly mimicked the pattern that went along with a life as a scribe. What *had* he been or done? What habitual patterns of behavior had left that distinctive and unusual record in his skeleton?

He separated the offending bones and laid them out in front of him: the innominates with their roughened ischial tuberosities; the bowed fibula; the finger bone with its marked ligament-attachment lines. To them he added a metacarpal that also had some unusually prominent areas of ligament attachment, and one other oddity that had puzzled him from the beginning: the skull with its unusual tooth wear pattern: incisors worn down almost to nubs, while the molars showed only moderate wear. Humans did their chewing with their back teeth; if you were going to get extensive attrition anywhere, it ought to be on the molars.

It was the second time he had looked at them all in a row like this, and once again he had the feeling that the answer was there, right in front of him, just out of reach. In finger-snapping distance, so to speak.

It was possible, of course, that there was no single explanation, that each trait had a separate, unrelated cause, but he couldn't make himself quite believe that. There was a configuration here, a constellation that taken as a whole made sense if he could only comprehend it. For the dozenth time he picked up the fibula, the phalanx, the inominate. He fingered them, turned them over, put them down. He sat on a high stool, his heels hooked over the rungs, and chewed ice from the coffee. He picked them up again.

Five minutes later he snapped his fingers.

At 4:10, a police constable with smudged glasses and only a few words of English came to get the report, which Gideon had typed on a forty-year-old Remington he'd found in a dusty office. After considerable protest and two calls to police headquarters the constable reluctantly agreed to take away the skeletal material, which Gideon felt would be better off in the police vault than lying around Horizon House, prey to who knows what new drollery.

Once the constable had left with his unwelcome burden,

Gideon washed up and went to the other workroom, where some of the students had regathered to number pottery and gossip some more about Haddon's death.

"Excuse me, is one of you Stacey?"

A young black woman with a scarf around her head looked up from the row of potsherds on the table in front of her.

"I am."

"Stacey," Gideon said, "do you suppose I could have a few minutes of your time?"

Chapter Seventeen

"Welcome in Egypt! Where you want to go?"

As soon as they'd stepped through the Horizon House gate they had flagged down (or rather been flagged down by) one of the string of caleche drivers who lounged along the curb, polishing the tin decorations on their carriages, chatting with each other, and smoking cigarettes.

"Shari Tahrir," Phil told him, heaving himself up to ride shotgun beside the driver while Julie and Gideon climbed into the hansom's regal passenger seats.

They had had predinner gin-and-tonics in Phil's room, where the window fan was marginally better (if noisier) than their own, and infinitely superior to the gurgling, rattling, next-to-useless air-conditioning that had been turned on in the main house the instant the temperature had hit a hundred degrees.

Julie, who had spent the day putting in volunteer labor at WV-29, TJ's dig across the river, had needed to be filled in on things, and an hour's discussion of Horizon House foul play, past and present, had left all three without much inclination to have dinner with the others in the dining room. (Please pass the salt. *Hm, I wonder if he/she is the one who bumped off Clifford Haddon.*) At the same time, they were sensing some reciprocal discomfort on the part of the others, as if their suspicions and Gideon's continued contact with the police were general knowledge, which they probably were.

That being the case, Phil suggested that they go "grazing" at some of his new *On the Cheap* finds—where the real people ate, and at no more than five dollars a head, tips included.

"But no lamb's eyeballs, agreed?" Gideon said now, as the driver set the well-decorated but swaybacked horse more or less in motion. "No fatted sheep's tails."

Phil turned in his seat to gaze pityingly down on him. "Julie, when did this man get to be such a wimp?"

"I can tell you exactly when," Gideon said. "Two years ago, in Madrid, when you took me to the tapas bars where the 'real' people went. A distinguishing characteristic of real people," he said to Julie, "seems to be a proclivity to be a little careless about waste disposal. We were up to our knees in shrimp crania, fish bones, and spit all night long."

Julie laughed. "Do shrimp have crania?"

"Sure they have crania. And they crackle when you step on them."

"But what about the tapas?" Phil asked. "Good or not good?"

"Not bad," admitted Gideon.

"Well, I suppose that was a fairly rough crowd," Phil admitted in his turn, "but nothing like that tonight. You may put your faith in me. We won't go anywhere that I wouldn't recommend to my readers."

"That's what worries me," Gideon said.

The driver, who had been waiting for a pause in the conversation, joined in with a dazzling smile. "I, Gamal. Horse, Napoleon. You go *souks*? You want to buy Egyptian rug, Egyptian hat? I show you best place, no extra charge."

Phil murmured a few fluid sentences in Arabic. Gamal, after registering his amazement, haughtily ignored them and gave his attention to nudging Napoleon along at a dignified pace befitting both its name and the weather. At a little after 6 P.M. the sun's rays were no longer searing anything they hit, but the evening breeze off the Nile had yet to spring up and the temperature was still an unseasonably warm hundred degrees. The feeble stir of air created by Napoleon's ambling along was welcome.

They drove into central Luxor on the jammed Corniche and were soon towered over by smog-belching trucks and sleek tourist buses with sinister black windows. Bicyclists darted death-defyingly around and between motor vehicles. Automobile-tired carts of vegetables dragged by slow, weary donkeys set off long fits of hysterical horn-blowing in their wakes, to which their nodding drivers, probably dreaming of the dinners awaiting them in their villages, seemed totally oblivious.

Gamal did what he could to add to the bedlam, frequently standing up to brandish his whip and berate truck and bus drivers, who replied with tooth-rattling air-horn blasts that detonated lively, long-lasting chain reactions in every direction. Bicyclists and pedestrians were hissed and screamed at by Gamal, who replied in kind.

Evening traffic, Gideon had noticed, was no thicker than morning traffic, but always a good deal crazier. Egypt in general seemed to be at its most relaxed in the morning, to undergo a steady increase in nervous tension through the day, and to be at its peak of frenzy in the evening. Phil's theory was that it was a combination of the steadily building heat, the ordinary frustrations of city life, and the cumulative effect of all those potent little cups of coffee the Arab world consumed, uncountered by the decompressing influence of alcohol in the form of the gin-and-tonics that European visitors were gasping for by late afternoon.

Just north of Luxor Temple they turned from the choked Corniche onto a crooked, shop-lined street not much wider than the caleche itself. Within two blocks they had left most of the traffic and nine-tenths of the tourists behind. "Pharaonic art," decorated papyrus mats, and painted heads of Nefertiti were gone from the shop windows, along with signs in French and English. The very shops and windows themselves had disappeared, to be replaced by a warren of open-air stalls—*souks*—with their wooden shutters folded aside to let in the breeze—and let out the aromas. The warm air was heavy with the ancient fragrances of the Oriental bazaar:

coriander, saffron, cinnamon, ginger, roasting lamb, baking bread.

Julie sat up and sniffed like a dog that hears its bowl rattled. "I'm *starving*. Aren't we ever going to eat?"

"Right now," Phil said. "Here," he told the driver.

But Gamal couldn't bring himself to let a good thing go without one more try. "No, no, I know much better place. More good prices, nicer peoples."

"Here," Phil said firmly.

Comforted by a substantial tip, Gamal capitulated and dropped them off near a blue donkey cart set up soup-kitchen style, with a perspiring old man and a young boy standing in a cloud of steam behind two dented, blackened kettles. There they ladled out bowls of stew to a crowd of men clutching grimy one-pound notes and an occasional woman hardy enough to elbow her way through the mob.

"*Madame, monsieur, les hors d'oeuvres,*" Phil announced. "Here we have the stand of Mr. Farag Shash, famous among those in the know. The best *fuul* in Luxor."

It was certainly the most popular. There were twenty people clustered around the wagon, with others taking the place of everyone who left with a filled bowl. Diners sat at seven or eight newspaper-covered folding picnic tables set up helter-skelter in the street, lapping it up and hissing for more, which was delivered by a second teenager in a stained *galabiya* who poured it out of a spouted metal jug. Others ate leaning against walls or simply standing up. It took Gideon, Julie, and Phil five minutes to work their way to the front of the crowd, plunk down their pound notes—about thirty cents—and then fight their way, spoons and bowls in hand, back out through the hungry gaggle around the cart.

"Whew," Julie said.

"I heard Bea grumbling the other day about how much better the Egyptians would get along in life if only they learned to stand in line," Phil said.

"Bea has a point," Gideon said. "Pardon my cultural absolutism."

Phil shook his head. "It's a good thing he likes bones," he said to Julie. "He'd never have made it as a cultural anthropologist."

They were lucky in getting a just-vacated table with three chairs, under a red, white, and green umbrella that proclaimed *Corona Extra, La Cerveza Más Fina*. The sheets of newspaper on the table hadn't been changed for a while, but the stew smelled wonderful, the setting was agreeably exotic, and Gideon was glad to be just where he was, doing just what he was doing, with just the people he was with. *Fuul* was the nearest thing to a national dish that Egypt had; a paste of mashed fava beans prepared in a hundred different ways. Gideon had tried a good dozen and had liked most of them, but he was ready to agree that Mr. Shash's version won hands-down.

For several minutes they ate in animated silence, wolfing down the mixture of beans, garlic, onions, oil, and spices. When they had eaten enough to slow down a little, Julie spoke pensively, having ruminated on their earlier discussion for an hour.

"So now we have two murders: Dr. Haddon and an unknown Egyptian—both of them, we think, having something to do with an Amarna head seen by Dr. Haddon, except that he never saw it because it was never there."

"Well, I've been giving that some thought," Gideon said. "I think it *was* there."

Phil looked up from his bowl. "There in the enclosure or there in the drawer?"

"Both, just the way he said. Think about it: why would he give us a detailed description—yellow jasper, five inches high, dug in 1924—of something that wasn't there? If he was trying to save face, wouldn't he have described one that *was* there, so he could show it to us when we got back to Luxor? Why would he go out of his way to promise to show us something that he knew wasn't going to be there to show?"

Phil considered. "How do you explain it, then?"

"Easy," Gideon said. "Haddon did see it in the enclosure, and later he saw it in the drawer, exactly as he said, because someone took it out of the enclosure and put it there. And then, afterward, someone—probably the same someone—came along and took it out of the drawer and put it someplace else."

"And why would this someone be doing these curious things?"

"I think it went into the drawer because that was where it belonged; it was a perfect place to 'hide' it as long as no one was looking for it. I think it was taken *out* of the drawer when Haddon started talking about having seen it and getting people excited."

Julie shook her head. "But I thought one of TJ's students checked and found out there was no record of it in the collection. Do you mean she was lying?"

"Stacey Tolliver, you mean. No, I'm pretty sure she was telling the truth."

"Well, then, if there was no such head in the collection—"

"But I think there was."

"This is getting pretty deep," Phil said.

No, it was ridiculously simple, Gideon told them. He'd spent some time with Stacey that afternoon in the old Lambert Museum office, looking at the way they kept their records. What he found was an ancient sixteen-drawer card file—the kind with curled brass pulls on the drawers—in which there were "object cards" for all the items in the collection. Each three-by-five-inch card consisted of a description of the item and its catalogue number, which was also painted on the object itself. The number 24.1 would mean that the item was the first object collected in 1924; 24.500 would be the five-hundredth.

"Sure, that's a fairly standard system," Julie said; she had administered two small museums for the Park Service and had kept up her interest in the field. "We use it in the Service."

"The difference being," Gideon said, "that yours is on computer. This one's on handwritten three-by-five cards that have a hole in the bottom for a metal rod that keeps them in place."

"Fascinating," Phil remarked to Julie, "and don't you just bet it's relevant?"

"It's relevant, all right," Gideon said. "All you'd have to do if you wanted to steal something and make it look as if it'd never been there would be to walk away with the object itself, and then stroll over to the card file and pull out the object card. That's it. There isn't any other record. And that's exactly what somebody did. Well, I think so; I'm ninety-nine percent sure.''

Julie smiled as she spooned up the last of her *fuul*. ''Only ninety-nine percent? Isn't that a little tentative for you?''

''Not anymore. I've learned my lesson. Considering the way I cleverly determined that a man killed five or so years ago was a four-thousand-year-old scribe, I thought maybe I ought to exercise a little more restraint in my deductions.''

''But there's a problem,'' Phil said. ''If you removed the object card, there'd be a gap in the numbering system.''

''Sure, but it wouldn't matter. There are hundreds of gaps in the numbering system already. Every time they gave something away to another institution the card was just tossed.''

''Mmm,'' Phil said doubtfully, concluding the subject for the moment. ''Everybody done? Time to move on. We still have four and a half dollars to go.''

After stand-up stops for thick, unflavored yogurt, pickled vegetables, and *tahina*—sesame paste—with fried bread chips, Phil led them to a *koshari* shop, a clean, plain, indoor restaurant. At the door they handed over fifty piasters—sixteen cents—and were given deep bowls, which they gave in turn to a bucket-brigade line of servers behind a counter. A layer of pasta was shoveled into the bottom of each bowl, then scoops of lentils, rice, tomato sauce, and fried onions. Another fifty piasters got them each a plateful of pita bread and a plastic bottle of Baraka mineral water.

They found a free end of a wobbly wooden table and joined a group of Egyptian men who paid them no attention but went on steadily and singlemindedly getting *koshari* into themselves, a few with forks, most with fingers and bread. The three Americans went at it with their forks, but with diminished enthusiasm; it was tasty but this was their fifth stop.

''No, no, no, no,'' Phil said pushing lentils around in his bowl, ''it couldn't be as easy as you said. No museum, even in those days, would have been idiotic enough to have a system that easy to fool. There must be some backup, some—''

''Actually, Phil, there are museums that still do it that

way," Julie said. She put down her fork. "There was a case only a few years ago where just the kind of thing Gideon is talking about happened. Somebody stole an Egyptian pectoral from a museum in Philadelphia. They also took the object card. This was in the early 1980s as far as anybody can tell, but it might have been even earlier. The thing is, without the card nobody had any idea it was missing until ten years later, and that was only because it showed up in another museum and it looked sort of familiar to someone."

"There you are, then," Gideon said. "It could have been done. I think it *was* done. The question is: why? According to Haddon, it was a run-of-the-mill piece, not that valuable."

Phil looked soberly at Julie. "Something tells me he's been giving this some thought too."

Gideon smiled. "You know what a composite statue is?"

Phil nodded. "Where different parts of it are made from different kinds of stone. The Romans did it."

"The Egyptians did it too," Gideon said, "but only in the Amarna Period. Usually, the head—and sometimes the hands and feet—would be one kind of stone, and the body another. As it happens, yellow jasper was one of the kinds used for the heads. As it also happens, although there are a fair number of heads and a fair number of bodies around, complete statues—the right body with the right head—are extremely rare. And extremely valuable . . . even with run-of-the-mill carving. Get it to the right buyer, and it'd be worth—well, maybe millions. So I was thinking—"

"That there's a body that goes along with that head," Phil said, "and somebody knows where it is. Or already has it."

"Exactly."

"Or could it be right there in the collection?" Julie suggested.

Gideon shook his head. "No, I went ahead and checked through everything, and there are only two partial bodies, neither of which could possibly go with the head.

"How can you know that?" Phil asked. "You haven't seen the head."

"Well, no, but Haddon said it was five inches from the crown to the base of the neck, so applying normal body ratios, and giving a little leeway to Eighteenth Dynasty artistic license, I figured that the body, from shoulders down, would be around twenty or twenty-two inches, and there's nothing close. But then, why should it still be there? It could have been stolen just the way the head was stolen. So the next question is—''

Julie was regarding him skeptically, her head cocked, the flat of her fork against her lip.

"Julie, do I take it you're not buying this?"

"Well, this is usually your line, Gideon, but may I respectfully point out that you are hypothesizing somewhat in advance of the facts? We still don't know that the head—let alone this body you've now conjured up—was stolen, or even that it was ever there. Simply because something could have been done doesn't mean it was."

Gideon looked at her. "Good God, I've created a monster."

"But I'm right, aren't I?"

Gideon sighed. "Yes, of course you're right. We *don't* know." He scowled at his half-finished mineral water, his enthusiasm draining away. "And if we did, what would we do about it anyway?"

Phil had a final forkful of *koshari* and pushed his bowl away. "Well, now, I just might be able to help in that regard. Things get around, you know. I could ask around, talk to some of my, ah, shadier Luxor friends, see if they've heard any rumors about an Amarna head coming on the underground market in the last few days. It couldn't do any harm."

Julie's eyes widened. "You have friends who would know things like that?"

"Real people," Gideon said.

"People who hear what's going on," Phil said. "Luxor seems like a big city, but if you separate out the tourist trade it's simply an overgrown village full of families who've known one another for decades or even centuries. There aren't many secrets."

Gideon folded his arms gloomily. "But what's the point? If I can't get the Egyptian cops interested in two murders, why should they get excited about a piece of an old statue?"

"Never mind the criminal police," Phil said warmly. "What if we can get the antiquities people interested? They carry a lot of weight with the government. Let *them* put pressure on Saleh to do something.''

Gideon took a slow sip of warm mineral water. "It's a thought."

"It's a thought to forget," Julie said. "Or don't you remember that Clifford Haddon's been murdered over this? Stay out of it, Phil; this isn't a game."

"That's good advice, Phil," Gideon said soberly. "Talking to the police is one thing. But stay away from the bad guys."

"Is everyone ready for dessert?" Phil asked brightly. "I know a marvelous place for mint tea and *muhalabiya*."

Chapter Eighteen

Sergeant Monir Gabra dislodged the last stubborn shred of lamb from between his teeth, dropped the toothpick into his wastepaper basket, and sank with a grimace into his chair. *Shwarma*—people were beginning to call it *gyros* now, in the Greek fashion—didn't agree with him the way it once did. It was the fat, he supposed. The older you got, the harder it was to digest, and it was certainly true that he wasn't getting any younger. He was going to have to stop going out to the stands for hurried lunches. His stomach couldn't take it anymore. And look at that paunch. Pretty soon Fawzia was going to have to make him lunches of *sandweeches* and put them in paper sacks the way she did for the children. He put a hand to his chest and burped softly, painfully.

"*Shwarma* again?" Asila said dryly from her desk just beyond the partition that made an "office" out of his windowless nook on the second floor of the old police building on Shari Bur Said.

Gabra grumbled something in response as he looked at the message slip on his scarred metal desk. How cheeky they were these days, the clerks. Even the old ones, like Asila. There she sat, fat and tawdry, in clothes that were too tight for an overweight woman of forty-five, smoking like a man and full of smart-aleck remarks. Nowadays they learned how to behave from watching "Dallas" on television.

The message asked him to call Major Saleh. He fought down a second burp and punched one of the intercom buttons. Nothing happened. He punched it again.

"It's broken," Asila said around her cigarette and over her shoulder.

He shook his head. *It's broken*. If Egypt ever needed a national motto, *It's broken* would get his vote. The intercom was broken. The swivel on his chair was broken. The electric typewriter was broken. The fan was broken. The paint to refinish the fly-spotted green walls was broken.

"Does the lift work?"

"At last report."

"God be praised." He walked dourly from his cubicle.

Asila looked up at him as he passed and suddenly lifted the corners of her mouth with her fingers to make a smile. "Hey, cheer up," she said as warmly as her brassy voice would allow. "He won't eat you."

He laughed. Ah, she wasn't such a bad old girl, really, compared to most of them. The best secretary on the floor, if he wanted to be honest about it, if you didn't care about lousy typing. And after twelve years he ought to be used to her manner. It wasn't much different from having a second wife on the job. Fawzia watched "Dallas" too.

He gave her gaudily beringed hand a pat. "I'm a pretty tough old bird," he said with a smile.

"Don't I know it!" she called after him.

In his third-floor office Major Saleh looked up from his work with a noble expression of devotion to duty and country that almost matched that in the picture of President Mubarak on the wall behind him.

"Ah, Gabra, I have something to delegate to you; something that requires sensitivity and discretion. I think you'll find it interesting."

"I'm sure I will, sir," Gabra said, but he sat down in the leather chair beside the desk with deep misgiving. From long experience he knew better than to expect anything good to come of it when Major Saleh started talking about delegating.

Twenty minutes later he was back in his cubicle with a three-page report from Gideon Oliver in front of him and a set of verbal instructions from Major Saleh. Gabra's assignment, in a nutshell, was to get this meddlesome and lunatic American busybody, as the major called him, out of their hair. He was to do it without offending Oliver or the other Americans, he was to do it without creating any fuss, and he was, above all, to do it without involving Major Saleh any further. The extremist crisis was growing; another tourist, a Dane this time, had been shot near the main ferry landing the previous evening, and the major's time and energy could no longer be wasted on fantastic intrigues, imaginary murders, and old skeletons.

But Gabra's could, of course. Ah, well, he thought philosophically—his stomach had settled and he was feeling more in tune with the world—wasn't this, after all, the very nature of delegation?

It was as the old proverb said:

Shit falls downward.

TO: Major Yussef Saleh
FROM: Gideon Oliver

1. INTRODUCTION

Today I reexamined a set of skeletal remains originally found in an abandoned storage enclosure at Horizon House on November 28. At that time they were mistakenly identified as being those of an archaeological specimen from the institution's collection, an error in which I concurred in an examination on November 29.

However, a later examination leads me to conclude that these remains are modern, belonging to an individual dead between two and five years.

2. BONES PRESENT

The partial skeleton consists of four ribs, one thoracic and two lumbar vertebrae, the skull (minus the mandible), the right scapula and humerus, the right second and third metacarpals, the first phalanx of the right index finger, the sacrum, both innominates, both femurs, both tibias, and the left fibula. No other bones were recovered.

Gabra yawned and lit up a Cleopatra King. This would be tough going even if his English were up to it.

3. CONDITION

No soft tissue was present. There is moderate environmental erosion and considerable evidence of rodent and canine gnawing, particularly at the long bone ends.

4. TRAUMA AND PROBABLE CAUSE OF DEATH

There is a ten-centimeter antemortem fracture of the right parietal running diagonally back from the coronal suture. This type of injury is commonly associated with falls. Total absence of healing indicates that death followed shortly after. It is therefore highly probable that cranial damage resulting from a fall was the cause of death. Naturally, other causes of death that might not show in the existing bones cannot be ruled out.

In my opinion, it is highly likely that foul play was involved. (See "Conclusions and Implications.")

5. RACE

The admixture of racial strains in these remains makes positive racial identification difficult. However, given the circumstances, the admixture of Caucasian, Mediterranean, and African attributes suggests strongly that the individual was Egyptian.

6. SEX

The subpubic angle and the angles of the sciatic notch indicate that the bones are those of a male.

7. STATURE AND BODY BUILD

Estimated stature, based on combined long bone lengths and using the regression formula of Trotter and

Gleser, ranges from 169 cm to 176.5 cm (66.5″ to 69.5″), with a likely height of about 173 cm (68″).

8. AGE

All epiphyses are fused, indicating that the skeletal system had reached maturity. The pubic symphyses, although damaged by carnivore activity, appear to be at about phase five of the Suchey-Brooks age determination system. This, combined with other indicators such as cranial suture closure and "lipping" of long bones, vertebrae, and scapula, suggest an age of about forty to fifty years, with forty-five to fifty being likely.

9. PATHOLOGIES AND ANOMALIES

The right malar was fractured sometime before death, possibly in childhood. Although completely healed, the bone did not set properly, and it is likely that the right cheek of this individual had a caved-in or "dropped" appearance.

Other than this, there is no evidence of anomalies or of pathological conditions beyond the normal bone deterioration and degeneration to be expected with an age in the late forties.

Gabra scowled and read the last section again. At fifty-four, he was all too aware that his teeth weren't what they had been, or his digestive system either. But was he supposed to believe that his very *bones* were going too? Of this he had never heard before. His wife's grandfather was still alive at ninety, and though the old man grumbled freely enough about his numerous ailments, Gabra could not remember him complaining about deteriorating bones.

He began to see some merit in Saleh's assessment of Gideon Oliver. Gabra himself had had dealings with a pair of forensic scientists once before and had failed to be impressed when they quarreled over the age and race of a decomposing corpse that had turned up along the river south of Qena. The only thing they had agreed on was the sex, but Gabra had hardly needed an expert for that.

And look at the mess the physical anthropologists had made with their famous examinations of Tutankhamun's mummy.

No, these experts had to be taken with a grain of salt. If Gabra's bones were "degenerating," no one was going to have to tell him about it; he would be the first to know.

The broken swivel in his chair clacked (or was that his hip joint?) as he shifted and went on reading.

10. POSSIBLE INDICATIONS OF OCCUPATION

There are a number of skeletal indicators that appear to offer clues as to the occupation of this individual, and may thus be helpful in his identification.

a. Bilateral osteitis of the ischial tuberosities; that is, an unusually craggy appearance of those portions of the hip bones on which most of one's weight rests when seated.

b. A laterally bowed fibula; that is, a slight side-to-side "bending" of the fibula, which is the thinner of the two bones in the lower leg.

c. Enlarged ligament-attachment areas on the phalanx (finger bone) and on one of the metacarpals (the bones in the body of the hand), along with evidence of osteo-arthritis of the metacarpals.

d. An unusually advanced state of wear on the upper and lower incisors, or front teeth.

Gabra huffed. He knew what an incisor was. He'd known what a fibula was too, or close enough to make no difference. Who did this Oliver think he was dealing with?

This unusual combination of traits resulted in some misinterpretation during my first examination of the skeleton . . .

Gabra hooted quietly. Leave it to one of these puffed-up scientists to describe a monumental blunder as a "misinterpretation."

. . . but further analysis of the individual characteristics has suggested a more plausible explanation.

The roughened areas of the hip bone, as determined earlier, are very probably the result of sitting for long periods on a hard surface. Similarly, the bowed fibula would appear to be a reaction to pressure on the lower leg exerted by years of sitting cross-legged. The roughened areas on the finger bones have been associated in the past with the firm grasping of a relatively thin object in the fingers.

What this object may have been is suggested by a close examination of the worn incisors, which reveals many small front-to-back serrations or indentations in the eroded biting surfaces of the teeth. These have been found to occur in other cases with long-term use of the incisors to hold and snap thread.

Add to this the fact that metacarpals like the one described here have been reliably associated with habitual forceful opposition of the thumb and index finger, and have in fact been referred to in the literature as "seamstress's fingers"—and a probable conclusion as to occupation seems justified.

In my opinion, the deceased was probably a tailor in life, practicing his trade in the old-fashioned manner, seated on a wide bench or on the ground in the cross-legged "sartorial" posture. I understand that this is a position still used by many Egyptian village tailors.

Gabra's mind had begun to drift. His eyes continued to move steadily down the lines like a donkey that keeps on trudging along after it has fallen asleep in its traces. But now he blinked, skidded to a halt, and went back to the top of the page. His mouth hung open as he read it for the second time. The burnt-down cigarette, pasted to his lower lip, dangled for a few seconds before he plucked it off and impatiently ground it out in the ashtray.

"A tailor!" he said aloud. Maybe Saleh had given him something interesting after all.

"What?" Asila said without stopping her unsteady, two-fingered typing.

"Asila," he called over the partition, "do you remember

that archaeological theft in the Western Valley a few years ago? At the Horizon House excavation?''

"Where the watchman was killed?'' Click. Clack. Click.

"Yes, it's never been closed, has it?''

"No, it's still open, but no longer active. Don't you remember? We were fairly certain that the el-Hamids were in it up to their eyelids, but when it came to proving—''

"Get me the file, will you?''

The typing finally stopped, or he thought it did. It wasn't an easy thing to tell. "What, now?''

"No, a week from next Thursday.''

She sighed mightily. Her chair creaked. Her copper-dyed hair appeared over the top of the partition, her penciled eyebrows, her mascaraed eyes. "What's all this excitement, a new lead?''

Saleh extracted the last cigarette from the pack on his desk and threw the crumpled container into the wastepaper basket.

"No,'' he said. "An old lead.''

He turned to the remaining two pages of the report, the part entitled "Conclusions and Implications.''

Gabra nodded to himself while he slipped the cellophane off another gold-striped pack of Cleopatras. At one hand lay Oliver's report, at the other the file that Asila had brought him. The details were coming back now. It had happened four years earlier, in the fall of 1989 at WV-29, an isolated Horizon excavation in the Western Valley. Thieves had raided it during the night. It was not a major site by any means and would not have engendered the formidable investigation it had, if not for the murder of a police constable who was working as night watchman. He had been doped, tied up, and gagged, and when the crew had reported the next morning they had found him dead, choked to death on his own vomit. Probably it had been unintentional, but it was murder all the same. Of a policeman.

What they had taken was a small, Eighteenth Dynasty sandstone sculpture, a headless statuette "in the Amarna style.'' It had been found only that afternoon and had not yet been measured or removed from the ground. The thieves had dug it up themselves. Gabra pulled a cigarette from the pack with his lips and flicked his cigarette lighter across its end while he rummaged in the clutter of papers (not all the clerks were as efficient as Asila) for the summary sheet. Ah, here. Signed by Saleh himself.

The investigation to this time leaves little doubt as to the involvement of the el-Hamids, the notorious and hereditary family of tomb-robbers from Nag el-Azab, where for several generations they have maintained a tailoring business as a front for their other activities.

Well, that was pretty much correct, except that the el-Hamids' tailoring was no front. But that was Saleh for you. The major's father had been a deputy minister and Saleh had grown up among the clean white villas and fragrant green gardens of Cairo's Maadi district. Despite years of police work, he had never really come to understand the poor. Gabra, on the other hand, had been born in one of the swarming tenements near the Bab el-Luk, the son of a donkey-cart driver; understanding the poor had come with his birthright.

The el-Hamids were legitimate tailors, all right, but who could survive as a tailor in Nag el-Azab? This dilapidated warren of alleyways was only a few blocks from the heart of oh-so-fashionable Luxor, but the styles didn't change as often on the muddy Shari el-Jihad as they did on the elegant Corniche. They didn't change at all, in fact. *Galabiyas* and *chadors* were store-bought, then worn until they fell apart, which was the point at which the el-Hamids came into the picture, patching them up for a few piasters, and sometimes repairing shoes into the bargain.

It was impossible to live on such work, and so decades ago the family had learned to eke out a precarious and marginal sideline pilfering second-rate artifacts from the isolated secondary sites across the river, sites that better-class tomb-robbers didn't bother with. He had dealt with some of them, not only on this case, but also at one time or another when they had been caught at their illicit trade, as they frequently were. (Clearly, three generations of tomb-robbing had failed to increase their proficiency.) Usually they were fined a few pounds or given a night in jail. Always they accepted their punishment with a shrug and went back the moment they were released to their tailoring and their stealing. Apparently their antiquities profits netted them more than the cost of their fines, because they certainly stuck at it. How much more was debatable. It was the rich dealers and middlemen—not the diggers who expended the sweat and took the risks—who came away with all the money.

But when had it ever been different? Now as ever, the poor man's jaw ached with the rich man's wealth. His own untutored father had ranted for entire evenings about the coming revolution, about the freedom of the masses, the righteous upheavals of a new order. And yet, all his life he had never been able to think beyond the occupation of cart-driver. When young Monir had told him he wanted to go to high school to prepare himself to be a policeman, the old man had been stunned. "Who will drive the cart after I'm gone?" he asked. "Who will provide for the family?"

Gabra pulled deeply on the cigarette and returned to the file summary sheet.

Nevertheless, it has been impossible to prove a verifiable connection to the el-Hamids. In addition, no witnesses of any kind have been found. Moreover, Abdul Nasr el-Hamid, the man thought to have been primarily responsible for the theft and the death of the guard, appears to have fled the area immediately after his crimes, possibly to the Sudan. And finally, a year-long search of the usual outlets for this type of antiquity, in which excellent cooperation was received from Police and Security Service branches in Aswan, Cairo, and Alexandria, has produced no usable evidence that a statuette similar to the one stolen has recently traveled in the usual channels, or even been offered for sale. Interpol was contacted as well, with negative results.

For these reasons, this case is being classified to inactive as of this date.

Major Yussef Saleh's gorgeous, flowing signature followed at the bottom of the sheet.

Abdul Nasr el-Hamid, Gabra mused, the killer-thief who

had conveniently run off to the Sudan. Or so they had all thought. But hadn't that been only because the rest of the el-Hamids had so stoutly maintained it? What the police *knew* was simply that he had disappeared, as if into the air.

Or into the old storage enclosure at Horizon House, Gabra said to himself, never to reemerge. He flipped through the file looking for Abdul el-Hamid's description; if Gabra himself had ever met the man, he couldn't remember it. Ah, here it was. Age, forty-six, height 172 cm, unusual facial appearance due to the right eye being lower than the left . . .

Well, well. Gabra's lips pursed. It seemed there might be something to this anthropology business after all. Maybe, like a lot of things, it depended on who was doing it.

Hair black, mustache black, eyes brown . . . He smiled. Not much help there from Gideon Oliver and his bones.

For another five minutes he browsed in the police file, then pushed himself away from the desk. He leaned back as far as the defective chair would let him, his fingers clasped behind his head, and blew smoke at the stained ceiling.

El-Hamid had had six earlier arrests for tomb-robbing and the like, but only a single conviction. When he wasn't stealing antiquities he worked mostly in the family shop. Occasionally he found a job in Luxor but never lasted long. He had, in fact, worked as a janitor at Horizon House for three months in its laboratory, but not at the time of the theft. He'd been let go two weeks previously over an accusation of petty thieving. Took it badly too, making enough of a scene so that a constable had to be called to eject him from the premises. There had been some thought that he might later have stolen the statuette more from revenge than anything else, but with him nowhere to be found, there had been no way to prove it one way or the other.

"Well, well," Gabra said. "Asila, will you get me Horizon House on the telephone? I want to talk to a gentleman named Gideon Oliver."

"It's broken," Asila said.

His good-tempered laugh must have surprised her. "Well, then, use the one in here."

Chapter Nineteen

"For you, Gideon," Bea said, holding out the telephone.

Gideon dabbed at his mouth with a napkin and walked around the end of the table, around Haddon's still-empty chair, to take the call. Lunch, which had begun at eleven o'clock on account of a full afternoon shooting schedule, was just ending and Bea, sitting closest to the wall table on which it was situated, had reached behind her to pick the telephone up, not pausing in her attentions to a cup of sherbet.

It was Mrs. Ebeid. "The police are calling for you again," she said. "Will you speak with them this time?"

"I would have spoken with them last time," Gideon said, "but I didn't hear the phone—"

"Dr. Oliver? I am Sergeant Gabra. I have been reading your report with interest. May we discuss it this same afternoon?"

Well, what do you know. Somebody at the police department actually gave a damn after all. Gideon swallowed his amazement.

"Sure, when would you like?"

The only thing he had scheduled was a one o'clock session with Forrest and Kermit to reshoot the previous day's interrupted segment on race, and he was more than happy to put it off, even at the cost of further frazzling poor Forrest. Maybe if he put it off enough times, Forrest would decide to forget about it altogether.

"Would one o'clock be convenient? I will come there."

"Perfect," Gideon said happily. "Why don't we meet in the library? I think we'll have it to ourselves."

"Very good."

"Sergeant? You've decided to pursue this then?"

"I would think so. And—" There was a pause. "Your views on the death of Dr. Haddon, which you attached to your report? I would be interested to hear more."

Gideon topped off his coffee at the urn and slipped into the chair beside Julie again. He'd thought he was finished eating but now he reached for a few more dates from the fruit bowl.

"Things," he said, "are looking up."

Sergeant Monir Gabra was a weathered, gravel-voiced man in his mid-fifties with most of one earlobe missing and an old knife scar on his cheek beside it to make clear how it had happened. He was wearing a brown woolen uniform, past its prime and closer in its styling to that of the el-Amarna private with the pinned-on stripe (not that Gabra's stripes were anything but firmly attached) than to the splendid outfit of the commanding general of River and Tourist Police. With his ample black mustache and glistening, foxy, slightly bulbous eyes, simply changing from the uniform into a *galabiya* would have let him pass with ease as a seller of dried spices or inlaid cigarette boxes in the *souks*.

All in all, Gideon had the feeling he was going to get further with the sergeant than he had so far done with his boss; a hunch that quickly proved accurate.

Under the high, groined ceiling of the otherwise deserted library, seated across one of the monograph-littered tables from Gideon, smoking one cigarette after another, asking frequent questions in his shaky English, he had listened to everything Gideon had had to say about the unidentified remains, about Haddon, about the Amarna head.

"Well then," he said when there wasn't anything more, "I think you are right. We have here a police matter."

Gideon, who'd come to the meeting not knowing what to

expect, felt like a spent runner who'd finally managed to pass the baton. From now on it was Gabra's job to do the worrying and suspecting.

"I'm happy to hear you say it. After my experience with General el-Basset, I wasn't quite sure what your reaction would be."

"Well, you must make allowances for General el-Basset," Gabra said. Did "And for Major Saleh" hang in the air, or was Gideon imagining it?

"Here we do things differently," Gabra said complacently. "Already we are making progress, you see. We have succeeded to identify the remains."

In one day? They did things differently, all right. "Who is it?"

As always, he was curious to know where he'd gone right and where he'd gone wrong in reconstructing the onetime owner of those bones. But this time he was leery too. He'd already botched this one once, and now he was thinking that he'd probably gone out a bit too recklessly on another long limb or two.

Gabra, who smoked like most of the Egyptians Gideon had met, which was to say incessantly, lit up again. "Did you know this, that since four years, on ninth of October, 1989, there was a robbery at site number WV-29, resulting in the death of a policeman?"

"No, I didn't. What does—"

"That the person believed to do this was one Abdul Nasr el-Hamid, who has worked in Horizon House until shortly before this theft and murder? That he has not been seen alive since this theft and murder? That this Mr. Abdul Nasr el-Hamid was forty-six years old and 172 centimeters tall, and that in addition to being a tomb-robber he was by trade a tailor? That his right eye was lower than the left?"

After a moment's silence Gideon let out a peal of triumphant laughter that would have shocked anybody but a seasoned cop or another forensic scientist. He was used to hitting nails on the head, but not all of them at once.

"I was lucky," he said.

"May we continue to have such luck," Gabra said. "Ah, the object that was stolen will interest you, I think. It was a small, Amarna sandstone statue—a statuette—that was without its head.'' He smiled. ''You see? A small Amarna statue with no head is taken from the excavation on the one hand . . . and now a small Amarna head with no statue is found in the enclosure on the other. Would you say these events are coincidence?''

Not unless somebody had just repealed Abe Goldstein's old dictum, the Law of Interconnected Monkey Business, they weren't. When that many queer, related things were going on around one another, they had to be connected: the headless body, the bodiless head, the death of Abdul Nasr el-Hamid in 1989, the death of Clifford Haddon four years later.

''There is more,'' Gabra said. ''This Abdul Nasr el-Hamid was a member of the el-Hamid family of Nag el-Azab, who have been known to commit tomb-robbing for many years.''

''I see. Sergeant—''

''*Ss,*'' Gabra said with his eyes focused over Gideon's shoulder. Gideon turned to see a highly agitated Arlo Gerber in the doorway, his wispy mustache twitching.

''Yes?'' Gabra said.

Arlo jumped. ''That man. I—I can tell you who he was.''

''Man?'' Gabra said. ''And you are . . . ?''

Arlo licked his lips. ''I am . . . ?''

Gideon helped him out. ''This is Dr. Arlo Gerber, head of the epigraphic unit.''

''His name was Abdul,'' Arlo blurted. ''He used to work here.''

''Oh, yes?'' Gabra said. ''That is interesting. And what did this Abdul look like?''

''Look like?'' Arlo was thoroughly disconcerted. He had come here to say something. He had planned it and rehearsed it, and Gabra had thrown him off his stride. Arlo's hands fluttered indecisively. ''He was . . . he had a . . .'' His hand went to his face and pulled the right cheek down.

Gabra glanced meaningfully at Gideon.

''I can also tell you who killed him,'' Arlo said.

''Ah,'' Gabra said softly, ''now this I would very much like to hear.''

''Well, it was, um—well, it was sort of—''

"Would you like to sit down, Dr. Gerber?"

"No thank you," Arlo said mechanically, at the same time seating himself in a wooden chair on Gideon's side of the table. He looked utterly flustered. "Could I please have one of those?" he said, gesturing at Gabra's Cleopatras.

"Certainly." Gabra held out the pack and lit Arlo's cigarette with a lighter. Gideon hadn't seen him smoke before.

Arlo's fingers shook as he brought the cigarette to his lips. He inhaled with his eyes closed. His color improved slightly.

"It was me," he said. "But it was an accident."

Well, it was and it wasn't. El-Hamid's death, as Gideon had thought, had been caused by a fall. But the fall had been caused by Arlo. Directly and precipitately. As Arlo told it, he had surprised el-Hamid one night, walking out the back door of the annex with an Amarna head.

"And when was this, please?" Gabra asked.

"October 16, 1989," Arlo said, like a man reciting the date of doomsday.

Gabra and Gideon exchanged glances. That made it just one week after the theft of the statuette at WV-29. Interconnected monkey business, all right.

"Proceed," Gabra said.

Arlo proceeded. He had shouted at the man to stop. Instead, el-Hamid had begun to run. Arlo, calling upon reserves that came as a surprise to Gideon, and had very likely come as a surprise to Arlo, had chased after him. As el-Hamid rounded a bend his foot had caught on something and he had fallen hard, striking his head on the stone base of a defunct fountain.

When Arlo realized that he was dead he had gotten frightened. He had dragged the body twenty or thirty feet to the unused enclosure, thrown the Amarna head in after him, and left them there, shielded from nonexistent passersby by the stucco walls and the piles of junk.

Arlo, whose eyes had been fixed on the floor as he spoke, looked up. "And that's about it."

Not by a long shot, Gideon thought.

Gabra didn't think so either. "Why did you become frightened? If all was as you say, you did nothing wrong. Why you have said nothing all this long time? Why do you come forward now?''

"Oh, well," said Arlo reluctantly, "that's a long story."

Gabra gestured with his cigarette. Time was no problem.

Arlo carefully laid his cigarette in an aluminum-foil ashtray and began. He spoke like a man who'd already been tried and condemned, hunched forward as if against the fetid damp of an Egyptian jail, with his hands squeezed flat between his knees.

It had started several weeks before the fatal night. There had been an outbreak of pilfering from the annex. It was an old and recurring problem at Horizon House. Nothing of significance; merely the sort of generic, everyday bits and pieces that might be palmed off to tourists for five or ten dollars. It had been going on in Egypt for millennia, and there always seemed to be more where they had come from. Still, Arlo said, one couldn't help but hate to see them go off to Topeka and Fort Lauderdale to gather dust on knickknack shelves next to Toby jugs and commemorative spoons. He had grown suspicious of Abdul, who had started there at about the time the latest rash had begun, and who, as a janitor in the annex, had easy access to the collection.

He had reported his suspicions to Haddon and a trap had been laid. The bait had been snapped up and Abdul had been fired, but not until after a horrible scene during which the Egyptian had refused to accept Haddon's decision and loudly accused Arlo, as Allah was his witness, of everything from offering him money to steal the objects to—and here Arlo flushed and lowered his voice—asking him to procure women and, er, ah, little boys, young children. It was too absurd for anyone to take any of it seriously, of course, and Haddon had called for a constable to send Abdul packing, but it had been terribly stressful for Arlo.

"May I have another cigarette?" he asked Gabra. His own, left untouched in the foil tray, was a cylinder of ash.

Gabra slid the open pack across to him along with the lighter.

"And you saw him next . . . ?"

Arlo had some trouble getting the cigarette lit but finally

managed. "I told you, that night at the back door of the annex, the night I—the night he fell."

"Died," said Gabra.

"Yes," Arlo said after a moment. "Died. When that happened, I—I suppose I panicked. How could I tell anyone what happened? I was afraid it would look as if I killed him because of his revolting accusations. I was nearly hysterical— I felt—I *heard* his head crack, you see—all I wanted to do was get out of there, get him out of sight, so I—well, you know the rest."

"No, not all," Gabra said. "Since 1989 you can easily dispose of these bones. Why have you not done it sooner? Why do you leave them all this time until they are discovered, which must happen eventually?"

Arlo's shrug was half-shudder. "I couldn't bring myself to touch him, or even to go back in there where he was. I think I made myself believe it had never really happened. I suppose I hoped somehow it would all never come to light."

"Yet you come forward now," Gabra said.

"Yes, because Dr. Oliver was working on it." Arlo raised his eyes to Gideon in mournful tribute. "I knew it was only a question of time before you found out who it was."

As compliments went, Gideon supposed, it wasn't bad.

"What will happen to me now?" Arlo asked. "Am I under arrest?"

"Please, just to be patient," said Gabra. "Dr. Oliver, I think you have things to ask?"

Indeed he did. He nodded his appreciation; not all cops were so collaborative. "Arlo, you're sure that what he was making off with was an Amarna head?"

"Oh, yes, there was no question. Dr. Haddon described it perfectly on the ship the other night."

"Yet you said nothing when the time was there," Gabra said.

Arlo hung his head. "No."

"When this all happened in 1989 you already knew about the theft at the site, didn't you?" Gideon asked.

"Of the statuette? Yes, everybody knew about that."

"And it didn't occur to you that the head might go with the body? That the two thefts might be related?"

"Of course it occurred to me," Arlo said with a brief spark of temper. "I told you: I was frightened. I just wanted to put it behind me, can't you understand that?"

Yes, Gideon could understand that. Faced with the prospect of an Egyptian prison he too might have wanted to put it behind him.

"Arlo," he said more gently, "let's talk about last Sunday night when Ragheb found the skeleton, all right?"

Arlo nodded cautiously.

"After everybody went to bed, you went back to the enclosure, you painted the numbers on the bones—"

Arlo blinked, transparently surprised. His fingers almost stopped trembling. "What?"

"You painted—"

"I most certainly did not."

Gideon blinked back. "You didn't paint the numbers? You didn't bury the original 4360? You didn't take the head?"

"Absolutely not," Arlo said, sounding offended for the first time. Accidentally killing a man was one thing; perpetrating a ludicrous escapade involving buried skeletons and faked numbers was clearly beneath his dignity.

"Well, who did?"

Arlo took a long, thoughtful pull on his cigarette. "Well now, how in the world would I know that?"

"The funny thing is," Gideon said, holding up his hand to refuse the three-foot-long flexible smoking-tube the waiter was offering him, "I believe him."

"As do I," Gabra agreed, sighing with his first burbling puff on the *narghile* that had been placed on the tiled floor beside their table.

At the sergeant's suggestion they had left Horizon House for a nearby outdoor café on Shari Mabaad after concluding their session with Arlo, who had almost wept with relief on being told by Gabra that he was not under arrest or in imminent danger of it, but was merely to keep himself available in Luxor for further questions, and to keep to himself what he had told them.

Arlo had done a cogent if not altogether coherent job of explaining himself. He had spent a terrible night after they had all gone out to look at the skeleton, he said, determining at dawn that he would confess and finally confront his fate that day. He had steeled himself to face Saleh and the wheels of Egyptian justice, and then he had been as flabbergasted as anyone else when the numbers were discovered on the bones the following morning. At first he had leaped at the idea that he had suffered some sort of hallucination four years earlier, that el-Hamid's death had never happened, that the skeleton really was that of F4360.

But even Arlo, who clearly had some considerable propensity for deluding himself, couldn't quite make himself believe that. In the end he had accepted the astonishing development as a kind of cosmic gift, like finding a winning lottery ticket among one's dry-cleaning stubs. He had gratefully accepted his salvation, had asked no questions, had looked no gift-horses in the mouth. He had been delivered from evil, and he had had no intention of upsetting things by trying to find out who had done it or why.

No, it wasn't very logical, but it did sound convincingly like Arlo.

"Somebody recognized that head for what it was," Gideon mused aloud now, "then killed Haddon afterward because he'd seen it too. The question is: who?"

" 'When the cow stumbles,' " Gabra said somberly, " 'many knives come out.' "

This gloomy particle of Eastern wisdom hung in the air while the waiter set down their orders: mint tea for Gabra, Turkish coffee ("Here we call it Egyptian coffee," Gabra had reproved him) for Gideon.

"Here's what I think," Gideon said. "I think the skeleton was painted to keep anyone from realizing it was one of the el-Hamids so that no one would make any connection to the theft of the statuette four years ago. That means that somebody besides Arlo knew all along that it *was* el-Hamid—either that, or knew enough to figure it out when the bones turned up. He also knew enough to make off with the head when he saw it.''

Gabra nodded, stirring sugar into his already sweetened glass of tea. "I too believe this to be so."

"If it is," Gideon said, "wouldn't your next step be to find out if there's been any new word of the head on the black market? Talk to the el-Hamids?"

"Yes, but to get information from these people is hard. Also, I think by now that this goes beyond the el-Hamids. It is too large a matter."

Gideon leaned forward. "I have a friend here, a Dr. Boyajian. He thinks he might be able to learn something from people he knows in Luxor, people who might have contacts in the illegal antiquities market—"

But Gideon had pushed a little too far, a little too fast. "Your friend is too much interested, I think," Gabra said curtly.

"I just thought—"

"This is a police matter, Doctor, a matter of . . ." He searched for the right words. "Of sensitivity, of discretion."

Glumly, Gideon took a sip of the thick, syrupy coffee from its small, squat glass. Was he running into another police roadblock after all? "What's so sensitive about it? Look, there have been two murders. There have been two thefts of antiquities that add up to a single piece of tremendous historical and monetary value. That piece properly belongs to Egypt, but if it's not already out of the country by now it's well on its way. I'd think—"

Gabra was shaking his head. "They will not talk to your friend, they will not talk to me. What we require is to have the help of a—a person with disguise, a—" He fumbled for words again.

"An undercover agent?"

"Yes, an undercover agent, a person to pretend to be a rich buyer of antiquities in search of an Amarna statue."

Gideon calmed down. "That's a good idea."

"We must have a person they do not know, a person who is familiar with Egyptian antiquities. We will have to speak with the antiquities authorities in Cairo. Unfortunately, this may take time—"

"How much time?"

Gabra hunched his shoulders while he used a pair of over-sized tweezers to adjust the brazier of burning charcoal that kept the tobacco alight. "A week, no more."

"A *week*? In a week there wouldn't be—"

"Perhaps three days. If we are lucky, tomorrow, even."

Tomorrow. *Bukhra.* Well, Gabra might be operating on Egyptian time, but Clifford Haddon's killer wasn't. "Sergeant, there's a murderer at Horizon House. He—or she—is still there, but the more time we give him, the more chance he has—"

"Dr. Oliver, believe me, I have this many times before. To rush in without good preparation is bad. A proper undercover agent must first be found. Then he must be explained the situation, he must understand—"

"How about me?" Gideon said, startling himself.

Gabra appraised him for a good twenty seconds, through two pulls on the *narghile*. For a single, teetery moment Gideon thought he was going to go along with the idea, but then he shook his head. "This is not possible."

"Why not?" Now that he'd adjusted to having made the suggestion in the first place, he was beginning to see some merit in it. The only part that daunted him was the prospect of telling Julie about it, but he'd work that out later. "They don't know me. I know a fair amount about antiquities. I think I could do a pretty convincing imitation of a collector or a dealer who didn't have too many scruples—"

"You don't know to speak Arabic—"

"Why would a rich American collector speak Arabic?"

"You have no false identification."

"You couldn't have some made up for me?"

Again, there was a flash in Gabra's eye, a brief, eager weighing of pros and cons, but again it dulled. "It is too dangerous," he said with finality. "Already one American is killed. No. We will wait for a proper undercover agent. In the meantime, I have plenty of questions for your friends in Horizon House."

"But—"

Gabra smiled and shook his head. "Go slowly, Doctor. You're in Egypt. May I tell you an old Arabic saying?"

"Sure," Gideon said with a sigh. Who knew, a few words of guidance from the Koran might be what he needed.

Gabra steepled his fingers and looked sagacious. "How does the camel fuck the ant?"

Or maybe not from the Koran. "How?" Gideon asked.

"With patience," Gabra said.

Chapter Twenty

"Fortunately," Phil said, "I have a plan."

Trust Phil to have a plan.

He had been lying in wait in the shade of a fig tree, angularly wedged into one of the wicker armchairs on the patio, when Gideon had returned from his talk with Gabra. He had listened with exclamations of excitement and interest to Gideon's accounting; his own researches, it seemed, had also led him to the shadowy el-Hamid family. He too felt an undercover agent was required. And he had a plan.

"What is it?" Gideon asked doubtfully. He hadn't much cared for Gabra's *bukhra* approach, but he wasn't wild about the idea of a Boyajian Plan either. "If it involves imitating an Egyptian police colonel, forget it."

"Ha, ha," Phil assured him, "nothing like that at all. As it happens, you're John Smith, a rich American antiquities dealer somewhat lacking in scruples. I'm acting as your agent." He glanced at his watch and unfolded himself from the chair. "Let's take a walk around the compound. I've been sitting here waiting for you since two-thirty. We meet them at five, which doesn't give us much time to get our act together."

"We—you—"

Phil had taken a couple of steps down one of the shaded

paths before Gideon got his voice and his legs going and caught up with him. "You set up a meeting with these guys for *us*?"

"Yes, I did," Phil said with pride. "No easy matter."

"How did we get into it? I thought it was the antiquities police you wanted to get involved."

"I know, but I thought we might as well cut out the middlemen. Do you know what these plants are? The spiky ones? I always like to throw a few plant names into my books. Promotes credibility."

"They're agave. Phil, what the hell are we supposed to be meeting them *for*?"

"Ostensibly, because you're looking for a few little gewgaws to add to your stock without the bother of applying to Customs, or paying import duties, or other such nuisances. Actually, to see if they've heard anything about the head that might be helpful."

"Phil, if you set this up, then you already must have talked to them."

"I did talk to them. Some of them, anyway. God only knows how large the entire clan is."

"Well, why didn't you just ask them about the head yourself, then?"

Phil shook his head and clucked. "I don't know, for a supposedly intelligent man . . . Look, Gideon, these things take a certain amount of subtlety, of—"

"I know. Sensitivity. Discretion."

"Correct. You don't just walk up to them and *ask*. You negotiate, you express interest in buying a few things, you make it worth their while. I can't do it because they know me and they know I don't have enough money to be a serious collector. But you—you're John Smith. I've told them just how rich and avaricious you are. They can't wait to meet you. It'll be fun, you'll see."

"And how am I supposed to bring this delicate mission off with my eight words of Arabic?"

"That's why you have me along," Phil said reasonably. "They think you're paying me a commission to interpret. So those are agave. Ugly buggers."

They smiled greetings at a workman who was serenely

pruning a leggy hibiscus trellised along an archway separating the main house from the annex.

"What if they ask for identification?" Gideon said.

Funny how he'd jumped from one side of the fence to the other in less than an hour. In the café, Gideon had been the one hatching plots and Gabra the one raising barriers. But working within the law and under its protection, collaborating with the sober, practical Gabra, had been a different prospect from trying to put over some harum-scarum deception with the breezily confident Phil.

"You won't need any identification," Phil told him. "These people aren't going to frisk you or demand proof of who you are. They're just diggers, poor bastards who hope to sell what they find for a few piasters. They're decent people at heart, trying to scrape by any way they can. They're not dangerous."

"Oh, right."

"It's the dealers, the exporters, the middlemen with the clean fingernails who are the vicious ones—because at that level there's real money involved. The el-Hamids and people like them aren't the violent type."

"Tell that to the guard they killed."

"Yes, well, there is that," Phil allowed, "but you must admit that was clearly unintentional."

"I'm sure that was a great comfort to him. Look, assuming I'd be crazy enough to go along with this, what would we do with this information we gathered? We'd pass it along to Gabra, right?"

"Of course. That's the plan. Now then: let's go up to my room. I have something I want to give you before we get started that should, ah, help put a good face on this, shall we say."

"I haven't said I'm going to do it," Gideon said.

"Of course you'll do it. I never had a moment's doubt. You just feel you ought to give me a hard time for form's sake. Really, I don't mind."

Gideon opened his mouth to argue but laughed instead. He wasn't sure just where along the line he'd swung over, but there it was, despite his objections: of course he'd do it. If the two of them didn't, who would? Besides—had he been spending too much time around Phil?—it did sound like fun.

"One question," Gideon said. "What's the hurry? Isn't five o'clock pushing it a little?"

"I thought it might be better to be off before Julie gets back from the site. I'm not sure she'd approve."

"I can handle Julie," Gideon said.

Phil just laughed, a spontaneous peal of genuine amusement.

They had circled the main complex a couple of times and now returned to the patio. Stepping into the shade of the second-floor balcony brought a slight but immediate reduction in heat; something like getting out of a broiler and into a low-temperature oven.

"You'll probably have to buy a few things from them to establish your credibility," Phil said, searching through his wallet as they climbed the stairs. "They'll want American dollars, not Egyptian pounds. I have fifty dollars, what about you?"

Gideon checked. "A hundred."

"That ought to be more than enough. These people aren't used to seeing very much for their labors." He handed his bills to Gideon. "Now look. We'll turn over anything we come away with to the police, but I don't want the el-Hamids getting into hot water over it. I know that offends your stern sense of justice but those are my terms. I trust it will be all right with you? In the interests of the greater good?"

"It'll be all right with me. I just hope we end up with something Gabra can use."

Phil unlocked the door to his room and went to the air conditioner to flick it on. "I think it would be best," he said, "if you wore a disguise. What I have in mind," he said, opening the top drawer of the bureau, "is a beard."

"Come again?"

"A false beard and mustache. Fortunately, your hair color is almost the same as mine. Ah." He removed a plastic bag with a dark mass inside.

"A *beard*?" Gideon said. "What, with wires to hook over my ears? How about a pillow for my stomach?"

"No, no, this is an up-to-date little item; never travel without it. I use it often, most notably in Damascus a few years ago to successfully convince a supercilious government official that I was a close relative of the president of Syria."

"Didn't you wind up in jail over that?"

"Well, yes," Phil said, "I suppose you could say that, but it wasn't the fault of the beard."

"Thanks all the same—"

"Gideon, it's quite possible that you've been noticed around Luxor. It's also quite possible that one of the far-flung band of el-Hamids is working at Horizon House even now. It wouldn't pay for you to be recognized. It might even be dangerous."

"Dangerous? These decent, everyday—"

"I'm not concerned about the el-Hamids. I'm concerned about word of your interest getting back here. Haddon was apparently murdered over that head—by someone who is now at Horizon House—or have you forgotten for the moment?"

Gideon was silent. He'd forgotten for the moment.

"I wouldn't want the same thing to happen to you; it'd probably be up to me to get *your* body back to the States too, and it's a damned bother." Phil pulled the room's single chair into the center of the floor. "Now sit down and let me get this thing on you. I've had practice."

Gideon sat.

While Phil pressed and repressed the silky mustache and goatee into place, they went over their strategy for the meeting. It took fifteen minutes, at the end of which Phil stepped back for an artistic evaluation.

He nodded his satisfaction. "I don't believe we need to bother with the false eyebrows. Shall we go?"

Gideon got up to look in the mirror over the bureau. He'd worn a beard years before and had thought it suited him, but that one, while close-cropped, had pretty much been allowed to grow where it pleased. This one was fussy and pinched, a finicky little topiary beard sitting on the front of his face like a mat.

"I look" he decided, "like a poodle."

"You look corrupt," Phil said approvingly, "as if you ought to be sidling around the Casbah with a fez on your head and six false passports for sale in your breast pocket. All in all, not a bad image to cultivate tonight."

"I'll do my best. Any other advice?"

Phil thought for a moment.

"Yes," he said. "Try and look rich."

Chapter Twenty-one

When Phil asked to be taken to the Shari el-Jihad the taxi driver had protested.

"No, you don't want to go to that place," he told them. "Not for tourist, only for Egyptian peoples."

But he had unwillingly complied, and Gideon soon understood his initial reluctance. Luxor, like most of the Nile cities, was laid out in parallel bands of decreasing prosperity. Along the river the Corniche was a glittering filament of affluence, but with every block traveled inland the glitter diminished and the squalor increased. Their driver, muttering disapproval to the last, took them beyond the *souks* in which they'd grazed the evening before and let them out in a narrow, unpaved maze of shoddy two- and three-story tenements, recently built but already stained and crumbling. Bleating goats wandered in and out of doorways. Chickens and gaunt, listless dogs scratched in the rutted dirt or ate street garbage. Somewhere nearby a donkey bawled and was answered by a second. The smells were of animals, excrement, and rancid cooking oil.

They were only seven blocks from the opulent Corniche; they might have been on another planet.

Phil led Gideon another half a block, past the guarded, appraising glances of weary, thin men and the hidden eyes of women covered in black from head to toe like shrouded statues, who watched avidly as they passed. Or so it seemed; the thick, dark veils made it impossible to tell what was happening behind them.

At the first corner they turned left into a livelier area; a warren of *souks* something like the one they'd had their *fuul* and *koshari* in the night before, but a level or two downscale; a sort of blue-collar version, so to speak. Street vendors hawked oil-soaked *fuul* and pita bread ("Not recommended for the timid alimentary canal," Phil said.), charcoal-grilled corn, and fantastically colored soft drinks. In a shop no more than five feet by eight, a man sat in a cracked leather barber chair having his hair cut under a single naked light bulb. Next door was a stall selling used television sets with chipped screens and missing knobs.

And next to that was their destination, a dingy, six-table café packed with men hunched over tea or coffee, arguing over Arabic newspapers, and smoking cigarettes or *narghiles*. Walking through the entryway produced an immediate reaction: conversations were suspended, heads were raised, every pair of eyes was on the exotically dressed strangers. The waiter, carrying a tray with two cups of coffee, stopped in mid-stride. Gideon's skin prickled. In the fug of cheap tobacco smoke, the men, who had seemed merely weary a moment ago, suddenly looked like a pack of assassins. Even the two elderly, white-mustachioed constables in mildewed black uniforms, who had interrupted their backgammon game to watch, looked sinister.

Gideon glanced uncomfortably at Phil. "Are you sure we know what we're doing?"

"Not really, no, now that you mention it. Oh, we're supposed to go to a room in the back; that much I know."

They crossed to the far wall under a continuing barrage of silent scrutiny. In passing, Phil said a few words to the waiter, who responded with a nod. Only when they pulled the rickety double-doors shut behind them did the hum of conversation resume.

They found themselves in a bleak, harshly lit room half as large as the outer one, with rough, colorless walls grimed by smoke and oily hands, and two inert, dust-covered ceiling fans. The only furnishings were a single round table and five chairs, with three waiting men seated on them. There were no greetings. One of the men, with a square-cut white skullcap that came down to his eyebrows and a curling black beard that rode up his sweating cheeks almost to his eyes and put Gideon's prissy little affair to shame, motioned them into the vacant chairs and made a curt let's-get-on-with-it gesture. He was Fouad el-Hamid, he said through Phil. The old man beside him was his uncle, Atef el-Hamid, and the young man was a cousin, Jalal el-Hamid.

Phil, smiling, launched into the opening speech that he and Gideon had worked out: he, Phil, was there to assist the famous antiquities dealer, John Smith of Cincinnati, who was interested in enlarging his Egyptian inventory. Mr. Smith was quite wealthy, and was willing to pay well for superior objects but did not care to have his time wasted with fakes or cheap trash. Naturally, he carried only a limited amount of money on his person, but if he were shown something that pleased him he could easily enough return to his hotel, where his traveler's checks were kept.

Gideon used the time to study the el-Hamids. Judging from his interruptions and rambling, self-serving comments, Fouad, who puffed regularly at a *narghile*, was going to be the spokesman. Atef el-Hamid, seated next to him, was a wizened elder wearing a carelessly bound turban made from a ragged swatch of plaid cloth. An immense, tobacco-stained white mustache—it would have been a handlebar mustache if it had been waxed—hung on either side of his frail chin. The old man smoked with a vengeance. Mustache, fingertips, and lips looked as if they'd been cured. Periodically he would hold two lighted cigarettes, one in each hand: the one he was just finishing, and the one he was about to start.

Jalal, the third member of the party, was about twenty, slim and darkly handsome, with a loose, unpleasant smile and a greased hairstyle last seen in America in *West Side Story*. He was the only one who wasn't smoking and the only one in Western dress—a shiny brown suit of eye-catching sleaziness, several sizes too tight and worn with a wilted white shirt and no tie. Once, when he noticed Gideon looking at him, he coolly, showily adjusted something that bulged behind his breast pocket.

As Phil wound up his presentation the waiter entered with coffee for everyone and a tray of flaky, sticky cakes.

Fouad nodded an indifferent thanks at Gideon and made a grab for the largest of the pastries. The other two just grabbed.

"It's on you," Phil explained, lifting his cup in salute. "Too kind."

"My pleasure," Gideon said, wincing as he sipped his own coffee, sugared as usual to the point of nausea for the American palate. Most American palates, at any rate; beside him Phil smacked his lips.

The preliminaries had been concluded. There was an air of anticipation around the table; time to get started. Gideon put down his cup, took a breath, and threw himself into the role of John Smith of Cincinnati, famous antiquities dealer.

"Do they have something to show me or don't they?" he asked Phil gruffly. "I have other things to do with my time."

Earlier they had agreed that they should say nothing in English that they didn't want the el-Hamids to hear. No secrets, no asides, nothing that wasn't in character. It was highly possible that they knew more English than they let on.

After Phil translated, the two older men conversed briefly and Atef el-Hamid reached under his chair, brought up a cane-and-rush basket that looked like something the infant Moses might have been found in, and set it on the table. It was full of crumpled wads of Arabic newspaper. The old man picked slowly among the wads, came to a decision, and removed the one he wanted. Squinting against the smoke from the cigarette between his brown teeth he pulled open the paper and took out a flat, crudely carved piece of wood a foot long and two or three inches wide, with a channel down the center and two circular depressions at one end. He gave it to Fouad, who passed it on to Gideon and watched him keenly while gobbling down another cake.

Test-time, Gideon thought. And he'd lucked out; he actually knew what it was.

"Scribe's palette," he said to Phil with weary disdain. "The groove was for holding the brush, these depressions were for the cakes of ink, one for red, one for black. Here, you can still see a little red. That would have been ground ocher. The black was carbon. The brush would be dipped in water and then rubbed on the cake of ink, like watercolor.''

Phil translated as he went along. The men's quick glances at one another told him he had scored. It was a good thing too; he had used up everything he knew about scribal palettes.

''They want to know if you're interested,'' Phil said.

''In this piece of garbage? Be serious.''

That was part of the plan too. He would begin the bargaining in the time-honored fashion, disparaging whatever was offered first. Anything else would have undermined his credibility.

The old man gave no reaction. The palette remained on the table while he pulled open another wrapping of newspaper. A few copper implements spilled out onto the table. One was an adz with an open collar for the haft. The others Gideon wasn't sure about; chisels, perhaps, or gouging tools.

The older men watched him guardedly. Jalal lay back in his chair, propped on the base of his spine, cocky and contemptuous.

''Want to make an offer?'' Phil asked.

Gideon brushed the idea aside. ''Please, don't waste my time,'' he said, with the closest thing to a sneer he could muster. ''This is crap.''

This is fun, he thought.

Both older men started talking angrily at the same time. Phil translated what he could: ''Old Kingdom . . . very rare . . .''

''What do I want with tools?'' Gideon interrupted loudly, well into the swing of it. ''What do they think I am, some damned carpenter?''

Fouad flashed an aggrieved look at him, grumbled something that Phil didn't catch, and went into a huddled conference with his uncle.

''Do you want to buy or not?'' Phil translated for them. ''They don't have time to waste either. Make them an offer or go play your games somewhere else. Perhaps you ought to offer something,'' he added on his own.

''I haven't seen anything to make an offer on yet. Don't they understand my customers are interested in *art*?'' He gestured at the objects on the table. "This looks like a garage sale."

Apparently Phil came up with an understandable translation. Fouad and Atef went into another huddle. The old man pushed his drooping turban back from his eyes, scratched his nose, and reached judiciously into the basket, hesitating first over one package, then another.

"I don't have all night," Gideon said abruptly. "Tell them to lay out what they have."

This created some protest—it was not the customary way—but in the end, the contents of the basket were laid out over the table. In addition to what had come before, there was a small ivory figurine of a woman, primitively carved and probably Predynastic, a set of miniature copper vessels and utensils, some tiny pots and basins that he took to be cosmetics containers, and a small blue and yellow vase that had been cracked and mended.

Everyone looked at him expectantly, even the prodigiously bored young Jalal. The old man had two cigarettes in his hands again, forgetting for the moment to smoke either one.

Gideon picked up the vase and tried to look as if he knew what he was doing. He scratched it gently with his fingernail, he pursed his lips, he frowned and stroked his jaw, not helping his case any when he encountered the furry thing on his chin and almost jumped out of his chair.

"This vase, where's it from?" he asked when he settled down again, thinking it sounded like the right kind of question.

Phil listened to their answer. "They don't tell where they find anything, but they say it's definitely from the time of Thutmose III."

"I don't think so," Gideon said as if he knew what he was talking about. "I think it's probably a modern forgery."

This produced an indignant explosion from Fouad, which Phil translated with fine gusto, slipping into first-person for the full effect.

" 'A forgery, you say? A *forgery*?' " Phil's hands sprang ceilingward in emulation of the Arab's. " 'How can you say a thing like that? The man who found it, who personally found it where it had lain three thousand years, is my own brother-in-law. Would my brother-in-law lie to me? Would we lie to you?' "

Gideon was searching for a firm but politic answer when Jalal spoke his first words in a husky, confident voice. Phil listened soberly.

"He says you're wrong, these aren't fakes, but, yes, they're run-of-the-mill, not high-quality. But he can show you much better things, not the kind of things you carry through the streets in a basket. If their business with you here is satisfactory, maybe he'll show you some finer things, more interesting things."

The old man remonstrated shrilly with the boy but was cut off by a sharp response that left him muttering. Gideon realized with surprise that if anybody was in charge, it was Jalal, half Fouad's age and a quarter Atef's. The boy continued to speak his piece, looking directly at Gideon.

"He wants to know what you're interested in," Phil said.

So. It was time to begin closing in on what they'd come for. Gideon put down the vase. "I have a number of clients who have asked me to look for Amarna Period art for them."

Jalal smirked. "Everybody wants Amarna art," Phil translated when he'd spoken.

"Everybody can't pay what I can pay. I represent some very wealthy clients. And I pay in American dollars. I'm particularly interested in statuary," he added casually.

Jalal continued to appraise him for several seconds after Phil interpreted, then uttered a few words.

"It's possible," Phil translated, "but afterward. First, this." He lifted an eyebrow toward Gideon. "I, ah, think this might be a propitious time to make an offer."

Gideon thought so too. He leaned forward to pick up the vase again. "Let's start with this. I might be able to find someone foolish enough to buy it. Shall we say, oh . . ."

Oh, what? He was completely in the dark. In this room, with these humble people, it was worth perhaps a fiftieth, maybe only a hundredth, of what it might sell for in the legitimate or pseudo-legitimate art market, but as to what that was, he didn't have a clue.

He took a stab. ". . . oh, fifty dollars."

The two older men went into a whispered conference, sibilant and heated. Fouad excitedly ticked off points on his fingers while his elder emitted streams of smoke, shook his head, and rapped the table. Jalal remained above it all with an apathetic, slack-lipped smile. After a while he looked at his watch—fake gold band, fake Rolex face—got up, and sauntered out, but not before a gangsterly, showy shrug of his left shoulder and another pat of his breast pocket to adjust what Gideon hoped was a fake gun in a fake holster.

It took a few minutes more before the other two came to a conclusion. The old man shoved his turban out of his eyes again, made his statement, and folded his arms.

"They say it's out of the question," Phil said. "They will accept one hundred and fifty, which they say is a very great bargain when you consider—"

"Okay," Gideon said. The men looked stunned. Phil looked a little pained too; apparently he'd hoped to get out of this with his fifty dollars at least partly intact.

Gideon put the money on the table, bill by bill, before the Egyptians, who were patently too astonished at their good fortune to speak. He knew well enough that this wasn't the way to bargain in the Arab world, but he was anxious to finish up. If they were going to learn anything about the Amarna head, he had concluded by now, it was going to be through Jalal. And he had the impression that the young man had left only temporarily, to talk to somebody or to make a telephone call, that he would be back with something to say, that progress might yet be made this night.

The men eagerly scooped up the bills, chattering away at Phil to tell the honored gentleman from Cincinnati that they had many more such beautiful items for sale, at equally favorable prices, and if the honored gentleman—

Jalal eased his way back through the double doors and cut them off with a word. They looked at each other, bobbed their farewells, and hurried toward the exit.

"They're forgetting their things," Gideon said. "All I bought was the vase."

"No, you bought everything," Phil said. "The basket too."

Gideon was flabbergasted. "For $150? The figurine alone must be—"

The young man cut in. Phil, instead of translating, got into an exchange with him.

"He knows someone who has Amarna things to sell," Phil said. He wants to take you to meet him. It's a man called Ali Hassan. Apparently he's a dealer, an exporter. According to our young friend, anything decent that comes out of Luxor illegally goes through his hands."

Bingo. "Terrific, what are we waiting for?"

"No, just you. I'm not invited." Phil's face had tightened. He didn't like the turn of events.

Gideon wasn't overjoyed either. "Just me? How am I supposed to communicate? I need someone who speaks English."

"Me, I speak English," Jalal said, not altogether surprising Gideon. "Let's go."

Gideon exchanged a worried look with Phil. He understood what Phil had been trying to tell him a moment ago. A dealer, an exporter—one of the vicious ones, in other words; one of the dangerous ones. But was there really anything to worry about? Why should this Ali Hassan, regardless of how vicious, have any reason to do him harm? Hassan's business was buying and selling illegal antiquities. And Gideon was John Smith, a rich American not overly burdened by ethical considerations who was looking for just the kind of things Hassan had to sell. Hassan would naturally be a little wary of a new face, but he would be licking his chops over profits to come, not planning assassination.

Or so he hoped.

"Just a minute," Gideon said. "I have to talk with my associate—privately, if that's all right with you." Circumstances had changed on them. Plan A, so airily devised an hour ago, was no longer in effect and there wasn't any plan B.

"No talk," Jalal said sharply. "We go now, this minute, or don't go."

He was on edge too. He didn't quite trust them, and Gideon thought he meant what he said.

Gideon looked at Phil, who shrugged. Gideon shrugged too. "All right."

"Get in touch with me as soon as you get back," Phil said.

"No talk," Jalal snapped.

The boy pulled a folded turban cloth from an inside pocket and shook it out. "For to go over you eyes. Sit down."

"All right," Gideon said again. Actually, this was a heartening development. If they didn't want him to know where he was going, at least that meant that they expected him to leave alive. Not that there was any reason, he repeated to himself, that they might want him otherwise.

"Wait a minute," he said as Jalal began to wind the cloth around his eyes. "If you take me through the café blindfolded everybody's going to see it."

"They see before," the boy said off-handedly.

Chapter Twenty-two

Jalal was right. The sight of a blindfolded man being led back through the café by the elbow was apparently nothing unusual. If anything it was less noteworthy than his entrance with Phil, because this time the conversations didn't lapse altogether, but only ebbed a little. Gideon wondered if the two elderly constables were still there and what they made of it.

Once in the street he was turned to the right for a few steps and bundled roughly into the back of a car, his knees jammed against the stiffened fabric of the front seat. Jalal got in next to him and said a few words in Arabic. A bearlike grunt came from the front, and the engine started up. The car smelled unlike the inside of any vehicle he'd been in in Egypt (except for the *Menshiya*): no fustiness, no mildew, no layer upon layer of stale sweat. What it smelled like was an automobile; a relatively new automobile. As they got under way he felt the cool puff of an air conditioner. That was a first too.

"Nice car," he said.

"Peugeot," Jalal said proudly.

Well, he thought with satisfaction, that was something he could pass on to Gabra later if need be. He set his mind to capturing other details of the journey, memorizing the turns and counting the seconds between them—one-Mississippi, two-Mississippi—but gave it up after the fourth Mississippi. There weren't any seconds between the turns. When they weren't lurching to the left they were lurching to the right. In this particular part of Luxor there weren't any nice right-angled corners to help get things clear in the mind, there were only twisting alleys that never seemed to straighten out.

All he could say for sure was that they drove that way, fairly slowly, for two or three minutes, then got onto a straighter, smoother road for another three or four, slowing once to jolt over some bumps. A railroad crossing? If so, they were headed east, away from central Luxor. Their speed picked up. Gideon was starting to get jumpy in spite of himself. It was well and good to conclude that the blindfold proved that foul play wasn't in the offing, but that had been in a lighted café on a busy street, with his pal at his side. Now the blindfold was over his eyes and he was alone in a car with a false beard pasted on his face, a gun-toting thug-in-training sitting next to him, and an unknown goon in the driver's seat, heading . . . where?

There was a sharp turn to the left—northward?—and a final, twisting, bumpy stretch of another minute or two. The car stopped. The driver came around, opened his door, and pulled on his shoulder.

"How about taking this thing off now?" Gideon said to Jalal.

"Soon. In one minute."

He got out, bracing himself for whatever might be coming, but he heard children at play, he smelled garlic and cooking oil. He relaxed a little; at least he hadn't been taken to the edge of some lonely desert ravine. He guessed they were in one of the sprawling villages that straggled along Luxor's uneven eastern edge, an uneasy buffer between metropolis and desert, between city slicker and wandering Bedouin.

He was guided by Jalal through a gate. The gate was pulled closed behind him, screeching over rough stone, and he was told, at last, to take off the blindfold.

He relaxed a little more. They were in a walled courtyard with a one-story house of whitewashed clay in front of them. On the right, against the wall, was a low table at which two women and a little girl squatted, scouring pots and pans with sand and paying the newcomers no heed. A partially collapsed outside stairway on the left of the house climbed skeletally to the roof. At its base was a low door.

"This is Ali Hassan's house?" Gideon asked.

Jalal's loose lips curled. "Mr. Ali Hassan does not live here. Only sometimes he do business here."

They went through the doorway—Gideon had to stoop—and walked through an unfinished and probably never-to-be-finished kitchen. On their right a middle-aged man sat at a wooden table glumly watching a laughing woman on a portable black-and-white television set two feet from his nose. Next to the sink an old woman was giving a piece of her mind to an unrepentant-looking goat, shaking her finger in its face while it tore at a juice carton with its teeth. The man glanced incuriously at the newcomers in his kitchen and went back to his television. The woman continued to address the goat.

A narrow flight of stairs against the rear wall took them up to the flat roof, on which they emerged into the usual disorder of the village rooftop: thick, vertically stacked bundles of reeds and sugar cane, disused farm tools, two rotting, smelly mattresses standing on edge, construction rubble in heaps, a doorless refrigerator—and a small cleared area on which stood a cot made up with sheets, a small, Formica-topped kitchen table, and an old cane-bottomed chair.

A short, heavy, olive-skinned man of fifty in a brown, Sadat-style suit and an embroidered, open-collared shirt rose from the chair and came toward them on little feet, lumbering and mincing at the same time, like a pygmy hippopotamus.

He extended a hand with rings on three fingers to Gideon. "How do you do, Mr. Smith? I am Ali Hassan." His voice was an odd, not-unfriendly growl, his accent a hodgepodge of Cairo and Marseilles, and maybe a touch of Belgrade too. Mr. Ali Hassan had been around.

"How do you do?" Gideon said. It hadn't been lost on him that "Ali Hassan" was the Arabic equivalent of "John Smith." Was it a couple of fictional characters who were greeting each other so politely? Maybe yes, maybe no. There were, after all, plenty of people really named John Smith, so why not an occasional Ali Hassan?

"The blindfold didn't inconvenience you? No?"

Hassan peered up at him, directly into his face, with unsettlingly bright, piggy eyes. "You understand. When it's someone I don't know, I have to take my little precautions. You can't be too careful these days. It's terrible, what goes on."

Gideon managed a tolerant smile. "I understand completely." Only with an effort did he resist a near-overwhelming impulse to make sure his beard was still on straight.

"So, come, sit down, Mr. Smith."

Gideon perched uncomfortably on the cot—the only other place to sit—while Hassan resumed his seat in the chair. He was a sleek, squat man, not quite obese but certainly overfed, with a flat, broad face and an ongoing, muttering chuckle from deep in the back of his throat. Jalal was motioned over and sent downstairs with a few brusque words.

Hassan smiled hospitably at Gideon. "I have sent the boy down to bring us some—"

Not coffee, Gideon prayed.

"—coffee," said Hassan. The rumbling chuckle was heard again. "Tell me, Mr. Smith, where are you staying? The Winter Palace?"

"The Hilton," Gideon said, thinking it sounded more like John Smith's kind of place. He regretted it immediately. A call to the Hilton would tell Hassan that there was no John Smith registered there.

On the other hand, so would a call to the Winter Palace or anyplace else. He was going to have to be more careful, take more time before speaking. What, he thought suddenly, was he going to do if Hassan asked for a business card?

"Next time," Hassan said, "try the Winter Palace; the old wing, not the new. Tell Mr. Shebl I personally sent you. Tell me, Mr. Smith, why haven't I heard of you before?"

This one Gideon was ready for. "This is my first Egyptian venture," he said smoothly. "Until now I've been active in the South American trade. Mostly Peruvian. Moche and Chimú artifacts, mainly."

"Oh, yes? Well, that's not an area I know much about."

A good thing too, Gideon thought.

Hassan folded his arms. "Now, what can I do for you?"

"I'm interested in art from the Amarna Period. Statuary, in particular. Jalal seemed to think you might help me."

"For yourself or is there a client involved? It helps me to know."

"A client," Gideon said carefully. "He's looking for something, not too large, for a place in his library."

"Ah, yes."

"I'm not at liberty to tell you his name."

That was good, Gideon thought. It sounded like something John Smith would say, and it established that secrets were acceptable between them.

"No, no, no, no, of course not," Hassan said quickly. "Sometimes it's best not to know these things. Well, here is our coffee."

Jalal had returned with two tiny cups and set them on the table. Then he had gone to stand off to one side, just at the edge of Gideon's vision, while Hassan sipped and Gideon pretended to. They made stilted, ceremonial chitchat for a few minutes—about the weather, of all things. An unchallenging topic in a land where 363 out of every 365 days were the same: hot, dry, and utterly cloudless. Hassan remarked that the evening breeze was pleasant. Gideon agreed that it was quite pleasant.

In truth, they weren't getting much benefit from the evening breeze. Hassan's precautions against Gideon's knowing where they were had extended to his having had the junk on the roof stacked in such a way that it formed a screen around the edges. Gideon could hear sounds of village life—the creak of a wooden cartwheel, the complaint of a cranky camel, the continuing shouts of children, the amplified call of a muezzin—but all he saw was mattresses on end and bundles of tall, dried reeds.

Jalal cleared away the cups and was sent back to stand just out of Gideon's sight again. Hassan rubbed his hands briskly together. Time for business.

"Well, I think I have some things to show you, Mr. Smith. A few things that have come my way lately."

"Fine." Gideon became a little easier. If Hassan trusted

him enough to lay out his goods, then an awkward demand for a business card wasn't likely to be forthcoming.

Hassan took a thick packet of cards from his breast pocket, separated a few, and offered them. Gideon came close to asking what they were before remembering that men like Ali Hassan didn't make a practice of publicly demonstrating their wares like the less discriminating el-Hamids. They carried Polaroids, not baskets of artifacts.

There were about a dozen, poorly lit and badly composed, and Gideon longed to rip through them in search of a yellow jasper head. Instead, he thumbed through them with agonizing thoroughness, peering at them in the fading daylight the way John Smith probably would have, one at a time, with pauses and nods and grunts, thoughtfully laying each one out on the table next to the one before, like a hand of solitaire. First were several miniature, whole statuettes of varying quality; then a few fragmentary heads—chins and lips, mostly—made of what appeared to be quartz and obsidian; then a statuette body of a seated woman made of coarser material, probably sandstone. And then two small, finely made faience figurines of animals: a goose and a fish.

And that was it. No yellow jasper head.

He put down the last picture. "These are quite nice, but I was hoping you might be able to find me—"

He paused, frowning, and turned back to the twelve photos spread on the table in two rows. He picked up the third one from the right in the nearest row. The sandstone figure. The headless body.

It was a female dressed in a simply depicted gown and seated on a boxlike support with hieroglyphic symbols carved into its side, her hands resting palms-down on her thighs. It was Amarna style, all right, early Amarna, just beginning to move away from the stiff, conventionalized pose of former times to the more relaxed, natural posture that would be a hallmark of Akhenaten's reign. Between the shoulders was a square-carved recess to accept the tang that would have projected from the underside of the separate head and neck.

A composite statue.

The hairs on the back of his neck stirred. Was it possible that he had gotten to what he was looking for by the back way? He had come looking for the head that went with the body. Had he found the body that went with the head? He felt his heart pick up its beat.

"I don't know, this might be fairly interesting," he said indifferently, flipping it back onto the table. "What can you tell me about—"

"Har, har, har," said Hassan.

Gideon looked up sharply. "I beg your pardon?"

"Har, har, har," said Hassan. He was sitting with his hands over his belly, the left wrist clasped in the right hand. His feet were flat on the floor and his shoulders were shaking. As far as Gideon could tell, he was genuinely amused.

Gideon waited.

Hassan used a handkerchief to wipe tears from the corner of his eyes. "I thought that one would get your interest. Oh, yes." The handkerchief was wadded up and stuffed away somewhere and with it went Hassan's sudden burst of mirth. "Let's not mince any more words. It's what you came for, isn't it? The statuette that was taken from the Horizon site across the river four years ago. I'm afraid I'm not at liberty," he added with heavy-handed sarcasm, "to tell you how it came to me."

He looked keenly at Gideon, awaiting a reaction.

Gideon felt himself floundering. Things had begun to spiral out of his control. No, apparently they'd always been out of his control; he just hadn't known it.

He spread his hands. "Why would I be particularly interested in that?"

Hassan leaned forward, a thick hand on each knee. "Please. Suddenly, from nowhere, you come to me with a story of a client interested in Amarna statues? And this happens to be, by coincidence, one week after a certain missing Amarna head at Horizon House is found again . . . and 'lost' again? You expect me to believe this?"

Gideon did his best to manifest wounded dignity. The pelt adhering to his upper lip didn't make it any easier. "I assure you, I don't know what—"

"Please, Mr. Smith, don't insult my intelligence. You know everything there is to know about the head. Do I look like a child?"

"I—all right, yes, you're right, I do have it," Gideon said, figuring that it had to be easier to put over a sham that Hassan believed in than one that he didn't. "I have it and I'm willing to make you a more-than-reasonable offer for the body." What, he wondered nervously, was reasonable?

Hassan sat back with a sigh, shaking his head sadly. "Mr. Smith, Mr. Smith. Really."

Now what? The safest bet seemed to be to wait him out.

It didn't take long. "Mr. Smith," Hassan said, his tone revealing sad disillusionment at Gideon's prevarication, "I happen to know that you don't have the head."

"I assure you—"

"Mr. Smith, I *know*. Now, I don't know what your plans are for getting it and I don't want to know. It's your business, so why should it concern me? I have the body, you want the body. I'm a businessman. If we can come to an agreement, it's yours. Very simple."

Gideon's mind was buzzing. If Hassan knew—truly *knew*—that he didn't have the head, then didn't that mean that he knew who did? And wasn't that the information this goofy charade had been designed to ferret out? Whoever had the head had surely killed Clifford Haddon. Or if not, if it had already changed owners, then he or she could certainly direct the police to whoever had.

Gideon smiled indulgently. "Tell me, Mr. Hassan, just who do you think does have it?"

Hassan wouldn't play along. "No games, please," he said tartly. "Here is my position. I'll be frank with you."

But being frank obviously took some forethought (not that Gideon was in any position to look down his nose over a little equivocation). Hassan got briskly to his feet, pulled a pack of Marlboros from an inside pocket, offered one to Gideon, who shook his head, and lit up. He walked the few steps that the cleared space allowed him to, handed the cigarette to Jalal after a single long draw, and turned to face Gideon, his hands behind his back.

"A certain person, an old business acquaintance, offered me $20,000 for it. I accepted. Now, I don't like to break an agreement once it's made, I'm not that kind of man, but the truth is, I still haven't seen the money. If you can double it, it's yours. Forty thousand dollars. I can give you two days.''

Well, at last Gideon knew what a reasonable price was: something under $40,000. This was bargaining time, and in Egypt that meant that when you were selling you started out at roughly three times what you thought you might come away with in the end.

He uttered an airy laugh. "Mr. Hassan, all I've seen is a photograph. I don't know that it's what you say it is, and even if it is, how do I know you have it?''

Hassan grinned mockingly back at him. "You're not interested? Well, well, maybe I should just put those pictures back in my pocket and—''

"Assuming that it's what you say, I might be able to go as high as $10,000," Gideon said.

"Har, har, har," said Hassan.

"Maybe twelve, if it's in particularly good condition.''

Hassan's grin turned sly, not an appealing sight. He came back and sat down again, his heavy thighs flattening under the pressure. "You know what I think? I think you *do* have, what should we call it, the final element, the last part.'' He raised his eyebrows and tapped Gideon conspiratorially on the knee. "Yes? Am I right?''

"Maybe I do, maybe I don't," Gideon said. What the hell were they talking about now?

"Oh, I think you do," Hassan said. The muttering chuckle had started up again, like an idling engine. "So this little item''—his stubby, beringed forefinger came down squarely on the photograph, one, two, three times—"is going to be worth a whole lot of money to you. What's a measly $40,000? You're lucky I'm not asking five times as much. Don't be so stingy, Mr. Smith.''

"All right," said Gideon, "$40,000 it is.''

Well, why not? Hassan was right: why be stingy? The money didn't exist anyway. The important thing now was to set up another meeting with Hassan, one that Sergeant Gabra would be in on too. Hassan knew who had the head; he might not be willing to tell Gideon, but he would tell Gabra.

"Well, then, isn't that more like it?'' Hassan said, reaching for Gideon's hand, grasping it, pumping it up and down. "This way everybody's happy, right? How will you pay?"

"I—" He caught himself. He'd been about to say he'd pay in cash, but would John Smith really have $40,000 with him? This was no time to blow things with a careless blunder. Besides, did he want Hassan and the Six-Gun Kid thinking he might have all that money on him the next time they met? No, cash was out, and so was a personal check; John Smith wouldn't be stupid enough to use one for contraband merchandise, and Hassan wouldn't be stupid enough to accept it.

Beyond that, Gideon was in muddy waters. He barely knew the difference between a money order and a certified check. In the Oliver household it was Julie who handled high finance.

"What would you suggest?" he said.

Hassan plucked at his lower lip. "Well, I don't think a foreign draft would be a very good idea, and a wire transfer would complicate everything, wouldn't you say?"

"Yes, that's very true."

"Your bank has a branch in Cairo?"

"Of course."

"Good. Then why not a treasurer's check?"

"Fine, good idea."

"That way," Hassan said, "you won't have to use your real name."

Gideon swallowed. "Mr. Hassan—"

The dealer held up his hand. "I know, I know. You assure me. Listen, Mr. Smith, or Mr. Jones, or Mr. Wilson, I don't know what your name is, and I don't care. I don't ask questions, and I don't answer them. There's only one thing I care about: can you raise $40,000 in the next two days?"

"I can raise it," Gideon said. "I'll have it for you by tomorrow afternoon. Where shall I meet you?"

Hassan sat back, still pulling on his lip. "Can you find the el-Fishawy café again?"

"Where I was tonight? Yes."

"Good. Six o'clock? You'll have the money?"

"Naturally. You'll have the statuette?"

"Naturally. He stood to shake hands a final time, rumbling contentedly, "Until tomorrow, my dear Mr. John Smith."

Chapter Twenty-three

"Not a chance," Julie said, squinting up at him from the umbrellaed folding table where she sat sorting potsherds under the flat, dazzling sky of the Western Valley. "I'm going with you."

"I'm just going back to the House to get *Red Land, Black Land* and a couple of other things before I go on camera. I'll be back by noon." He smiled and put a finger on the bridge of her nose. "Your nose crinkles when you squint, did anybody ever tell you that? It's that sexy little *pyramidalis nasi* of yours that does it."

She shook her head, unmoved by these blandishments. "You're not going anywhere by yourself, pal. You're on probation." She reached under the table, slung her bag over her shoulder, and stood up. "All right, let's go."

Gideon laughed. It had been this way since he'd returned to Horizon House the previous night after his meeting with Ali Hassan. He had come back to their room after a blindfolded ride to Luxor to find her standing there with Phil, pale with worry and close to tears. Phil, also concerned about him, had just used the telephone downstairs to call police headquarters, hoping that Gabra, with traditional Egyptian disdain for normal working hours, might still be at his desk.

He was, and Phil had been about to leave for his office when Gideon appeared.

Instead, all three of them had taken a taxi to the police station, Julie asserting her determination not to give them a chance to get into any more trouble on their own. She had pressed herself close to Gideon's side during the ten-minute drive, mute and fragile, and he had kept his arm around her, brimming with contrition and with love. "I'm fine," he murmured into her ear again and again. "I'm fine, Julie."

By the time they pulled up at the station she was herself again.

"One suggestion," she said as they walked up the steps.

Gideon looked at her.

"You might do better in there without the beard."

"The—?" He snatched it off his face.

Gabra had been in a bad mood to begin with, and he had been stonily unamused by their story, but eventually Phil's enthusiasm—he was back to thinking it had been a jolly adventure—had swayed him, and he had begun to see the good side. A simple plan quickly evolved. Undercover law enforcement people in sufficiently disreputable-looking *galabiyas* would begin drifting into the café at 5 P.M., an hour before the meeting with Ali Hassan, and station themselves at several tables. Gabra would be in a car a block away. As soon as Gideon came in and sat down with Hassan, the police would quietly appear at the table and it would be over before it began. No complicated sting operation, no money changing hands, nothing dangerous at all. Even Julie's mind had been put at ease.

But not so much that she had let him get out of her sight since. At first he'd grumbled about it, but the truth was that he loved it when she fussed over him and she knew it, so there wasn't much point in grumbling.

They had breakfasted at Horizon House with the dig crew at 5 A.M., then joined them on the public ferry to the west bank, where they'd been picked up by the two Horizon vans stationed there and taken the eight desolate miles to WV-29. He had spent a peaceful, lovely two hours helping her with the sorting until TJ had come up and offered him a tour of the dig.

Reserved at first, she soon became a spirited guide, leading him through the maze of tumbled mud blocks and square pits that made up the Eighteenth Dynasty workers' settlement. Around them diggers both Egyptian and American scraped away with everything from hoes to teaspoons under the sharp eyes of the site supervisors. Students wandered self-consciously around with clipboards or fiddled endlessly with surveyors' tools and tripod-mounted cameras.

Gideon found it hard to pay attention. His thoughts about TJ, and to a lesser extent Jerry Baroff, had been uneasy since Gabra had told him about the four-year-old theft of the statuette body. That had happened on TJ's watch; she had been the dig supervisor then as now. Yet in all the past week, with everything that had occurred, she had never mentioned it. Why not? How could the possible connection between the body and the head have escaped her of all people? Gabra had seen it in a flash. So had Gideon. So would anybody.

And why had she so readily—so adamantly—accepted as fact Stacey's determination that there had never been such a head in the collection? It hadn't taken Gideon very long to find sizable room for doubt. He had no good answers for these questions, and he didn't like the direction they had taken him. Somebody at Horizon House was a murderer, but he preferred that it not be TJ, thanks all the same.

"This building here was shown in Lambert's records as a brewery, but actually it was a butcher shop," she was saying. "You know how we know? It's fascinating: the—"

"Wasn't there a theft here a few years ago?" It had come blurting out on its own.

TJ stopped, her arm still extended, her finger still pointing at whatever she'd been pointing at.

"Did I miss something? What's that got to do with anything?"

"I understand it was an Amarna statuette."

"That's right. Just the body." She looked at him quizzically, then took him a few dozen yards to the left, to the neatly excavated remains of a rectangular hut where two Egyptian workmen were protecting the eroded tops of the mud-brick foundations, using paintbrushes to lay on a ce-mentlike goop out of a bucket.

"It came from here," TJ said. "This was a sculptor's studio. It was probably something he was working on. The bastards were on it like vultures the very same night we found it. Why? What's the sudden interest?"

He hesitated. "Oh, I was just thinking about the head that Haddon saw and wondering if the two of them—"

She flung up her hands with a laugh. "Christ, you never give up, do you? Gideon, believe me—truly—there *was* no head. Haddon was just doing his usual number, trying to cover his poor old rear end. What does it take to satisfy you?"

More than that, he thought, and yet he was marginally reassured. Conceivably, it *was* as simple as that—that TJ really, sincerely believed that Haddon had never seen the head, that there wasn't any head to see, that it was first a delusion and then an invention. She hadn't made a connection between the body and the head because she had never for a moment believed the head existed. It was possible, he supposed. He hoped it was true.

"Come on, I'll show you the rest of the place," she said when he didn't answer, and led him off. She was polite and enthusiastic and Gideon asked intelligent questions, but an edge had come between them again, and he was glad when she looked at her watch, mumbled apologies, and went back to her clipboard and her graduate students.

On his way back to the sorting area he passed the camera crew on its next-to-last day of shooting. They were taping activities at one of the more interesting excavations, a building that had been a well-equipped bakery, and Kermit was arguing sourly with the local site supervisor because the young man wouldn't let him set up directly on the excavated clay floor. Nearby, restless as a chained bear, Forrest shambled back and forth wearing an oversized Panama hat with a jaunty red band, trying to bite what was left of his nails.

"Hi, Forrest, how's it going?" Gideon said without thinking.

He should have known better. "Don't ask," Forrest mumbled and then told him: Half of yesterday's taping was going to have to be reshot because some bozo on the ferry had knocked a box of cassettes into the river the previous evening. Cy was being sulky because Kermit had overruled him on a complex shot that Cy had spent an hour setting up, and Kermit was acting sulky because Forrest had overruled *him*. Patsy wasn't acting any sulkier than usual but she had diarrhea, which meant they had to stop for ten minutes between every shot while she made a run for the can. The whole thing was coming apart in their faces.

And Haddon had screwed things up beyond redemption, not to speak ill of the goddamned dead, by picking a hell of a time to fall into the Nile. Corners were going to have to be cut, interviews were going to have to be scratched—

"Sounds really tough, Forrest. Um, am I still on at noon?" Hope had stirred. Had the director been hinting that Gideon's session would have to be dropped?

No such luck. "God, yes," Forrest said, shocked, "We need you more than ever. What are you supposed to be talking about?"

"Racial composition in ancient Egypt," Gideon said reluctantly. "We were going to reshoot the session I was doing with Kermit the other—"

"No, screw it," Forrest said, scanning his wilting and dog-eared shooting schedule and making a few more smudgy pencil marks on it, "we don't need that, let's forget that one."

That was something, anyway.

"How about if instead you do the hour on village life you were going to do tomorrow? That'll give me tomorrow to—"

"I don't think so, Forrest. I'm not ready. There were some things I was going to look up in the library."

Forrest gnawed his two-inch-long, much-gnawed stub of yellow pencil. "I could probably switch you from noon to two o'clock. Would that give you enough time? Kermit will have a fit, but, what the hell, screw Kermit too."

"You mean you wouldn't need me at all tomorrow?"

"Right, finish it off today."

Gideon considered. It would rush him, but it would also mean a day with Julie tomorrow, an entire free day on their own, the only one they'd had since coming to Egypt and the only one they were going to get.

"You're on," he said.

Which was why he and Julie were now climbing into one of the white Horizon vans to be taken to the ferry dock. The driver, a smiling new hire named Gawdat, slid the side door closed with a clunk, ran around to the front, climbed into the driver's seat, turned the key, and started them up the steeply inclined road.

They drove past the ruined foundations of what everyone said was the set from an old movie, although no one knew its name, then around the base of Monkey's Spine, the curious, humpbacked knob that loomed over WV-29, and then onto the long escarpment that led to the main road to the Nile. Once on the escarpment, an enormous panorama spread out on their left. They were at the very edge of the great plateau of the Western Desert, riddled with canyons and dropping away, foothill by tawny foothill to the distant Nile, a dull brown band between two narrow strips of green as sharply defined as if they'd been drawn on a map. Beyond the farther strip the desert began its slow climb again, desolate and sterile, and continued far beyond the range of their sight, for almost three thousand terrible miles, the largest desert in the world, across the whole of Libya and Algeria and Morocco . . .

"I forgot," Julie said abruptly.

Gideon turned from the window. "Leave something back there?"

"No. I forgot all about it. In all the fuss. The ledger." She put her hand on his arm. "Yesterday."

"Maybe complete sentences would help," he said.

"I found the chronological ledger," she told him as if he were being particularly dense. "I went looking for it and I found it."

He sighed. "I think I missed something."

"You missed the chronological ledger, is what you missed."

"That's not too surprising. What's a chronological ledger?"

It was a register, she explained excitedly, in which new

accessions to a museum were recorded as they came in, as an adjunct to the object cards. It had occurred to her that there might have been such a register in Lambert's time, that it might still be around, and that a record of the head that Haddon had described, the head that was at the center of every strange thing that had been going on, might be in it.

She squeezed his arm. "And it was."

Gideon shook his head, still bewildered. "Do you mean a field catalogue, a site notebook? But they wouldn't have been using one here in 1924. It wasn't part of the standard archaeological method yet. Cordell Lambert wasn't Howard Carter."

"I'm not talking about archaeology, I'm talking about museumology." She started rummaging in her duffel-sized canvas purse. "I went into the old office in the annex before dinner yesterday and browsed around. There were some dusty old ledgers down on the oversized shelves."

"I never saw them."

"You'd have to be looking for them. They were in there with the bound periodicals. Anyway, they were the Lambert Museum's chronological ledger from 1920 to 1926. Damn, where is that thing? Ah. . . ."

She pulled out the soft leather pocket notebook that was always in her purse, the one that he'd given her on her promotion to supervisor so that she would have her own little black book. "Here it is. '21 March, 1924. Head of—' Here, you read it."

He snatched it from her. " 'Head of young woman or girl, inscribed, made of yellow jasper . . .' This is it, Julie!"

"Really?" she said mildly. "You know, I wondered if it might be."

He laughed and read on. " 'Height five and one-eighth inches to base of neck, not including one and one-quarter-inch tenon for insertion into mortise joint in shoulders.' " This was it, all right. The head Haddon had seen, the head he'd described. Something like an Ali Hassan–type chuckle rumbled around inside Gideon's chest. " 'Chipped left ear and some abrasion of tip of nose. Slightly elongated skull shape, possibly for mounting of wig.' "

He slapped the notebook against his palm. "Julie, this is great. It confirms everything we—"

He stopped in mid-sentence, scowled, and tore the notebook open again.

"Look at this," he said wonderingly. " 'Head of a young woman or girl, inscribed . . .' " He slapped his forehead. "Where's my mind been? I should have figured this out days ago, before we ever got back to Luxor!"

"I'm afraid I've missed something," Julie said. "What is it that we're talking about?"

"Remember my telling you how Ali Hassan was leering at me and muttering about 'the final element, the last part'?"

"Yes, but—"

"I know what it is, I know what he was talking about!" He sobered. "My God, no wonder this thing was worth killing over. If—"

The van, which had been bobbing timidly along the sandy road the last time they'd noticed, suddenly rocked heavily to the right and went through a jolting series of bumps, throwing Julie against Gideon and knocking the notebook to the floor.

"Hey, take it easy," Gideon called to the front, "we're not in any hurry, we—"

Another tooth-rattling set of shocks bounced both of them two inches off the seat. The notebook jumped about on the floor. Everything else on the seats—Julie's purse, their hats, somebody's clipboard, somebody's jacket, a couple of empty soda pop cans—was flung to the floor. In front of them Gawdat hung rigidly on to the wheel with his left hand, fighting to keep his turban from toppling off with his right.

"What is he doing?" Julie said anxiously. "This can't be the way to the ferry."

It wasn't the way to anywhere. Two hundred yards in front of them, so bright it hurt to look at, was a squat, rugged cliff of weathered limestone eighty or a hundred feet high, blocking their way like a dam. On either side of the van, but much closer, similar stone walls closed in, craggy and forbidding.

A box canyon, Gideon thought. He's driven us into a box canyon. What . . .

"Gawdat," he said sharply. "Stop the van. Right now. Turn around and—"

The rest of the sentence was jarred out of his mouth as the van bucketed on. His teeth clicked painfully together. Gawdat turned panicky eyes on him for a moment—Gideon saw white all around the pupils, as in a frightened horse— and stepped on the gas, rigidly clutching the wheel with both hands now while his turban went flying. Julie and Gideon grabbed at whatever they could to keep from being tossed into the air. Limbs flopped, heads knocked against the padded roof.

"Damn it," Gideon managed to get out, "you're going to—"

They were thrown forward against the backs of the front seats as the car juddered to a standstill, so that Julie and Gideon wound up falling all over each other in the narrow space, like a pair of Keystone Kops, knees in ribs and elbows in eyes. When they floundered up unhurt, they were in time to see the turbanless Gawdat bolting back across the desert, with the skirts of his robe held high and his brown knees pumping, finally vanishing into a warren of boulders at the entrance to the canyon.

The springs of the van resettled themselves with a last, abused sigh, and then there was utter silence, unnerving after all the tumult. Around them, pale dust slowly settled back to earth and sifted in through the open windows and driver's door. The odor of gasoline was thick in their nostrils—gasoline and the strange smell of the Egyptian desert; flinty-clean and fusty at the same time, redolent, so it seemed, of ancient tomb chambers, and camel dung, and Bedouin camps that had been set down and pulled up a thousand times over the ages.

"Well, that was certainly exciting," Julie said, pushing her shirt into her jeans. "What now?"

Gideon considered. "If there was a phone booth we could use it to call the auto club," he pointed out. "If there was an auto club."

She gave him the look it deserved and slid to the right end of the seat to scan the barren, silent rock walls through her sunglasses.

He knew what was on her mind—the same thing that was on his: two days before, two English tourists had been shot to death by extremists in a remote canyon near the Valley of the Kings, only a few miles from where they were now. They had been in a hired van. The driver had mysteriously disappeared.

But there was something else on his mind too: a new thought, closer to home but no less nasty. Like Julie he searched the clefts and outcroppings, but without his sunglasses—they were back on the bureau at Horizon House, damn it—it was next to hopeless. The clefts were too many, the shadows too deep, the glare on the sun-bleached rock too blinding. He wiped a sheen of sweat from his forehead and pushed the fly-window open as far as it would go. The temperature had dropped to a seasonally normal eighty-five degrees, but under the desert sun the flat-roofed vehicle had begun to heat up the moment they had stopped, even with the driver's door and all the workable windows wide open. Already he was imagining that his tongue had begun to thicken, the back of his throat to turn gluey.

"What we need," Julie said, continuing to scan the cliffs methodically, side to side, down one face and up the next, "is a plan."

He laughed. "My sentiments exactly. What do you say—"

"Look there." She pointed upward and a little behind them. "On top, you see that formation like a—a long set of organ pipes?"

Gideon squeezed his way past her knees, crouched in the space next to the passenger door, and peered out, shielding his eyes against the blaze of sky and limestone. "Yes. . . ."

"Just to the left of that and down a little, there's a kind of hollow—"

Near his cheek something pulsed in the air, a vibration, a flutter, as of an invisible bird wing; a queer sensation he knew he'd never felt before. At the same time something thudded into the mess on the floor, and a fraction of a second later there was a *crack* from outside, followed by a diminishing grumble of echoes. Gideon had been half-expecting it, and still it took a blank, shocked moment to register. They were being shot at. Hurriedly, he pulled a similarly stunned

Julie roughly away from the window, to the other side of the van.

"Are you all right?" he asked with his heart in his throat. "It didn't—?"

She shook her head, her black eyes round. "No . . . I'm all right. "I think it went between us."

And without much room to spare, he thought shakily. Through the open window with about four inches on either side.

She was still staring at him. "I saw him," she whispered. "I saw his face! I saw the gun—I couldn't believe he was really going to shoot at us. Gideon, it's—"

"I know. Forrest Freeman."

"Yes! You saw him too?"

No, he hadn't seen him, but he knew. It was Forrest who had the head, Forrest who had killed Haddon, Forrest who was up there now with a rifle—his trusty Anatolian boar-hunting rifle, no doubt—bent on killing them.

"You *knew*!" she said with a flare of exasperation. "How long have you—"

"About a minute and a half. Julie, I'd say this would be a good time to come up with that plan. We can't just wait here for him to come and get us."

"Agreed."

Their eyes roved over the interior of the van. What they were looking for, Gideon hardly knew, but *something*—a decoy, a trap, a weapon . . . In the space behind the rear row of seats he found a jack, the handle of which was an angled tire iron about fifteen inches long. He pulled the iron out of the jack and hefted it. It would make a formidable club but how much help it was going to be against a rifleman shooting at them from behind a rock eighty feet above their heads was—

"I don't believe it!" Julie exclaimed. "The key!"

He followed the line of her pointing finger and there—amazingly, wondrously—was the ignition key, trailing a six-inch piece of wood with a red enamel 2 painted on it, fixed firmly in the ignition slot. In his agitation Gawdat had either been unable to get it out or had forgotten about it altogether.

They looked at each other. They had a plan after all: they could *drive* out of the box canyon.

"Okay, then——" he said.

The small, unopenable window in the passenger door exploded, scattering glass shards. A thread of dust puffed from the seat, exactly where Julie had been sitting moments before. For a couple of seconds they sat wordlessly, not moving, anticipating another bullet, but none came; only the single, desultory shot, as if Forrest merely wanted to let them know that he hadn't lost interest.

They let out their breath. "Well, the angle's the same," Julie observed coolly, looking from the shot-out window to the hole in the seat. "He's still in the same place."

Gideon nodded. "It overlooks the entrance to the canyon. He figures he can catch us if we make a run for it."

"Let's hope he can't."

"At fifty miles an hour, I doubt it."

The angle of the shots—which would be the same as the shooter's angle of vision—also made it clear that Forrest couldn't see them and wouldn't be able to see the driver's seat either. But all he had to do to change that was to climb down twenty or thirty feet. And that he would surely do, more likely sooner than later.

So it was time to go. He squeezed her hand and snaked between the front seats, sitting quietly for a moment to make sure he knew how the floor-mounted gear lever worked and just where the clutch and gas pedals were. He didn't expect to have much use for the brake. He thought about pulling shut the driver's door, left open by Gawdat, but decided he was better off not sticking his arm out into the open.

"Better get down, Julie. Get on the floor."

He pressed on the clutch pedal, shifted reasonably smoothly from third gear, where the fleeing Gawdat had left it, to neutral, turned the key in the ignition, and held his breath. The engine hesitated, chittered, and caught. He shifted into first and stepped on the gas pedal. The car pitched forward, stopped, pitched, stopped, pitched—

"The emergency brake!" Julie shouted.

"Where the hell is it?" he yelled back, bumping his head

as they jerked along in a sort of automotive seizure, but before he could find it something beneath the floorboard gave way and the van sprang powerfully forward at last, gathering speed. He shifted to second.

"You okay?" he called over his shoulder.

"Oh, fine," came Julie's voice from the floor. "Having a wonderful time."

He thought he'd heard at least one shot over the start-up commotion but apparently the startled Forrest had missed, and now they were quickly putting distance between themselves and him.

That was the good part. There were several bad parts.

First, they were headed *into* the canyon, not out. To get out of it he was going to have to get the van turned around and come barreling back through the entrance, right under Forrest's nose. He didn't like it, but he didn't see that there was any choice.

Second, the promised fifty miles an hour was out of the question. They were going to have to do it at no more than twenty. The canyon floor wasn't made for anything less than a half-track, and he didn't dare shift above second gear for fear of getting stuck in the loose, rough terrain. And even if he chanced that and got away with it, he'd wind up breaking their necks or cracking their skulls at anything faster. Already they were bouncing crazily along again, the way they'd been when Gawdat had been driving. And they were tipped precariously to one side, hugging the sloping, rocky scree at the base of the cliffs; it was the only way to get enough room to turn the van around without having to slow down even more, or backing up.

The canyon, he knew by now, was keyhole-shaped, widening to a two-hundred-yard arc at the rear, and constricting to a narrow bottleneck at the entrance, over which Forrest held sway from his perch. Whatever else you said about him, Gideon thought, you had to admit he knew how to pick his canyons.

The plan, then, was to continue on this arc along the foot of the cliffs, until he had enough of a turning radius available to head back toward the entrance.

And through it, with any luck.

"Uh!" The sound was wrung from him as the right front wheel jounced over a pile of stones and dropped into a foot-deep hollow. The van tipped over so far that the open driver's door slammed shut on its own. Metal screeched against rock as the undercarriage bottomed, but somehow the van scrabbled its way out. Gideon tasted blood where he'd bitten the inside of his cheek.

But they were still moving.

"Get ready now," he called back, wrestling the wheel, "I've got enough room to make the turn. I'm just going to get it pointed toward the opening, step on the gas, and pray."

"Amen," Julie said.

They were about a hundred yards from the entrance; they would be in Forrest's sights the whole time, head-on, with Gideon himself in plain view. But what else was there to do? They couldn't stay in the canyon, and if they tried leaving the van and scaling the walls a leisurely Forrest could pick them off in the bright sunlight like moving targets in a carnival shooting gallery. *Ping*, they'd go, and fall over like growling bears or quacking ducks.

And Forrest would get the prize.

Gideon swung hard toward the right, put just a little more pressure on the gas pedal, and clutched the jerking wheel to keep the van headed straight for the opening. With all the rolling, lurching, and jolting that was going on without any help from him, he didn't see any need to worry about evasive tactics.

The first shot was fired as he came full around, facing the entrance. There was an inconsequential *snick* from the front of the vehicle just below the window and a seemingly simultaneous thud as the bullet struck the floor on the passenger side, about three feet from Gideon's right leg.

Why, those things can go right through metal, Gideon thought indignantly. Like butter. What the hell, it hardly seemed fair. On the other hand, that was the fourth shot Forrest had taken at them now, and they were still in one piece. *Crack*, there was another; he saw the dust spatter twenty feet in front of the van. Was Forrest panicking, getting less accurate rather than more? He hunched down lower on the seat and pressed as hard as he dared on the pedal. Seventy yards to go . . . sixty-five . . . He began to let himself think about Life After the Canyon.

He never heard the next shot strike, didn't really see it strike. One second he was trying to decide whether or not he could risk taking the van over the rocks rearing up in their path. The next second the windshield was honeycombed by a thousand glittering little fissures that turned the landscape into a kaleidoscope. Immediately the steering wheel fought him harder, pulling at his arms as if it knew that he was blind, that it had the upper hand now.

"Hang on!" he yelled or tried to yell, pawing with his foot for the brake, but a scrunching shock sent him helplessly up in the air still clinging to the wheel, like a kid bounced off a seesaw and hanging on to the handle for dear life. Then, for a breath-stopping moment the entire van was airborne, coming down heavily on its rear wheels and careening on, slowed now but tilted wildly to the right, on two wheels; so much so that Gideon, flung like a bundle of laundry into the passenger seat corner, saw only sky through the driver's window on the other side.

We're tipping over, he thought. "Brace yourself!" he called. "We're—"

And over they went, the van falling sluggishly onto its right side and then, slowly, surprisingly, continuing to roll, as if someone were pushing it down a hill. For an impossibly long moment it hung, balanced and seemingly struggling, before it tumbled onto its top with a terminal, metal-crumping *whomp* that smashed the remaining windows, popped the crackled windshield out of its mounting, and crumpled the left rear half of the roof like so much tinfoil.

Gideon ended up on his back on the ceiling along with everything else that was loose, including Julie, who was sprawled beside him under a welter of seat cushions, clothes and other junk.

He reached instinctively for her with his hand. "Julie, are you okay?" Years of dirt and sand that had been tramped into the van fell onto their faces like dry rain.

"Ugh. Yes. Phooey." She was spitting dust. "Nothing that a few weeks in traction won't fix. What about you?"

"Yes, fine."

Well, pretty much. The van had tipped slowly enough to let him prop himself against the roof and the back of the front seat before it had turned completely over, but the tire iron— he'd brought it up front with him—had gouged him in the thigh, which had hurt a little, and somewhere along the way he had bitten his cheek again in the same spot, which had hurt like hell but wasn't anything serious. He realized abruptly that the engine was still running and quickly reached down— reached up, rather—to switch off the ignition, then cautiously peeked through a corner of the space where the windshield had been to check their bearings.

They were in a kind of nook or cul-de-sac, a mini–box canyon off the main box canyon. Apparently the van had swerved into it, then flipped when it rode up onto the sloping talus at the foot of the cliffs, rolling into the troughlike center of the little bay. A good thing too; only twenty or thirty feet ahead of them—all around them, in fact—were truck-sized boulders that had fallen from above, a collision with any one of which would surely have resulted in more to complain about than a bitten cheek.

There was another good thing: the hollow from which Forrest had been firing was out of sight around a spur of rock, and if they couldn't see where he was, then he couldn't see where they were either. That, Gideon assured himself, was what the laws of geometrical optics said, and who was he to question the laws of geometrical optics?

Not only that, but geography was cooperating too. They were on the same side that Forrest was on; behind him, so to speak. The perpendicular spur that thrust out from the cliff to create their little bay was a promontory of the same massive organ-pipe formation in one of whose upper hollows Forrest had been crouching to fire. But that was at the other end of it, and to get from there to here, to a place where he could see them again, Forrest would have to go the long way around, *behind* the sinuous outcropping, because on the canyon side it reared up, sheer and columnar, with no visible path or ledge around it.

The problem for Forrest would be that he had no way of knowing that the van had turned over, since he couldn't see the bay. As far as he knew, it could come rattling back out at any moment, spewing nuts and bolts like a cartoon car and heading full-tilt for the entrance again. And if he was stuck behind the outcropping when it did, there would be nothing to stop their getting through. On the other hand, he could hardly keep his position at the canyon's mouth because Gideon and Julie might already be scrambling up the bay's back wall and out of his grasp.

In other words, Forrest Freeman had himself a predicament. And if Forrest Freeman's past behavior was any indication, what he would do would be to worry for a while before doing anything else. That meant that they ought to have seven or eight minutes before he showed up above them with his rifle; five minutes while he dithered and another two or three while he worked his way around the promontory, if that was what he decided to do.

Gideon turned back to Julie. "Let's get out of this thing. We'll stand a lot better chance out there—there are caves and outcroppings all over the place—than we will waiting in here for him to come pick us off."

"I won't argue with that," she said. "I think the front window's the easiest way out. Go ahead, I'll follow you."

"Right." He pulled himself through, glanced warily at the deserted cliff top, and reached back in to help her get out.

She was up on her right elbow with a puzzled look on her face, tugging awkwardly at the junk that lay over her extended left foot. "Ow. Damn."

"Julie, what's wrong? Are you hurt?"

"No . . I don't think so. My ankle's caught. . . . *Damn!* There's this stupid bar . . ."

"I'll give you a hand." He clambered back in, hauling himself to her side on his elbows.

"No, it's not going to work," she said, straining at her foot. "Damn!"

A glance made the problem clear. When the van had flipped, two of the three passenger seat rows had come loose, and one of them had fallen over Julie's leg and been wedged firmly into the buckled ceiling. The steel reinforcing bar that ran along its base had come down across her ankle, pinning her hiking-booted foot to the crushed roof.

He tried to maneuver her foot out of its steel-rimmed trap

without success—there wasn't enough room to move it—then tugged fruitlessly at the bar.

"You're lucky you didn't lose your foot," he said.

"That's me," she said grimly, "lucky Julie."

He made her lie back, then managed to get both arms around the seat, pulling from his cramped position and putting all the strength of his legs and back into it. It didn't budge, didn't feel as if anything short of a crane could get it to budge.

He fell back. "Can you get your foot out of the boot?"

"I don't know." She fumbled at the laces, blocked by the mass of the seat. "No, it's hard to get hold—"

"Here, let me—"

Her hand came down on his wrist. "Gideon, there's no *time!* He could be here any minute. You go!"

"And leave you?" He laughed, but he felt as if something had punched him in the throat. "Forget it." He went back to her boot laces.

Her fingers dug into his wrist. Her face was very close. "Gideon, go! It's our only chance."

"But—"

"I'll be all right. *We'll* be all right. I know you'll think of something."

"I—Julie, I—"

"Go, already!"

Chapter Twenty-four

I know you'll think of something.

He had been unable to reply. He'd stroked her cheek, pulled himself back out of the car, and run for the cliff. And he had scrambled up the rocky wall with the mindless, pumping strength of a desert animal, seeming to throw himself from outcropping, to boulder, to crevice, to ridge, every second expecting to see Forrest appear on the rim above him, rifle in hand.

Forrest.

How could he not have realized it? He should have put it all together in Abydos, when TJ had told him about the ornaments missing from the el-Amarna Museum. But he hadn't; not until they were practically in Forrest's sights, not until Julie showed him what was in the ledger. "Head of young woman or girl, inscribed . . ." that is, of course, *engraved*. With hollows for the insertion of faience eyes, channels for eyebrows of gold, perforations for golden earrings, drilled holes for a wig of delicate golden strands . . .

Hadn't Arlo stood right there in the museum and flatly told him the damn things weren't jewelry? Of course they weren't jewelry. They were *inlays*; gold and faience inlays and decorations to adorn the head of an Amarna statuette. And when everything was assembled—head, inlays, and body—whoever had them would have something that no one else in the world had. An intact, complete Amarna Period statuette. Museums and collectors had burned to own one for decades, but none had ever been recovered.

No wonder the head had been worth killing over. And no wonder Haddon had had to go. He'd seen the head. He could describe it accurately. And if he could describe it, then eventually, when it came on the market as it surely would, it could be traced back to Horizon House and to the people who were there at the time. So he had to be disposed of, and disposed of before returning to Luxor, where he was chafing to show it to everyone in sight.

It wouldn't have been hard for Forrest to murder the old Egyptologist. Haddon liked his after-dinner drinks and after-dinner monologues; finding people to sit through them was his problem. Forrest could easily enough have gotten himself invited to Haddon's stateroom. Once there, how difficult would it have been to use Haddon's bathroom at some point and emerge with four or five crushed-up antidepressant pills? How difficult to find a way to slip them into Haddon's brandy or Scotch?

A little later he had probably taken a midnight turn around the deck with the notoriously insomniac Haddon. Groggy and stumbling by now, Haddon must have collapsed, hitting his face on the grating. The burly Forrest had lifted him over the railing, and it had been over. Or it would have been over but for that unseen little platform.

So many things should have given him away. It was Forrest, not Haddon or Bruno or anyone else, who had insisted on going all the way downriver to Amarna despite the press of time. Why, except that he knew that the inlays were there? And then there had been the disappearance of the head from the drawer between the time Haddon saw it and the time TJ called Horizon House to ask about it. Who had removed it? It might have been anyone back in Luxor, of course, but surely the likelihood was that it was someone closely connected to whoever had killed Haddon and was therefore on the *Menshiya*. TJ's student Stacey Tolliver was possible but farfetched. That left Kermit Feiffer, Forrest's assistant director.

Forrest and Kermit were in it together then, and maybe the rest of the crew too. And take it a step further: maybe they'd been in the antiquities-smuggling business on the side for years, acting as conduits for the el-Hamids' loot, profiting from their absurdly low prices. Hiding small objects in with the taping paraphernalia would have been child's play.

And there was something else, now that he thought about it: why would someone who hated Egypt as much as Forrest did keep coming back?

Well, it wasn't an airtight case, but everything added up.

Not that he was in need of an airtight case at this point. It was Forrest Freeman who'd been trying his damndest to blow them apart for the last fifteen minutes, and that, he rather thought, made the rest of it moot.

He pulled himself the last few feet onto the rim of the cliff—no sign of Forrest—and rolled quickly behind the scant cover of a few scattered boulders. The adrenaline that had propelled him up the wall had drained away, leaving him spent and trembling, hardly able to catch his breath, his pulse pounding in his ears. Flat on his stomach he sucked in air while sweat ran from his face onto the sandy gravel. He had scraped both knees coming up, and the palms of both hands. One of his fingernails had been ripped half-off. He didn't remember any of it happening. And his hip had been bruised by the tire iron he couldn't remember sticking in the back of his belt. He adjusted it, muttering, thinking it was doing him more damage than it was Forrest.

He pulled in a last, long breath through his mouth and got cautiously to his hands and knees, his strength seeping slowly back. He could see the van eighty feet below him, as pathetic as a beetle with its legs in the air. The thought of Julie in there, caught by the foot, defenseless . . .

He jerked his head. It was Forrest he had to worry about. Once he had taken care of Forrest Julie would be all right. What "taken care of" meant, he had yet to figure out, but something would come to him.

I know you'll think of something. He hoped so.

Staying low, he scrambled for better cover about thirty feet further on: a column of limestone that had collapsed and fractured into a jumble of massive slabs. From between two of them, he scanned the pale, eroded plateau in Forrest's presumed direction, squinting in the needle-sharp light. To his surprise a white Horizon van stood about two hundred yards away, and directly beyond it, no more than a mile off, was the familiar, humpbacked Monkey's Spine that marked the location of WV-29. Between the two he could make out, for much of the way, a portion of a "desert freeway," one of the sandy tracks used by night-driving truck drivers who had their own reasons for keeping far from the main roads.

That explained how Forrest had gotten here first. When Gawdat had started off on the roundabout route that would bring them to the entrance to the sunken canyon—it had taken a good twenty minutes—Forrest had simply hopped into the other van and driven straight to the cliffside, only a mile—

He ducked. There had been a flash of white about fifty yards in front of him, along the back of the organ-pipe formation. White and red. Forrest's broad-brimmed Panama hat. Gideon dropped onto his belly and peered through a heap of crumbled limestone. Forrest was coming toward him, rounding the edge of a rocky column and scooting sideways down a sandy incline, one hand steadying himself against the rock, the other holding the rifle.

Crablike, Gideon backed further into the three-foot space between the tilted slabs. He didn't think he'd been seen; Forrest's face had been down, his eyes on his footing, and the brim of his hat had probably blocked his vision.

Probably.

He could hear him now, big desert boots scrunching on the gritty soil. Forrest had no choice but to come this way to get to a spot where he could overlook the van; on this part of the cliffs the organ-pipe formation at Gideon's back sidled up almost to the rim, leaving only a six-foot-wide space for passage. Right in front of Gideon.

And when he came, Gideon would be coiled and ready, his eyes fixed on the place where Forrest's legs would appear. The instant he saw him he would spring, bowling him over, going for the rifle with both hands and wresting it out of the startled Forrest's grasp. He would take Forrest to the van he'd come in, lay him down in the back and lash him to something, and find the road that led down into the canyon.

In an hour he and Julie would be on a patio in Luxor sipping something cool, and Forrest would be learning firsthand about the Egyptian system of justice administration.

Assuming that all went well.

He got into position on fingertips and toes, a sprinter's crouch. With his eyes on the pathway and his muscles so tense they vibrated he waited. And waited.

Two minutes passed. His neck began to ache. His shoulders and back were stiffening; he had probably taken more of a mauling in the van than he'd realized. He adjusted his position, easing the strain on his neck and hands. Forrest didn't come. Another minute went by. No Forrest.

Sweat dripped from the end of his nose. Had he been seen after all? Had he boxed himself in? Was it Forrest who was doing the waiting-out, sitting at his ease—

His ears pricked. He'd heard something; the *chink* of metal against stone. Not coming toward him, but already past, toward the canyon rim. Somehow Forrest had gotten by. But how could . . . a frightening image of him out there, taking his time, drawing a bead on Julie through one of the van's windows, brought him swiftly out from behind the rocks with the tire iron in his hand.

It took him a few seconds to find Forrest. He wasn't on the rim with Gideon, but about fifteen feet below it, on a projection that Gideon hadn't noticed before even though he had to have climbed over it on the way up; a slanting shelf about a hundred feet long that ran from the cliff top, well behind where Gideon was standing, to peter out about seventy feet above the canyon floor. Forrest was hunkered down behind some boulders near the lower end of it with his back to Gideon, methodically surveying the area below. The rifle was held beside him, propped on its butt. Clearly, he was concerned that they might have gotten out of the van; equally clearly, the idea that Gideon might already have gotten up the steep walls and be behind him had never crossed his mind.

Frankly, it seemed improbable to Gideon too. He didn't have a particularly good head for heights, and looking at that fissured, near-vertical cliff face now was enough to make his legs watery. God bless the autonomic nervous system, he thought; always ready to kick in when you needed it. He hoped it was getting ready again.

He began to edge quietly forward, crouching low, placing his feet with care to avoid any friction. He had about fifteen feet of downward-sloping limestone to go to the rim of the cliff. Then a sheer six-foot drop to Forrest's level and another ten or twelve feet—the width of the shelf—to Forrest himself. It was the last dozen feet that were going to be the hard part. Assuming he made it without being seen to the edge of the cliff, what then? If he hurled himself down at Forrest, could he possibly reach him? He didn't think so. Well, on a bounce maybe, but that wasn't going to do the trick.

He gripped the tire iron. Flung end-over-end it would be a wicked missile, easily capable of cracking Forrest's skull. But one try was all he was going to get, and he wasn't close enough yet. He crept onward, freezing when Forrest straightened up. But the director, unwaveringly confident, didn't bother looking behind him. Instead, he settled down into a more stable position on one knee and brought the rifle forward, propping his left arm on one of the rocks and adjusting his aim. Gideon began moving again.

Forrest took off his hat, wiped his forehead with his fingers and put the hat on again. He sighted along the rifle, swung out the handle of the bolt and slipped it smoothly back and forward, chambering a new cartridge with a well-oiled click. Gideon picked up his pace. Julie wasn't visible through the windows, but even a chance shot through the floor of the upturned van could easily hit her.

But Forrest wasn't settling for chance shots; he seemed to be taking careful aim, repositioning his torso, shifting his elbow, getting his orientation just right. Standing on the rim now, behind and above him, Gideon could sight down the barrel at almost the same angle that Forrest had. He seemed to be aiming at a place just forward of the rear axle, at—

The gas tank. The sonofabitch was trying to—

"*No!*" Gideon yelled, heaving the iron at the white hat. With almost the same motion he launched himself after it. It was a long jump and he put into it everything that he had against Forrest: the heat, the pain, the fear, the blood in his mouth, the hammering in his chest. And above all, above everything, Julie. He plunged from the rim like an avenging angel, arms outstretched, fingers reaching.

The iron missed its mark by three feet, zinging end-over-end above Forrest's head and out into the canyon.

Gideon missed by two.

He fell short, coming down in a sprawling three-point landing on one hand and both feet, his momentum carrying him into Forrest, or rather into Forrest's rifle. At Gideon's shout Forrest had spun to his feet and tried to bring the gun to bear on the howling thing falling out of the sky on him. But he hadn't been fast enough. The barrel of the weapon, still being swung around, smacked Gideon hard in the ribs below his left arm. With a grunt he clamped his arm down on it, then got his other hand around it too, a few inches further up the barrel, butted up against Forrest's left hand. He shifted to get a grip with both hands and pulled.

Forrest hung on, staggering momentarily before he set himself. They stood, straining and glaring at each other with their faces a couple of feet apart, like fencers with crossed swords. The tire iron clanged distantly on the rocks below. Forrest's face was scarlet from the strain, his cheeks distended. The tendons in his neck were popping. Gideon supposed he looked about the same.

"This is crazy, Forrest," he said through clenched jaws. "Don't make it worse on yourself . . . let go."

Forrest kicked him in the hip with a size-twelve, lug-soled desert boot. Gideon stumbled backward over a rock and went down onto the seat of his pants, clinging to the barrel with his left hand and twisting furiously to keep the muzzle pointed away from him.

Forrest kicked at him again, catching him under the arm and tugging on the rifle at the same time. Flinching with pain and dragged over the stones by the heavier Forrest, Gideon held grimly on, forcing the muzzle to the side. Letting go would be the end of everything, for him and for Julie. The bullet was in the chamber, the gun was cocked, and Forrest's finger was on the trigger. A quick, simple squeeze was all it would take for Gideon's death. Julie's wouldn't be long in following.

Somehow he managed to scramble to his feet again, helped inadvertently by Forrest's hauling on the rifle. But although he got his other hand on the gun again, his grip had slipped down almost to the muzzle. If not for the metal tag of the front sight, digging agonizingly into the fleshy heel of his hand, he would have lost hold altogether. He was winded now; that last kick had taken something out of him, and Forrest's greater weight was grinding him down as the larger man continued to wrench at the rifle. His arms had begun to tremble. His fingers were wooden.

Why, I might lose, he thought dully. *This man might actually kill me, kill Julie.*

Forrest was fresher. Forrest was heavier. And Forrest had hold of the right end of the gun.

Breathing hard, Forrest seemed to sense a weakening. "God . . . damn . . . you," he croaked, his broad back arched with the strain, his nostrils flaring, "let—"

Gideon let go.

Forrest flew back like a man shot out of a cannon. There was no cry or curse, no futile scrambling for balance, no expression of horror. His eyes, fixed on Gideon's, showed only a dawning surprise. His mouth remained as it was, formed for the "g" in "go." Two quick, stumbling backward steps and over the edge he went.

Over the edge and down, not in the parabolic arc that Gideon anticipated but *down*, like a safe falling out of a window. A moment later, out of sight, the rifle went off, mercifully overriding the sound that Gideon was listening for but trying not to hear. On his knees he edged to the rim and looked over in time to see Forrest sliding limply to the sand from the inclined top of a ten-foot-high boulder. The lolling neck, the impossible position in which his head came to rest, made it amply clear that the craniospinal junction had been severed.

So it was over. About Forrest he felt nothing; no triumph, no misgivings about taking a life, no soul-searching over whether there might have been a better way. Already he wasn't sure if he'd meant for Forrest to plummet over the edge when he let go or if he'd just been trying to gain the advantage.

Either way, he didn't much care. It was done, that was all, and he was alive and Julie was alive. Wearily, he wiped his hands on his pants.

Twenty yards away from Forrest the white Panama hat with its red band spiraled gently to the canyon floor.

Chapter Twenty-five

"Fascinating," opined Rupert Armstrong LeMoyne. "An incredible story, just fascinating." He shook his head, staring into the softly crackling log blaze. To the side of the brick fireplace, beyond the windows of the faculty club's cozy bar a few spatters of gray, early-January snow, probably the last of the winter, swirled dismally over a murky Lake Washington.

"But why in the world," he continued after a reflective sip of white wine, "would this Forrest Freeman person want to kill *you*?"

"Obviously, that's something nobody's ever going to know for sure," Gideon said. "My guess is that he heard about my offer of $40,000 and thought it was for real; that I was actually after that statuette. I suppose he thought I was bent. Like him."

"Mm, yes, I see. That makes sense."

As far as it went, Gideon thought. But what could Forrest have thought his motivation was? Gideon, after all, didn't have the corresponding inlays or head, so why would he have been so ready to shell out $40,000 for a sandstone body that wasn't much of anything in itself? But maybe Forrest hadn't worried about motivation. From his point of view, the fact was that Gideon was *doing* it, whatever the reason, and that was enough.

"No," Julie said, turning from her own contemplation of the fire, "I can't imagine anybody seeing you as a crook. You're too straight-arrow. I think that business with Hassan made Forrest realize that you were on to him, or about to be."

"Yes, that makes sense too," said the agreeable Rupert.

"Either way," Julie said, "you obviously had to go. Unfortunately, since I was with you at the time, I had to go too."

"Well, now, wait, Gideon," Rupert said. "You were in disguise that night. Nobody knew your name. How did he find out it was you?"

Gideon laughed. "Come on, a mysterious American named John Smith? With a stick-on beard? In Phil Boyajian's company? A story like that, with a few more details from Jalal or one of the others, wouldn't have been too hard to crack."

"Well, in any event," Rupert said, "it all worked out in the end, and that's what counts."

So it had, thanks largely to Sergeant Gabra. The setup with Hassan had been executed perfectly, even without Gideon's presence (Gabra had forbidden it after he and Julie had gotten back in the second Horizon van and given him an account of the events in the Western Valley). By the next morning, Gabra had all the pieces: the body, the head, and the box of inlays, the latter two thanks to Kermit Feiffer, who admitted to having been an on-again-off-again smuggling accomplice of Forrest's over the years, but who expressed dubious shock at hearing that Haddon's death had not been accidental. After a long session with Gabra and a night in the Luxor jail, Kermit had welcomed the opportunity to produce the objects, to tell everything, and to swear never again to set foot in Egypt, all in exchange for a promise of immunity from prosecution.

Forrest, Gabra confirmed, had been a conduit for the el-Hamids for years. He would offer them a little more than they could get anywhere else in Luxor and then smuggle it out of the country in his equipment cases to sell for ten or twenty times what he'd paid. According to Kermit, four years earlier, when he had been a cameraman on Forrest's PBS documentary, they had approached the director with the sandstone body recently taken from WV-29, asking what was for them a preposterously high price. Forrest said no.

Ah, they explained, but this particular statuette was from a newly excavated portion of the same ancient sculptor's studio that a certain Amarna head, now lying forgotten in a drawer at Horizon House, had come seventy years earlier— the now-aged Atef el-Hamid himself had been on Lambert's dig as a boy-laborer—and they had good reason to believe that the two were parts of a single sculpture. Moreover, there was another branch of the family at the village of el-Till, near the ruined site of Akhetaten, with whom they were in periodic contact. Information from this branch had long ago led them to conclude that the inlays that had been made for this Amarna head were at the Tel el-Amarna Museum, unrecognized and unrecorded, having been excavated long ago from an ancient metalsmith's studio in Akhetaten.

Surely, they said, a resourceful man such as Forrest, armed with this knowledge, could manage to get his hands on the head and the inlays. When added to the body that they were offering to sell him, he would have an art object of fantastic value, which was why they were asking such an admittedly extravagant price.

Six hundred American dollars.

Forrest was skeptical. They already had the body, didn't they? If they were so sure about the inlays and the head why hadn't they themselves stolen them? Why hadn't they stolen them years ago? They responded with wounded pride. To take something from a museum would be stealing, and the el-Hamids were not thieves. Removing an object from the ground was an entirely different matter, however. Who could claim before God or the law to own what had lain beneath the desert for ten thousand years? But steal from a museum? Never.

Forrest, who also preferred not to sully himself or his staff with stealing if he could pay someone else to take the risks, pressed them to reconsider their convictions. He would pay $800 if they would get him the head as well as the body.

Never, said the el-Hamids, not even for $1,000.

But when he got to $1,200—almost four times the average annual wage—one of the family, Abdul Nasr el-Hamid, made it clear that his own ethics might not be quite as rigid as those of the others, and that he had little love for Horizon House. Moreover, having worked there for a little while, he knew his way around.

An agreement was reached, but when two weeks passed without hearing anything more, Forrest made contact again. He was told that Abdul had unaccountably disappeared, failing to show up after his foray to Horizon House. Forrest assumed they had simply found a better buyer, and accepted the situation with a shrug. That was the way the game was played. The matter was dropped.

Four years later, with Forrest and Kermit back at Horizon House for *Reclaiming History*, it was picked up again. When Arlo, Jerry, and TJ walked into the crew's late-night pizza party with a tale about the remains of a body in the storage enclosure, a light had clicked on. Forrest had gone to check for himself and had found the head. In the seven hours before Gabra and Saleh were due to arrive, he and Kermit had painted the numbers on the bones, buried the real F4360, and put the head in the most logical of places: its own drawer. By now, knowing more about Horizon's nonexistent security precautions, they were more at ease about retaking it later. All Forrest had to do now was reinstate the visit to the el-Amarna Museum to get at the inlays, buy the body from Ali Hassan, who had gotten it from the el-Hamids, and remove the head at his pleasure. He would realize enough money from the statuette's eventual sale to finance whatever films he wanted to make for the rest of his life; no more *Reclaiming History*s or *Joy of Spring Bulbs*. Kermit was to get twenty percent of the profits. And they would manage it all without leaving a single clue or even a single lingering question behind.

Except, as they were shortly to find out, that Haddon had seen the head.

"You know, Gideon," Julie said, "now that I think about it, there's one part of this I've never gotten straight."

Gideon smiled. "Only one? Congratulations."

"Amarna and Luxor are a long way apart—"

"Two hundred miles."

"So what were the head and body doing in a sculptor's studio near Luxor—Thebes, it would have been—while the inlays were being made in another studio way up in Akhetaten?"

"Good question," Gideon said. "I think that's what kept me from putting it all together for so long. But you have to remember, this was right at the time the capital was being moved. What probably happened is that the stonework was commissioned while they were still in Thebes, and then the finish-work was done in Amarna, after the move. Or maybe the metalsmith was given the job in Thebes and moved to Akhetaten before he finished it."

The date inscribed on the statue—1350 B.C. by modern reckoning—supported this, being about the time of the capital's transfer. The statue itself was now known to be that of a noblewoman of Akhenaten's court named Semet.

"Well, it all worked out for the best," said Rupert, understandably anxious to impress this point on Gideon, who still bore some of the bruises he'd gotten in the Western Valley. "The Gustafsons," he added, purring, "are *very* well-satisfied."

The Gustafsons weren't the only ones. Sergeant Gabra had had his picture in newspapers from Novosibirsk to Nova Scotia and had received a commendation from the president of Egypt for retrieving a priceless piece of his country's patrimony. And, as Gabra had delightedly told Gideon, he'd managed to do it without having to arrest a single American!

The restored statuette of Semet, glowing with refurbished gold, would go to a place of honor in the Cairo Museum. First, however, in gratitude for the part played by the Horizon Foundation, it was to have a brief tour in the United States. At Bruno's request, the first stop would be the Burke Museum on the campus of his alma mater, the University of Washington.

To celebrate this coup, Rupert had arranged today's luncheon for officials from the university, the Horizon Foundation, and the Egyptian embassy. And Julie and Gideon. Bruno was to make the after-lunch speech.

"And speak of the devil," Rupert said, "here he is now."

Bruno and a few of the other guests, having just come in from a reception at the museum, were clustering at the bar. Bruno, catching sight of them, came smiling to their table, martini in hand.

"Ah, just the people I wanted to see."

There was news on several fronts, it turned out. First, gifts and donations to the foundation were up almost twenty percent, no doubt attributable to all the recent publicity. And demand for *Reclaiming History*, its editing complete, was beyond anything they'd hoped, which boded well for the future.

Second, TJ, whom everyone had been expecting to accept the directorship of Horizon House when it was offered, had amazed them by turning it down.

"I can't say I'm really surprised," Gideon said. "She's an archaeologist, not an administrator."

"She put it another way: 'I'd rather be down on my knees in dirt than up to my eyeballs in crap.' "

On the other hand, Bruno told them, Arlo, who had been expected to turn down the directorship if offered, had also amazed them—by accepting.

"You know," Gideon said, thinking about it, "that just might work out."

"I think Arlo will do fine," Julie said. "All he needs is a chance to spread his wings."

"I just hope he has wings," Bruno said.

And third, he continued, third, some *really* exciting news. In the late spring he would be taking another film crew to Giza, Saqqara, and Medum. Stimulated by the success of *Reclaiming History*, he was producing a documentary of his own, something he hoped would be a lasting contribution to Egyptology: the first completely scientific and unbiased examination of the powers of pyramids. Did they know, by the way, that new studies had shown that sleeping in a pyramid could extend the human lifespan by fifteen percent and also inhibit male-pattern baldness? That keeping butter in a pyramidal container could keep it fresh indefinitely?

"I don't suppose," he said, rolling his chair a little closer to Gideon's, "that, um, you'd be interested in coming along to narrate? Another exciting, no-expenses-spared trip to the Land of the Pharaohs?"

Gideon laughed and waved over the bartender for another round.

"Talk to me after I've healed up from the last one," he said.

Welcome to the Island of Morada—getting there is easy, leaving . . . is murder.

Embark on the ultimate, on-line, fantasy vacation with
MODUS OPERANDI.

Join fellow mystery lovers in the murderously fun MODUS OPERANDI, a unique on-line, multi-player, multi-service, interactive, mystery game launched by The Mysterious Press, Time Warner Electronic Publishing and Simutronics Corporation.

Featuring never-ending foul play by your favorite Mysterious Press authors and editors, MODUS OPERANDI is set on the fictional Caribbean island of Morada. Forget packing, passports and planes, entry to Morada is easy—all you need is a vivid imagination.

Simutronics GameMasters are available in MODUS OPERANDI around the clock, adding new mysteries and puzzles, offering helpful hints, and taking you virtually by the hand through the killer gaming environment as you come in contact with players from on-line services the world over. Mysterious Press writers and editors will also be there to participate in real-time on-line special events or just to throw a few back with you at the pub.

MODUS OPERANDI is available on-line now.

Join the mystery and mayhem on:
- America Online® at keyword MODUS
- Genie® at keyword MODUS
- PRODIGY® at jumpword MODUS

Or call toll-free for sign-up information:
- America Online® 1 (800) 768-5577
- Genie® 1 (800) 638-9636, use offer code DAF524
- PRODIGY® 1 (800) PRODIGY, use offer code MODO

Or take a tour on the Internet at
http://www. pathfinder.com/twep/games/modop.

MODUS OPERANDI—It's to die for.